CHURCHILL'S S.O.C.K.S

SPECIAL OPERATIONS CADET KIDS

MEZ BLUME

RIVER OTTER BOOKS

First published 2020 by River Otter Books

Cover Illustrations by Edward Bettison

PB ISBN: 978-1-8380079-0-4
EBook ISBN: 978-1-8380079-1-1

In loving memory of Kenneth 'Grandpere' Stead and
'Aunt Terry' Bergeron
without whom Kenny and Esme could never have come to life

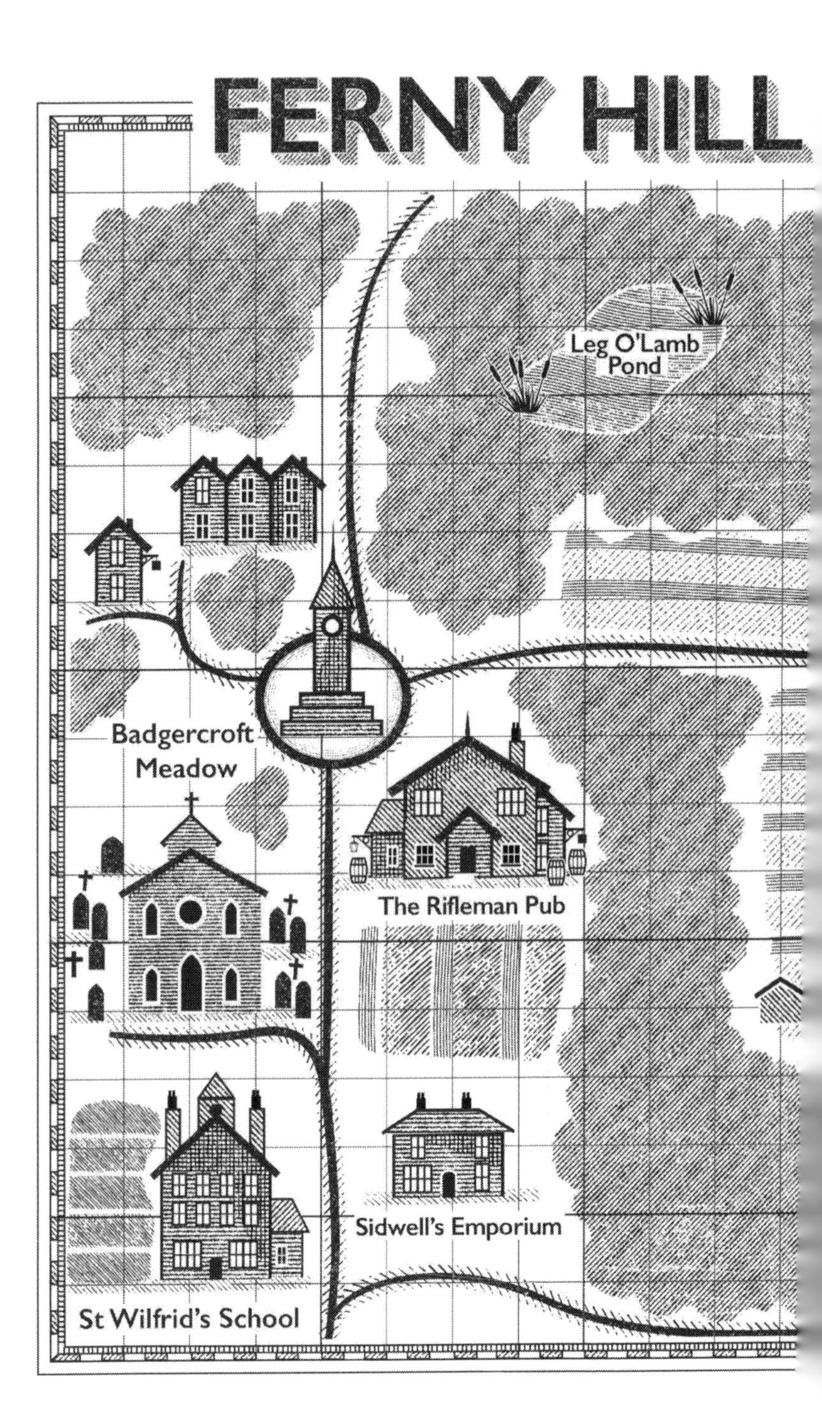
FERNY HILL
Leg O'Lamb Pond
Badgercroft Meadow
The Rifleman Pub
Sidwell's Emporium
St Wilfrid's School

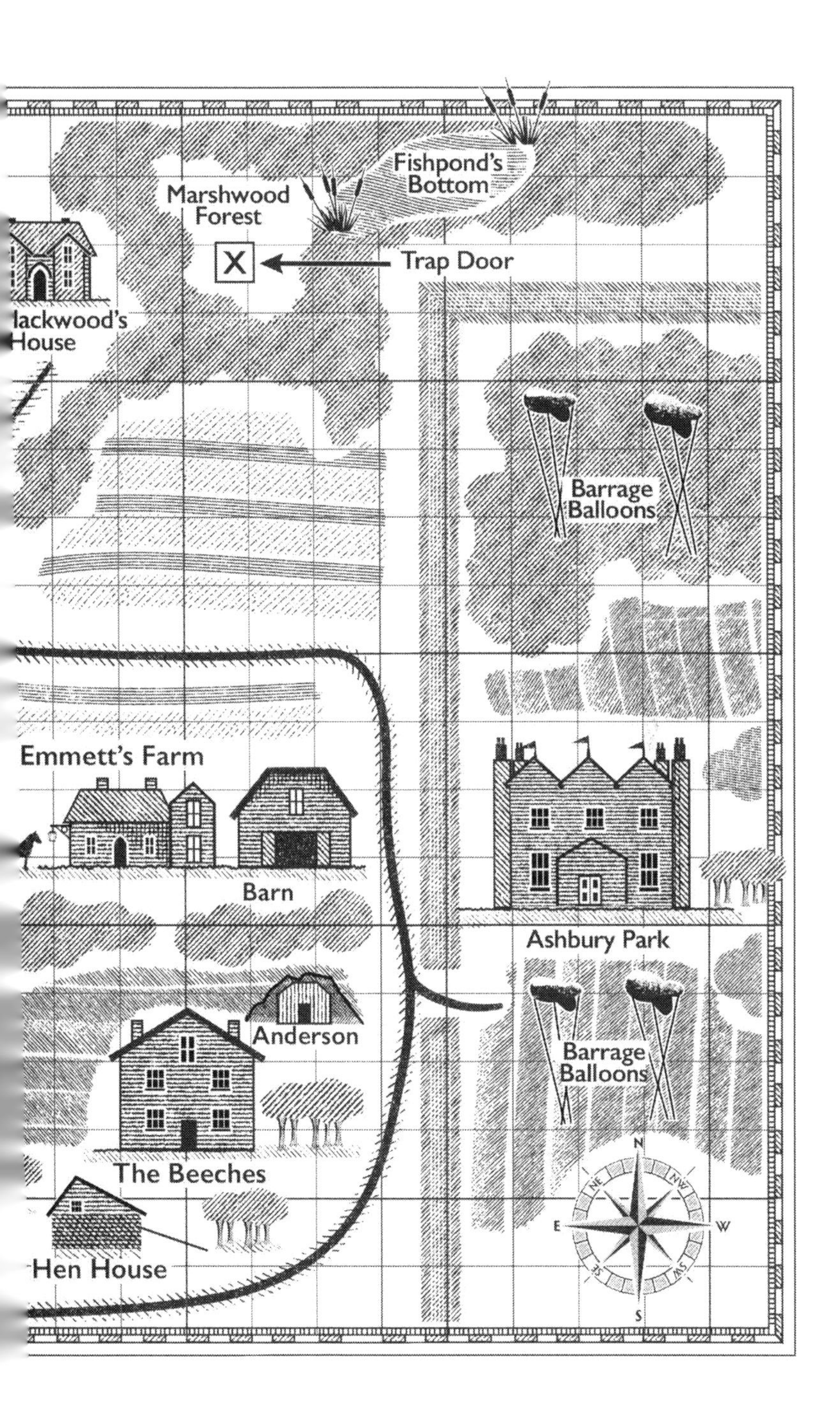
Fishpond's Bottom
Marshwood Forest
X
Trap Door
lackwood's House
Barrage Balloons
Emmett's Farm
Barn
Ashbury Park
Anderson
Barrage Balloons
The Beeches
Hen House
N
NE
NW
E
W
SE
SW
S

TERMS

Billeting – *the practice of civilians housing military personnel and evacuee children in WW2 Great Britain*

Dead Letter Drop – *a hidden location in which civilian spies would leave messages that would then be secretly collected by couriers, coded, and transmitted across a wireless*

Dogfight – *a battle between fighter aircraft, often requiring expert flight manoeuvres*

Hurricane – *a single-seat fighter plane; larger than the Spitfire and with bigger guns able to attack enemy bomber planes*

Special Duties Branch – *a secret network of British civilian observers and wireless operators; part of Churchill's British Resistance operations*

Substation – *an underground bunker operated by a civilian wireless operator; a.k.a. an OUT Station*

Messerschmitt – *the favourite fighter plane of the German Luftwaffe ('Air Force')*

Spitfire – *a single-seat fighter plane used by the Royal Air Force (RAF); known for agility; best in a dogfight*

Wireless – a *radio that could both send and receive a signal; used by Special Duties operators and the British Army in WW2*

PEOPLE

Adolf Hitler – German dictator and leader of the Nazi Party who started WWII in hopes of growing his empire by squashing those he considered his enemies

Colonel Colin Gubbins – appointed by Churchill to form the British Resistance Organisation; later promoted to Major General and knighted for his service

Lord Haw-Haw – the British turncoat who broadcast Nazi propaganda from Germany to the United Kingdom during WWII

Neville Chamberlain – Great Britain's Prime Minister who declared the country at war with Germany on 3 September 1939; resigned 8 months later

Winston Churchill – became Prime Minister in May 1940 and led Great Britain to victory in 1945; later knighted

SLOGANS

Dig for Victory – *encouraged citizens to plant 'victory gardens' to supply food during rationing and boost morale*

Keep Mum – *don't blab about secret information, because you never know who may be listening*

Make Do and Mend – *encouraged civilians to mend old clothes rather than buy new ones, since clothes were rationed as well as food*

PROLOGUE

"Granny Ivy! Granny Ivy! There's a secret tunnel in your garden, and we found it!"

The woman sitting beside the wood stove lowered her newspaper as her little granddaughter skidded through the doorway, her face flushed and her chubby little hands black with soil.

"A tunnel, you say?" the woman asked, removing her reading spectacles with interest. "Whereabouts in the garden?"

The little girl took a deep breath, then plunged into her explanation: "It's behind the chicken shed, beside the rose trellis. We were playing hide-and-seek, and I saw it first and told the others and Dan threw a pebble down it and it just kept going and going all the way to the middle of the whole earth, or maybe China! We heard it hit the bottom!"

Her grandmother suppressed a smile. "I see. And what's happened to your hands?"

"We tried to dig all around the tunnel so we could see

where it went to, but then Danny's shovel hit something hard under the ground, and I told him he shouldn't dig anymore, because what if it *was* the middle of the earth, and he said that was silly, but I said it wasn't and I was going to tell."

Though Granny Ivy's curly hair was grey with age, she stood with a youthful spring. "I'm glad you did, Lila. I'd like to see this secret tunnel for myself!"

Lila took her grandmother's hand in one of her smudged ones and led her to the door, where they both pulled on pairs of wellies. Granny snatched down a camping lantern from a hook before stepping out into the sunlit garden.

Behind the henhouse, an older girl sat on her heels, digging up dirt with a chicken feed bucket and dumping it in a heap, while the oldest of the three—a boy of thirteen or so—went at the hole with a shovel. When he saw his little sister returning victorious with Granny Ivy in tow, he stopped, awkwardly holding the shovel behind his back. The older girl dropped her bucket and bit her lip.

Granny Ivy placed her fists squarely on her hips. "You've done quite a job here, the three of you."

The boy diverted his eyes to his soil-covered shoes. "We should've asked first before we dug up your garden. Sorry, Granny Ivy."

"Well, I'm sorry too, Danny." She paused, and two oldest children exchanged an anxious glance. "Sorry you've wasted so much time and effort digging up that hole in this hot sun when there's a *much* easier way into that tunnel!"

The three children looked at one another, astonished.

The corner of Granny Ivy's mouth turned up in a mischievous grin. "Yes, I know all about it. It's a secret I've kept for many, many years now, since I was a girl growing up in this house. But as you've discovered it, I think it only fair I show you the entrance."

The middle girl looked dubiously over at the pipe coming out of the ground beneath the rose trellis.

"Oh no, not that, Sue." Granny Ivy chuckled. "That's what you call a dead letter drop. I'll tell you all about that presently. The *real* tunnel is all underground, beneath this hard surface you've hit on, and the best way to it is through the henhouse. Of course, we'll have to brave the chickens and probably a lot of old spiders' webs to get to it. Still care to see?"

The children nodded, all the more eager for the challenges in store.

"Good." Granny Ivy nodded once with the air of a sergeant. "Then follow me, troops."

Lila held tightly to her brother's hand as Granny Ivy forged a pathway through the flustered, squawking chickens, right to the very back of the long, dark henhouse. The children shot uncertain glances at one another as she brushed away heavy cobwebs and placed her palms against the back wall, feeling the boards up and down.

Presently, they heard her say, "Ah, that should do it, with just a little bit of elbow grease..." She wedged her old but nimble fingers into the cracks between the boards and gave a yank.

To the children's amazement, the plank lifted right off the wall, revealing a small room hidden behind. The only thing inside was a wooden bench with a hole in the middle of it.

Danny peered in, then quickly pulled back again. "Wait a minute. Is this some kind of outside toilet?"

"A privy is what we called it. Don't tell me you've never seen one?"

The children responded with a look of distaste.

"You mean people used to have to go to the loo in the henhouse?" Lila asked.

"Not usually in the henhouse, no. But everyone who lived in the country had to go outside to get to the loo in those days, unless they were very rich, like the family up at Ashbury Park. But this particular privy is a special one."

"Erm, Granny Ivy..." Danny had a deeply concerned look in his eye. "The entrance to the secret tunnel isn't through the loo… is it?"

"No…" Granny's eyes twinkled, "and yes." She turned to face the privy bench so they couldn't see her private smile. She was enjoying every moment of her grandchildren's horrified suspense. "Now just you watch."

She reached up, took hold of a metal hook on the back wall, and gave it a twist to the left. Lila gave a little gasp as something hidden in the wall went *click*.

Granny turned to Danny. "Now then, my strapping young man, just get a grip under the lip of that bench and give it a good shove upwards. It's likely to be a bit sticky after all these years, so don't hold back. Yes, that's it. Now hoist!"

Danny pushed with all his might, his cheeks blown out and his face going purple, until at last, the whole bench began to lift slowly upwards with a wonderful, mechanical sound of squeaky ropes and pulleys.

"Now you can let go and stand back," Granny instructed. The bench had nearly risen right up to the privy ceiling.

The four of them stood back, Danny panting and the girls gawking as if their brother had just cracked open a loaded treasure chest. Where the bench had been was now a square hole in the floor with a ladder descending into the dense, musty darkness below ground.

Lila tugged at Granny's trouser pocket, her eyes wide. "Do the chickens know they've got a secret tunnel in their house?"

Granny clucked. "Well if they ever suspected it, they never told a soul. Chickens are many things, but tell-tales is not one of them. Now, I think I had better go first down the hatch and give you the 'all clear' before you follow." She clicked on the lantern she'd brought along and set it down to one side of the hole before reaching right out over the empty space to grab the top of the ladder.

"Careful, Granny!" Dan put a hand out to steady her, but she stepped down onto the top rung with the ease of an acrobat.

"Never you worry, my dears. I've been going up and down this ladder in my dreams for the past fifty-odd years. It's eight steps down, if my memory is true."

Granny's fluffy grey hair disappeared into darkness, and for a moment, the children held their breath, hearing only strange shuffling noises. Then, at last, came Granny's voice with a cavernous echo.

"Just pass me down that lantern, would you, Danny?"

He did, and after a moment's inspection, she gave the 'all clear' for the children to follow her down the ladder while she held up the lantern for them. Once they'd all reached the rock-hard floor below, they stood gazing at one another's up-lit faces, their breath hanging in visible puffs from the heavy atmosphere. Both Lila and Susan clung on to Granny's arms. It was shockingly musty and humid underground after they'd all been soaking in the clear summer sunshine just minutes before.

Granny held the lantern aloft, casting its light from wall to wall, which were made of thick cinder blocks and wiggly sheets of rusted metal that domed over their heads like a train tunnel.

"Why, bless my soul. It's hardly changed! Except for a few extra resident spiders, of course."

"It's enormous down here! It's at least as big as the whole henhouse," Susan exclaimed, striking up enough bravery to venture several steps away from Granny. "And look, there's a table over here, and some benches hanging from chains in the wall! And a rusty old kettle... and some candles! Granny, did someone live down here?"

"Well, not exactly *live,* though we spent enough time down here for a season."

"Who's *we*?" Susan asked.

But before Granny could answer, Dan—who had come to inspect the table for himself—called out, "There's another door behind this table!"

"Ah, well spotted!" Granny approached, moved the kettle and candles to the floor, then pocketed some old sweets wrappers littering the table top. "That Kenny." She shook her head. "He always did love his pineapple creams." Once the table was cleared, she folded it and benches against the wall. "The room we're in now is called the Map Room, but the most important room is in here." She turned another metal hook sticking out above the second door, then pushed the whole thing open. "This is the Radio Room."

They all piled into the much smaller room.

"But where's the radio?" Lila asked.

Granny shone the lantern light on a niche in the stone wall. "It's not here anymore, but it used to be just there. The wires for the signal went up that hole there, then right up a great big chestnut tree which used to stand just behind the henhouse, so we could send our transmissions for miles.

"And this hole down here—" Granny shone the light on a square opening at the bottom of the wall with chicken mesh over half of it, forming a kind of built-in basket. Inside it was a tennis ball. "*This* is part of the dead letter drop I mentioned to you up above. Do you remember that pipe under the rose trellis?" The children nodded. "Well, that's where someone would drop the ball, then it would come out down here, where the radio operator would pick it up." She reached into the opening for the buff-coloured tennis ball. Then, she gave it a squeeze so an invisible slit opened like a mouth. "Inside the ball would be the day's messages on special edible paper, just in case the messenger got caught and needed a quick way to get rid of the evidence."

Lila stuck her tongue out in disgust. Granny smiled and continued. "The radio operator would take them out, code them up, then transmit them over the radio."

Dan, who had studied a fair bit of history at school, was

beginning to put two and two together. "But Granny Ivy, *why* do you have a secret bunker with radios and secret message pipes in your garden? Were you some sort of spy?"

Granny made a face of pretend alarm. "Now why would you say a thing like that?" She winked.

"Look! There's a big dusty book over here!" Lila pointed excitedly to a notebook resting on a stool in the back corner. "Only, you pick it up, Granny. I'm afraid of spiders."

They all crowded around the stool. Granny took a handkerchief from her pocket and gently wiped it across the book's cover, uncovering big block letters across the front.

Lila, who had recently learned to read, traced each letter with her chubby finger. "S-O-C-K-S. Socks. Huh? A book about socks?" She scrunched up her little nose and turned to Granny with a lost expression.

"That's right. S.O.C.K.s. Special Operations Cadet Kids." Granny tapped each letter of the acronym as she said the word it stood for. Below it, a date was scribbled: *Summer 1940*.

"That's during the Second World War!" Dan exclaimed. "We just studied about it last term." He gave a little gasp as something dawned on him. "So… this is a war bunker?"

"You're getting warmer, Dan." Granny's eyes twinkled in the lantern light.

Feeling hot on the trail of some discovery, Danny egged on his grandmother. "But you said *kids*. There weren't *kids* in the war, were there? I mean, surely grownups did all the important, dangerous things." He said it as a statement, but there was a hopeful uncertainty about his tone.

"As a matter of fact," Granny answered, "it was everybody's war. Grownups and children alike. After all, none of us wanted Hitler taking over our country… our homes. We all had our part to play."

"What was it like, Granny Ivy? What was your part?" Susan asked in an awed whisper, as if they spoke of sacred things.

A soft smile formed on Granny's lips. It crinkled the corners of her eyes, which seemed to be looking not into the darkness of the room, but far, far away—into another time and place. "It was a wonderful time for us children. The adults were all too occupied to notice much what we did, so we ran completely free—waging our own war, fighting make-believe battles with the Huns, collecting shells and shrapnel from the fields, watching the Spitfires' acrobatics in the sky above... The war opened the world up to us. Not one of us was ever the same after that first summer."

She paused and took a deep breath, as if returning to the present moment from her distant journey to the past. The faces of her grandchildren were solemn, their eyes bright and hungry for more.

"What I am about to tell you," Granny began in a most confidential tone, "I have never told a soul in all my life, and only a very few people living today know anything about it. But I think it's a tale that deserves telling, and I hope you will remember it all your lives. But," she eyed them pointedly, "you must first take the S.O.C.K.s oath, just as I did when I was a girl. Do you agree to it?"

The children all nodded, and Susan gulped loudly.

"Good. Raise your right hands and place your left over your hearts. Your other left hand, Lila dear. There you are. Now repeat after me." Gingerly, Granny peeled open the notebook's cover. The pages, brittle as dried autumn leaves, crackled at her touch. She found a page titled 'S.O.C.K.s OATH' and read it out—line-for-line—pausing after each so the children could repeat it:

S.O.C.K.s OATH

On my honour, I will do my best
To do my duty to God, King, and Country;
To defend Great Britain against her enemies;
To keep myself alert and ready for action;
Never to desert my post or betray
my comrades-under-cover.
Cross my heart
hope to die
Stick a needle in my eye
(Kenny added that ↑)

Once done, she nodded. "Well then, troops, it's a long story to tell, and I fancy telling it in the light of day with a glass of lemonade at hand. What do you say? Up and out!"

1

A NOT-SO-HAPPY BIRTHDAY

2 SEPTEMBER 1939

"But it isn't fair! How come Ivy gets to stay up with the grown-ups? She's just a kid."

Ivy resisted the urge to stick her tongue out at her little brother. That was childish behaviour, and she was no longer a child.

Mother knelt down to wipe the birthday cake sugar from Kenny's top lip. "It is fair, and you'll think so too when you turn thirteen and are allowed to stay up for the nine o'clock news. Now up to bed. Esme, you too. And tell your father goodnight."

Ivy watched the two youngest Briscoes—'the Imps', as she called them—hug their father in turn before moping up the stairs to bed, Esme dragging her tatty old stuffed dog behind her. How strange it felt not to join them in the bedtime procession as she had done for the past twelve years.

It had always been a Briscoe family tradition that once a child turned thirteen, he or she incurred the distinguished privilege of sitting up with the 'grown-ups' for the nine o'clock news. This elite club of grown-ups included Father and Mother and the two eldest Briscoe children. Ivy's eldest brother Ernie was 'eighteen going on forty', as Father liked to boast, and Vera was in the blossom of sweet sixteen-hood.

Ivy had looked forward to her initiation as one of the grown-ups for yonks, but now she felt strangely shy as she took her seat on the settee beside the wireless. Her father offered her a 'nightcap'—a tiny glass of sherry, just enough to taste and no more. She looked at Vera beside her, absently twirling a lock of her perfect, honey-coloured hair whilst flipping through the pages of *Women's Illustrated*. Ivy wrinkled her nose up at the pictures of doe-eyed fashion models. She averted her eyes to Ernie, who sat across from her with a newspaper draped elegantly across his knee, sipping his sherry with poise. She tried to sip likewise, feeling suddenly very out of place, as if she'd snuck into a private club with its own secret code of behaviour she didn't know. Right on cue, Ernie looked up from his paper and gave her a wink as he lifted his glass.

"Cheers, little sis." Ernie always knew how to make her laugh at her own awkwardness.

Once their mother returned from putting the little ones to bed, Dr. Briscoe clicked on the wireless and took his seat in the big armchair beside the hearth. There were some silly adverts, a song or two, and then at last the newscaster's voice broke through, fast and furious. One word repeatedly struck against Ivy's ear like iron on an anvil: *Hitler, Hitler, Hitler.*

That name had been on every newspaper headline and every broadcast, poisoning conversations in the streets, shops, and church. Now here it was again. Like a bad omen, it cast a shadow wherever it was uttered. As the broadcaster announced that Hitler had positioned the German army to invade Poland, that eerie shadow stole into the room until all the fun of the evening—the birthday cake, Ivy's new riding boots, Kenny's jokes and all the laughter—seemed a million miles away. Ivy felt a truly deep sense of sympathy for the Polish now that Hitler had not only threatened to invade their country, but had also gone and spoiled her thirteenth birthday.

When, at last, the sombre voice on the radio gave way to a jingle about Velvex toilet paper, Mrs. Briscoe stood up and angrily clicked it off. "Lord help us, I should be glad never to hear that odious man's name mentioned again for as long as I live." Her Irish accent always became more sing-songy when she was flustered.

"I'm afraid, my dear," Dr. Briscoe replied in his soft, steady tone, "that we are only just beginning to hear mention of that name." He sipped his sherry and nodded to himself. "It's come to it now. Great Britain is on the brink."

On the brink of what? Ivy wanted to ask. But everybody had gone so solemn, she held her tongue, not wanting to sound the ignorant baby. Instead, she lay awake that night, tossing and turning in bed as her mind roved over the enigmatic words of the newsreader.

The next day was Sunday. As Dr. Briscoe had to visit several of his patients that afternoon, the Briscoe family rose early and walked up to the Ferny Hill parish church for the early communion service. Back home, the family sat silently around the dining table, eating their scrambled eggs and thick brown bread with butter. A stiffness like a freshly starched school shirt fell over the room. It affected all of them; even jovial Kenny sat silently, swinging his legs and looking from parent to parent.

Ivy could not place where it came from. Was it the solemn words of the vicar who had warned them of trying times ahead? Or was it her father, intently reading the Sunday paper whilst smoke rings chugged from his pipe like a blustering steam engine? Or perhaps it was her mother, who gazed in a far-off way out the window and fiddled with the claddagh charm at her collarbone.

Only when the mantle clock chimed the hour, eleven o'clock, did Dr. Briscoe look up from his paper. "Have you finished, children?" He addressed the younger ones. "Shall we all move into the parlour?"

Ivy took her usual seat on the settee and hugged her knees close to her chest. Kenny and Esme wrestled with Spud, the family's Jack Russell terrier, on the hearth rug while Vera showed Mother a dress pattern she *just had to have* from her magazine. Ernie set the dial on the wireless, then took his seat in his usual armchair.

At last, radio gibberish gave way to the eleven fifteen news. All ears zeroed in as Prime Minister Chamberlain's dulcet voice came slowly and reluctantly through the speaker. The words he spoke buzzed like electricity, but Ivy couldn't quite take them in. They sounded too unreal.

"This morning the British Ambassador in Berlin handed the German Government a final Note stating that, unless we heard from them by eleven o'clock that they were prepared at once to withdraw their troops from Poland, a state of war would exist between us. I have to tell you now that no such undertaking has been received, and that consequently this country is at war with Germany."

At war? How could her country be *at war*? Dr. Briscoe had gone to war for Great Britain, but that was so many years ago! Something that happened in history, not now.

The Prime Minister droned on: "I know that you will all play your part with calmness and courage..."

Now, Ivy felt the words as if they'd been shot from an arrow straight at her. She glanced over at Ernie, who sat upright, his fists clenched. She, too, sat up a little straighter.

As soon as the radio announcer's voice signalled the end of the Prime Minister's speech, Dr. Briscoe stood and abruptly switched off the wireless. He turned to face his family, his expression grave but cool.

"But what does it mean, Father?" Vera asked, her lip quivering ever so slightly.

"It means that whatever happens, we've got to stick together and do our duty to God and country. Whatever the struggle. Whatever the cost. That goes for every one of us. If we do that, by God's grace we'll win this war against evil. Do you understand, children?"

"Yes, Father," they answered in chorus. And Ivy knew she meant it, though she hardly knew what *it* was. If her country and her family were to be at war, then she would find her part and do it with all her heart. She, Ivy Briscoe—though she wasn't a mathematics whiz like Ernie or a beauty like Vera, a comedian like Kenny or a baby doll like Esme—would find a way to do her bit and make them all proud.

2

WAR COMES TO FERNY HILL

In the weeks that followed, the war stayed at bay. Ernie returned to university for Michaelmas term. Vera travelled each day to the girls' grammar school in Tunbridge Wells and came home each evening with her bag of books, along with some new dress or lipstick she'd bought in town to show her mother. Ivy and the Imps carried on at the local village school, St Wilfrid's. As ever, Ivy stole every spare moment to do what she loved best: ride her old mare Nelly over the meadows in the crisp, autumn air.

But soon enough, that war crept its way like a thief in the night into the quiet Sussex village of Ferny Hill.

"Why, it's the Briscoe gang!" Ivy and the Imps stopped in at Sidwell's Emporium most days after school to buy sweets, but Mr. Sidwell always acted surprised to see them. "What'll you have today, you lot?"

Ivy stepped up to the counter. "Two scoops of strawberry and one toffee, please."

"Well, well, it must be a special occasion. Ice creams on a

Tuesday? That's a rare treat!" Mr. Sidwell raised an inquisitive eyebrow.

Ivy shrugged. "Not really." In fact, the occasion for the ice cream was that Sister Tabitha, the head teacher at St. Wilfrid's, had sent poor, tender-hearted little Esme into tears on the playground in front of the whole school, just because she couldn't tie her own shoes. Ivy still stewed inside at the memory of the cranky old woman's jibe: "Really, I'd have thought the daughter of a *famous* doctor would have learned to tie her own shoes by the age of seven! Or is Dr. Briscoe too busy with his work to teach you a little common sense?"

Ivy had overheard the whole thing, and she'd stormed right up to Sister Tabitha and given her as good as she'd given the little girl. "At least he taught her not to be a big bully and pick on people littler than her!" The words had torpedoed out of her mouth before she'd even considered the certain consequences.

She had paid dearly for them and spent the rest of the afternoon in solitary confinement, writing out the Ten Commandments. *It was worth it though,* she thought with a private smile, thinking back to the shocked gape on Sister Tabitha's face and the sudden (though short-lived) burst of laughter from the other children.

"Here you are." Ivy's mind returned from the memory as Mr. Sidwell passed out the ice cream cones. "That'll be one shilling, please."

Ivy stopped short before handing Mr. Sidwell the coins in her hand. *Had the price of ice cream gone up so much?* She dug deep into her pockets to pull out the last of her pocket money for the month and placed it glumly in the man's open palm. After all, a promise was a promise.

Mr. Sidwell plonked the precious coins in his cash box and chimed, "You enjoy every lick now, you hear? Those might just be the last ice creams you taste for many months to come!"

Kenny's eyes widened with horror, and he froze mid-lick to ask, "How come?"

"There's a war on, sonny! Didn't you know? Mark my words, they'll be rationing everything soon, and sweets and treats will be the first things to go."

Kenny looked down at his toffee cone as though he held the holy grail and licked it slowly and solemnly all the way down the country lane that led home.

But Mr. Sidwell's prediction of ice cream shortages was not the last shock of the day.

TOOT! Toot, Toot!

The earsplitting automobile horn made Ivy whirl around. She immediately reached out and pulled Esme off the road just in time as a whole caravan of enormous blue trucks trundled down the narrow lane. Some of the drivers rolled down their windows and gave them a friendly salute.

Kenny whooped and saluted back. He jumped up and down, trying to see inside the truck beds, but they were covered over with tarps. The three children watched as the leading truck turned right and drove through the great stone gates of Ashbury Park, the enormous old country house just across the lane from the Briscoes' home. After what seemed like an age, the last truck turned the corner.

Two men in military uniform hopped out of the back and pushed the gates closed behind them.

"Golly!" Kenny whistled through the gap in his front teeth. "This is my best day all year!" And he tossed the last bite of his ice cream happily into his mouth.

He was still grinning when they walked up the drive at their home, The Beeches, named for the giant copper beech trees that surrounded it like sentinels. He burst right through the kitchen door and wasted no time in shouting out: "Mother, Mother! The whole army has come to Ferny Hill!" while Spud danced around his ankles in adulation.

Mrs. Briscoe was up on a stepladder, hanging the new blackout curtains she'd sewn over the kitchen windows. When she turned to greet them, her smile fell into a grimace. "Esme, good heavens! What on earth is all over your face?"

"Strawberry ice cream," Esme answered innocently. "Ivy got it for us at Sidwell's."

"Mother!" Kenny butted in. "Mr. Sidwell says ice cream is running out because of the war! It's not true, is it? The Germans can't take all of it, can they?"

"I wouldn't lose sleep over it, Kenny." Mrs. Briscoe came down from her stepladder and bent over Esme with her apron to wipe away at the pink cream covering her freckled nose, mouth and chin. "Oh Ivy, what possessed you to buy ice creams so close to supper? You'll all have spoiled your appetites!"

"It was a treat, Mother," Esme spoke up in defence of her sister. "Because of what happened at school—" She stopped abruptly when she caught Ivy's wild gestures to *be quiet*. The last thing Ivy wanted was for Mother to find out about her run-in with the head teacher. Mrs. Briscoe always chided Ivy for her temper, though at least she admitted it came from her side of the family and their 'lively Irish blood'.

"And what happened at school?" Mrs. Briscoe asked, looking from Esme to Ivy with demanding eyes.

"Oh…" Ivy faltered. "It was just that…"

Esme suddenly gasped. "Oh Mother, Susie Watson's got a cat, and it's had kittens, and can't I have one, Mother, oh please?" Ivy could have kissed her scatter-brained little sister at that moment for saving her.

Vera, who had just walked in and was hanging up her coat, jumped into the conversation as if it belonged to her. "Ezzy dear, you know we can't keep a cat. Mother is allergic."

Ivy rolled her eyes. She hated it when Vera tried to sound like Mother, even if what she said was true. So what if Vera was clever and knew how to put on grown-up airs? She was still only three years older than Ivy.

Ignoring Esme's deflated pout, Vera propped herself up on the table and prattled on about her own affairs. "Did you hear, Mother? Evie Thompson's father is in the RAF, and she told me today that they're setting up a training camp right here in Ferny Hill!"

All at once Kenny leapt into the air, nearly jumping out of his skin, so eager was he to tell his tale. "We know! They nearly ran us over in the lane, and the officers saluted and everything!"

"Isn't it just a dream?" Vera continued, as if Kenny were a fly in the room. "Ferny Hill filled to the brim with handsome young men! There'll be dances, shows…" Ivy made a disgusted *ugh* which Vera decidedly ignored and carried on dreaming out loud. "Finally, something's *really* happening in this sleepy old village, and I'll hardly be around to enjoy it."

Mrs. Briscoe, who was taking a stack of plates from the sideboard, turned swiftly to frown at her daughter. "What do you mean by that?"

"Oh... well, you know. What with my studies, and exams coming up, and..."

Ivy watched her sister's lily skin turn pink as she fumbled for an answer. Vera had clearly said more than she'd meant to about something.

Just then, Dr. Briscoe came through the door. He greeted them all, then pulled Mrs. Briscoe into an embrace and scooped Esme up into his arms to plant a kiss on her now shining cheek. But Ivy couldn't help noticing how worn down he looked. For the past week, not only had he looked after his usual patients in Ferny Hill and the surrounding country villages, but he'd also had to oversee clinics in town for the men joining up for the war. Her father had never much liked talking about the Great War he had fought in... except for the parts to do with his meeting and marrying a beautiful Irish nurse at a Belgian hospital. But as to his own part, he rarely even let them look at the Victoria Cross medal he had won for bravery in battle. He kept it stashed away in a box in the top of the china cabinet.

Mrs. Briscoe must've noticed the look in her husband's eyes as well. She promptly clapped her hands together to call the troops to order. "Right. Get upstairs and wash up for supper, the lot of you."

As Vera swished and the Imps walloped up the stairs,

Ivy lingered just outside the kitchen doorway, where she could hear her parents' hushed voices.

"What's ailing your mind, Noel?"

Dr. Briscoe gave a long sigh. "Johnny Emmett joined up today. Infantry. He'll be shipped out to France by Christmas."

"Johnny? But he's only a boy! Only our Ernie's age! Surely there are enough men—"

"They *are* men, Kathleen. You know as well as I: the last war was fought by boys their age, and this one will be no different."

"Those poor Emmetts. What anxiety Lorna must be suffering." Mrs. Briscoe paused. "But what about Ernie? Oh, Noel, you don't think he'll have to go?"

"It's not a matter of having to, Kathleen. If I know Ernie, he'll want to go."

Ivy walked up the stairs in a daze. She washed her hands and her face in the basin without even feeling the wetness, then gazed blankly into the mirror, not bothering to try and tame the wild brown strands that had managed to escape her plaited pigtails. Ivy never gazed into the mirror to admire her own reflection; that was Vera's pastime. Ivy knew well enough she would never be rewarded with the pleasing picture of perfect skin, brilliant blue eyes, and glowing honey locks the mirror offered her sister. Her own reflection had always disappointed her: freckles, frizzy hair, cheeks that still clung to their puppy fat even though the rest of her body had thinned out like salt-water taffy that's been stretched. But now she looked, hoping her reflection wouldn't let her down in this moment of need.

Her own plain brown eyes gazed blankly back, offering no solace at all. *But Ernie can't…* She couldn't say the rest of the words. So far, the war had existed *out there,* across the Channel and on the wireless. It was the business of soldiers and pilots and sailors, but not her own brother—the person who, after her father, Ivy admired most in the world. She knew they would all have to play their part, but she had never imagined any of them would actually go into the fighting itself.

If anyone but her father who had said it, she'd have laughed. But Dr. Briscoe never exaggerated. Against her own better judgment, she looked at the anxious face in the mirror and reassured it in a thin whisper: "It surely won't come to that. Ernie won't go to war."

3

A SPITFIRE CHRISTMAS

"Do you think Father Christmas will still visit us during the war?" Kenny asked Ivy apprehensively as the three youngest Briscoes foraged for pine cones on the forest floor. Christmas decorations were scarce that year, and Ivy had thought up the brilliant idea of making their own with a little help from the woods.

Esme, who had been using her pinafore as a basket for pine cones, lost her grip on the skirt, letting all her cones plummet to the ground. "Oh he will, won't he, Ivy?" Her little chin quivered at the horrid thought of no Father Christmas.

"Of course he will, sillies." Ivy bent down to help Esme gather her fallen cones. "It's just, he mightn't bring *as many* toys and things as usual."

"Phew!" Kenny whistled through his tooth gap. "I sure hope he can afford to bring me a pair of skates. I won't complain if that's the only thing I get," he said nobly, then added, "and a pocket knife."

"What about you, Ezzy?" Ivy asked, climbing up into a

yew tree to break off a few of its evergreen sprigs with bunches of little red berries.

"A cat that won't make Mother sneeze," Esme lisped, and skipped off down the forest path.

The final days of school before the Christmas holidays ebbed away so slowly, it felt as if they would never end. Each day, the children at St Wilfrid's practiced the Nine Lessons and Carols they were to recite for the villagers on Christmas Eve. They also practiced 'the war game'. The older children knew it was no game at all, but an air raid drill, so they would be ready if the Germans dropped poisonous gas bombs on Ferny Hill. But the teachers gave them strict instructions to pretend as if they were all having a jolly good time playing this 'game' so as not to frighten the little ones. By mid-December, they'd practiced both carols and the war game so many times that Ivy's dreams began muddling the two; one night she dreamed she was singing "Oh Tannin *Bomb*" in a gas mask, bunched up under a Christmas tree!

At last, the final day of school came, and the Briscoe children hurried home for the annual digging up of their Christmas tree. They found Dr. Briscoe already in the garden with his spade. The children helped him lift the tree out of the ground, then set it—dirty roots and all—into a great big pot.

"What's that?" Kenny asked, pointing to a heap of metal and sand bags propped against the cellar door.

"It's called an Anderson shelter, my boy. It's a cozy little place to all huddle together for safety when the air raid sirens go off," Dr. Briscoe explained, wiping his brow.

"Like a secret fort?" Kenny asked with his snaggle-toothed grin.

"Precisely. Only not entirely secret. We'll be sharing it with the Emmetts, you see."

Kenny looked a little crestfallen.

"And you shall have the privilege of helping me build it once your brother gets home," Dr. Briscoe put in, making Kenny's grin return even bigger than before.

Ernie was due home the very next day. Ivy had soldiered away all week, making paper chains and pine cone garlands. She was determined this Christmas would be cheerful and 'just like always'. The house would be lovely and Christmassy when Ernie arrived home for the holidays; they would all be together and have the merriest time.

Since the day she had eavesdropped on her parents, no more had been said by anybody about Ernie going to war... or if they did discuss it, it was never when Ivy was around to hear. But the possibility had still pestered her mind like a sore tooth. Johnny Emmett had gone, just as Dr. Briscoe said. And when her father came home from his clinics each evening, he'd rattle off a list of names to his wife—all young men whose families the Briscoes knew... young men he himself had approved as healthy and fit to go off to war.

As if that wasn't enough to unsettle the Briscoe home, Vera's secret at last came out. She announced one night at the dinner table that she had joined the Women's Auxiliary Air Force, or WAAF as they called it. They had come recruiting at the grammar school, and her professor had recommended some of the brighter girls for training to become operators. He had commended her especially. So—she informed her mother and father in her most grown-up manner—she would not return to school in January, but would leave for Oxford just after Christmas.

Mrs. Briscoe's temper flared up at this bit of information from her 'still only sixteen-year-old daughter'. But, surprisingly, Dr. Briscoe supported the idea and brought Mother around to it... only after she had done quite a lot of storming about Vera 'throwing away her future' and being 'just a child, after all'.

"It's much more important that our children do their duty than make top marks, Kathleen," he reasoned, gently but firmly. "And don't forget that you, my dear, were hardly older than our Vera when you left Ireland and volunteered in the last war. Moreover, you landed in Belgium, right in the middle of the action! Vera will only be deployed as far as an office right here in England."

"But that's just it, Noel! *I* never returned home! Or don't you recall that a dashing English doctor swept me off my feet and made me agree to be his wife before I could say no?"

Dr. Briscoe gave her one of his irresistible smiles, but she turned her back to it. "I don't doubt that mixed in with her noble sense of duty is a hope of finding a wee bit of romance all her own."

"If that were her primary aim, she could find it right here in Ferny Hill, couldn't she?" Mrs. Briscoe retorted. "But our Vera has got an ambitious spirit. She'll not settle for a lieutenant if she can have a captain."

"So long as he's a respectable captain…" Dr. Briscoe stopped short when his wife gave him one of her looks.

This storm had raged whilst Vera was out at a charity Christmas dance at Ashbury Park. By the time she came home, Mother had made her peace with the idea and spent the rest of the evening recalling tales of her adventures as a young girl in the war effort.

Ivy had gone to bed that night feeling grumpy. It was too unfair. Vera got to go off and do something *real* for the war. Meanwhile she, little Ivy, would be stuck at school playing 'the war game' with babies. If only she were sixteen…

But I wouldn't be just a stupid old operator, she told herself. *I'd do something* really *important.*

Her grumpiness disappeared the next morning when she sat up and remembered what day it was: the twenty-third of December. Ernie was coming home! Like Christmas come early, there he was, just after dinner. He admired the homemade decorations to the Imps' glowing pride—and Ivy's too, though she tried not to show it. That night, they all roasted chestnuts; and on Christmas Eve morning, they ice skated on Leg O'Lamb pond on Emmett's Farm. Nobody bothered that there weren't as many chocolates or electric lights. The Briscoes were all together. It felt like everything was going to be just fine.

In the afternoon, Dr. Briscoe went on his rounds, and Ernie and Kenny were given the task of digging the new Anderson shelter. Ivy wanted to help, but Mrs. Briscoe had given her a dozen jobs to do in the kitchen—silly jobs like pressing the good napkins and polishing the special silver that only came out at Christmas and Easter. Vera was rolling pastry and going on and on about the dance at Ashbury Park, and what Colonel So-and-So's wife had worn, and how many times she'd been asked to dance... Ivy could listen no longer. As soon as she'd polished the last silver teaspoon, she burst out the back door without waiting for further instructions and found the boys in the back garden.

The shelter, a domed metal hut dug halfway into the ground, was nearly finished. She happily joined in patting down cold handfuls of earth all around it. Kenny, every inch covered in dirt from his sandy hair to his boots, was in the middle of telling Ernie how he had earned a second-class badge at Scouts and was *sure* to earn his first class before he turned eleven.

"What about you, Ivy?" Ernie welcomed her into the conversation. "Going to be the first girl in Sussex to earn first class in Scouts?"

Before Ivy could answer, a rattling, humming sound turned all their eyes towards the sky. It grew louder until Ivy felt her bones rattling; then two planes ripped through the clouds, trailing long ribbons of smoke behind them.

"Spitfires!" Ernie shouted over the noise as the planes doubled back, then swooped, then dove in unison like barn swallows at dusk. Kenny waved and hurrahed until the planes sputtered off towards the horizon; then he ran to the house to tell the others, leaving Ivy and Ernie still squinting up into the sky.

"Can you imagine what it must feel like sitting in that cockpit, flying at that speed? Like riding the wind!" Ernie answered his own question.

Ivy closed her eyes and tried to imagine it. "It must be like galloping, only even better."

"I'll say!" Ernie continued painting the picture. "Facing the enemy head-on in the air, a battle in the sky. It's the stuff of ancient mythology, isn't it?"

Ivy's imagination turned sinister. She pictured the German pilots, their inhuman, bloodthirsty faces glaring behind cockpit glass. She looked at Ernie, his jaw set, his wistful eyes still fixed on the planes, which were now mere specks against the wintery, white sky.

Suddenly, like coming out of a dream, he turned, caught her eye, and smiled. "Say, sis, how about a Christmas Eve ride after supper, just you and me?"

Ernie and Ivy were the two best riders in the family, and the only ones who owned their own horses. Ernie had coached Ivy when she first learned. It had always been their special thing.

"Sure, I'll race you. Nelly's been getting a lot more exercise than Napoleon since you've been off at university. Hope you're prepared to eat humble pie for pudding!"

"I'm sure you two will be a speeding bullet, just like those Spitfires." Ernie tossed a clump of dirt at her as they headed for the house.

It was a glorious night for riding. The clouds had cleared so that the gibbous moon bathed the meadow in a soft blue veil of light. The frosty air filled Ivy's lungs as she lowered her head and soared.

"Come on, Nell. Don't let up!"

She gently kicked at the mare's broad sides, white and glowing in the moonlight. When she could see the oak tree on top of the hill, she threw a glance over her shoulder. Ernie, almost invisible in the darkness on his black steed Napoleon, was gaining on them. With a last all-out sprint, she and Nelly thudded past the tree, their finish-line, just ahead of her brother, then pulled up to a trot beside him.

As the two siblings and their horses caught their breath, panting great puffs of smoke into the air, the rumble of plane engines once again shattered the silent night. This time it was three, and they streaked across the sky directly over the riders' heads. Off across the hills, in the direction the planes flew, enormous blimps hovered like giant sea cows over the pastures.

"What are they?" Ivy asked.

Ernie's eyes were still glued to the planes, but at Ivy's question, he turned them towards the eerie, white giants. "They're barrage balloons. Odd seeing them hovering there in the dark, isn't it?"

"But what are they for?"

"Well, as I understand, they're there to stop enemy planes from landing on open fields. Of course, they won't stop an invasion, but at least they'll make it a little more difficult."

"But do you really think Hitler will try to invade us?"

"He'll try, all right. But he won't succeed. Not if I can help it!" Ernie cast her a smile of such pure hope and confidence, Ivy almost believed he could stop a German invasion single-handedly if he wanted.

She stroked Nelly's strong, sinewy neck for courage. "You're going, aren't you?" She looked up and was surprised to see the apology in his eyes.

"I wanted you to know first, Ivy. Even before Mother and Father. I've joined up with the RAF. Can you believe it? Me, a pilot!" he said with Kenny-like enthusiasm.

"But you... you've never flown." It was all she could think to say. Picturing her brother in his college sweater and his mop of messy hair behind a glass cockpit was difficult.

"Well no, not yet. But they teach you all that in training, see. I start right after Christmas."

There was a moment's silence between them. Ivy carried on twisting bits of horse mane around her fingers; she couldn't look her brother in the eye, couldn't let him see how little and lost she felt. At last she muttered, "But... but wouldn't you rather wait until they call you? I mean, you don't *have* to go..." She stopped, ashamed of what a coward she must sound.

"I *want* to go, Ivy. I *want* to do my duty. I *want* to defend our family, our home. Just think of all the glorious tales of war throughout history, of all the men who've fought to protect this land. Wellington, Nelson... why, even Father! And now it's happening in our time. Hitler looks across the Channel at us and thinks we're just a bug to be squashed. If we don't stand and fight, who will? Don't you see, Ivy? This is *our* hour."

While he spoke, her confused heart stirred and began to beat faster, and finally gave a surge when he said her name —as if she was part of this glorious war as much as he was. She looked up at her brother. Perched on top of Napoleon, his head held high, eyes glistening in the moonlight, Ernie was like a knight... like the portraits of victorious generals of old. And though part of her still wanted to rant and scream "No, you can't! It's not fair!", she didn't. She swallowed back her protests and nodded.

Ernie's familiar smile returned as he reached out to gently grip her shoulder. "That's a brave girl. I knew you'd understand."

She did understand. Ernie had to go. But it still ached.

4
THE BRISCOES AT WAR

Just two weeks later, the Briscoe family stood on the station platform, a heap of tears and soppy kisses. Ernie had traded in his old tweed trousers and college sweater for a smart RAF uniform, and even combed his hair down. He looked just like a grown man, but he still put on his old sloppy boyish grin when he rustled Kenny's hair and scooped up Esme to plant a big kiss on her tear-moistened cheek. Last of all, he clasped Ivy by both her shoulders and gave her an appraising look.

"Buck up, would you, sis'? You mustn't be too jealous simply because I get to see Paris and maybe even Berlin and you've never been as far as London. I'll send you a post-card, after all."

She knew he was teasing, trying to get a smile out of her. Reluctantly, she gave in, and he pulled her into a back-breaking embrace. "That's a sport. I know I needn't tell you to be brave. You always are." He gave her a light knock on the chin with his fist, then slung his knapsack over his shoulder and turned to board the train.

As Ivy waved to her brother and watched the train grow smaller and smaller until it faded into the unknown, her heart was a muddle of immense pride and intense pain. But she wouldn't allow the thought of never seeing Ernie again to have even a little space in her head. She would fight off the fear by staying busy and doing her bit.

I will be brave, Ernie, she silently promised.

The very next week, what was left of the family returned to the platform, this time to see Vera off. She had traded in her lipstick for a smart WAAF uniform which made her look ten years older. Ivy was surprised to feel a great big lump climbing up her throat when Vera hugged her goodbye.

That night, Ivy crawled into bed with an empty feeling in the pit of her stomach. She rolled over and stared at Vera's empty bed, its frilly pillows still showing the imprint of the giant hair rollers her sister insisted on sleeping in each night to give her hair 'body'. Ivy had never understood that. After all, why would anybody wish for curls? Nature had bestowed them on her, and she'd have given anything to swap them for a nice, easy bob.

She had never understood a great many things about Vera—like why she had recently taken to wearing scent. Ivy couldn't stand the stuff. It made her sputter and gag every time she walked into the bedroom after Vera had splashed it on. But now, somehow, she missed its fragrance and sniffed the air, hoping to catch some little lingering waft of it.

Just like the Briscoe family, the final days of 1939 seemed to flutter away like the last, clinging leaves of the old beech trees. 1940 kicked off as one of the coldest Januaries on record; yet inside Ivy, the desire to *do* something—first kindled when the war began—grew into a burning, steady blaze. Not only had Ernie and Vera found their places in the war effort, but everyone else who'd stayed behind in Ferny Hill had a part to play as well. Mrs. Briscoe volunteered as an ambulance driver and helped Dr. Briscoe cover his rounds when he was busy at the clinics. Farmer Emmett had volunteered as an air raid warden, and Mrs. Emmett ran a canteen for the officers stationed at Ashbury Park. Even Father Bertram and some of the sisters from St Wilfrid's had been spotted manning the big anti-aircraft guns during an air raid drill.

The new school term began with a chapel service. Father Bertram talked to the children about the war being 'everybody's war'. It was a very grand talk for a group of runny-nosed village children. Ivy felt her heart drumming when the priest told them in all seriousness that "defending democracy is the job of every single one of you." She only wished he had told them *how* they were to defend democracy.

In their lesson afterwards, each pupil shared what his or her family was doing to aid the war effort. Susie Watson's parents were 'digging for victory' by planting a turnip patch. Ronald O'Shea's were salvaging paper. For the Millers, it was collecting aluminium pots. Caroline Tufts shared proudly that she and her mummy had mended all of her daddy's old socks so he needn't buy new ones as long as the war lasted.

"Well, Ivy?"

Ivy's head jerked up. She had been so absorbed in watching a plane out the window, wondering whether it was the sort Ernie was learning to fly, she hadn't even noticed it was her turn to share.

"Hmph," was all Sister Tabitha's reply to Ivy's silence.

At the withering look on Sister Tabitha's face, Ivy went red-hot and sat up straight in her chair. "My brother is going to be a pilot in the RAF, my sister is a WAAF operator, my mother drives an ambulance, and my father makes sure the troops are healthy," she rattled off defiantly.

Sister Tabitha, who had been carrying a grudge ever since her last run-in with Ivy, was not to be so easily silenced. In her shrill voice that sounded like a crow with laryngitis, she responded, "You have told me what your brother and sister and parents are doing. I believe the question was, 'What are *you* doing to help your family and country win the war?'. Perhaps some of us are too preoccupied with our own thoughts to bother."

Before Ivy could fire back, the head teacher clapped her hands and said, "Off you go, children. Get into your age groups. It's time for the war game."

Ivy stewed inside for the rest of the morning. It was as if Sister Tabitha had known exactly which button to push to turn on Ivy's temper full throttle, and she had pushed it with satisfaction.

I'll show her, Ivy assured herself a hundred times. *But how?*

The first flicker of an idea came at midday. On Mondays, the sisters collected money from each child for that week's school dinners. All the pupils gathered as close to the big pot-bellied stove as they possibly could for warmth as Sister Ursula took out the bucket.

"This week, we'll also be taking a charity collection," Sister Ursula explained in her mousy voice. "It's for the Spitfire fund, helping our government to build lots of new airplanes for the war, so I hope you'll all be very generous."

As the plate passed around, coins plonking one after the other, the idea plonked into Ivy's head. She didn't want to 'dig for victory' or salvage paper and pots, or 'make do and mend' old socks, or any of the mundane jobs that children did. But perhaps she *could* raise money—lots and lots of it—to help build Spitfires! It wasn't exactly brave, but at least it was more important than planting turnips.

The coins continued to plonk, and Ivy imagined herself high on a platform, receiving a medal for single-handedly raising enough money to buy a whole squadron of Spitfires. She imagined Ernie sitting in the front row, applauding her.

Ivy heard not a word of lessons that afternoon. Her mind was too busy roaming over a hundred different ways to make money.

5

A GOOD IDEA GONE BAD

"A bake sale? Whatever put that idea into your mind?" Mrs. Briscoe eyed her middle daughter suspiciously. Previously, Ivy's few half-hearted attempts at baking had all ended in disaster. Even Spud had turned up his nose at her Eccles cakes.

"It's for the Spitfire fund. And don't worry. I won't be doing any of the baking. We'll ask for contributions."

"Contributions from whom?" Mrs. Briscoe crossed her arms over her chest as if to say, *Don't even think about it.*

Ivy had her answer ready. "From Mrs. Emmett. She already bakes for her canteen, so I'll just ask her to bake a bit extra to donate to the cause."

"Ivy Briscoe, Lorna Emmett is a generous woman, but you know she's also wildly busy running that farm and the canteen. If she agrees to this notion of yours, I expect you to repay the favour by putting in some hours milking the cows and gathering eggs." She turned back to the pot she'd been scrubbing, then turned again to add, "And I suppose I can throw together some jammy biscuits to contribute to your sale."

Ivy grinned. She knew her mother to be as competitive as Ivy herself, and not to be outdone in generosity by Mrs. Emmett.

The next task was to convince the Imps to help her get all the cakes and biscuits up to the village common, where she would set up her stall. She found them building a tent in their bedroom and tried to make the prospect as appealing as she could. Esme was over the moon to help, but Kenny required some negotiation.

"I can't help. I have to go to Scouts. If I miss, I might not get first class by the spring jamboree."

"But isn't helping others part of being a First Class Scout?" Ivy pointed out. "And what sort of charity could be more important than building Spitfires for the war?"

Kenny cocked his head to one side and thought about this for a moment. "Can we keep the money in a bank account with my name on it?" he asked eagerly.

Ivy was a little taken aback by the question. "What for?"

"I have to have at least a sixpence savings in a bank account before I can get my first class badge."

Ivy struck out her hand. "Fine."

"Yippee!" Kenny gave the hand two stiff jerks, up and down.

The next morning, Ivy and Kenny passed through the hedge that separated The Beeches from Emmett's Farm. Mrs. Emmett had promised her a rum cake, a batch of scones, and one of her famous cherry tarts as contributions to the bake sale. As they came around the front of the house, a most unexpected sight stopped them in their tracks. A truckload of girls—all about Vera's age or older, in city dress and even high-heeled shoes—was unloading on the Emmetts' front lawn.

"Hi there, Ivy. Kenny," Farmer Emmett greeted them. "Come to see our army, have you?"

"What sort of army is *that*?" Kenny asked Farmer Emmett, more stunned than disappointed.

Farmer Emmett chuckled. "Women's Land Army. These fine gals have come from towns and cities to work the fields while the young men are off fighting."

There was another job taken. *Oh well, these Land Girls can have it,* Ivy thought. It was true, taking eggs from cranky hens required courage, but it was hardly going to win the war.

"But are they all going to live here with you and Mrs. Emmett?" Kenny prodded, looking from the gaggle of girls to the snug little farmhouse, then back at the girls with uncertainty.

"Lord save us, no!" The farmer put a stout hand on his belly and laughed good-naturedly. "They've all been arranged billetin' with families up in the village. No, Mrs. Emmett and I have some lodgers of our own coming to stay. Should be arriving in a few hours' time."

"Who's coming? Ow!" Kenny hopped on one foot. Ivy had kicked him. He never knew when to stop pestering people with nosy questions.

Thankfully, Farmer Emmett had the jolly disposition of old St Nicholas, as well as the round belly that shook when he laughed. "Evacuees from London!" He raised his eyebrows importantly as if he'd told them pirates were coming to lodge at the farmhouse. "And not just any! These two are the nephew and niece of the Misses Ashbury. But as they can't stay at Ashbury Park, what with all them officers shootin' off grenades and the like, the misses asked if we'd have 'em here, and of course we said we would, now Johnny's room is empty..." He trailed off; then, more to himself than the children, added, "It'll be a mercy to poor Lorna to have some lively youngsters in the house these days."

Ivy caught the unfamiliar sad note in the farmer's voice, but as she had no ready words of comfort, she said something about their mother telling them to hurry and pulled Kenny by his collar around to the farmhouse's kitchen door. He gaped all the while at the flock of females giggling in the garden.

The news of the evacuees roused Ivy's curiosity. Had Farmer Emmett not sounded so forlorn, she would've stayed longer in hopes of Kenny asking more questions about the new lodgers. She had met a few evacuees; a trickling of them had come from the coast last term, and more were due to arrive from London when school resumed that autumn. So far, the new children had been pretty ordinary, though their accents sometimes twanged.

But these new children were relatives of Meriwether and Delilah Ashbury. The two spinster sisters had inherited the huge estate of Ashbury Park when their father, an Earl, had died. Rarely did the lofty ladies make an appearance in the village; they had hired hands for all that, and Farmer Emmett oversaw their vast farmlands. The Ashburys existed in a different world to the ordinary folk of Ferny Hill. Ivy tried and found it impossible to imagine such people living in the farmhouse next door.

The kitchen was empty. Mrs. Emmett was busy

passing out coveralls to the girls in the garden, but Ivy and Kenny followed their noses and found the puddings easily enough, all laid out and still steaming on the sideboard.

"Thank you, Mrs. Emmett!" Ivy called out to the farmer's wife as they passed back through the hedge in a balancing act of baked goods.

Back in the kitchen at The Beeches, Ivy gave orders to the Imps. "Now, you two arrange these in the crates while I go to the cellar for the folding table." Kenny and Esme saluted.

A few minutes later, after wrestling her way around a hat stand covered in old horse riding kit, a broken bicycle, and her father's golf clubs, Ivy finally returned triumphant from the cellar with the folding table and her mother's tartan tablecloth in tow. She had an old wooden piggy bank tucked under her arm for collecting the money. She kicked open the cellar door and nearly tripped over something lying in the corridor, which turned out to be Spud, sprawled on his side.

"Spuddy, what are you doing in the house? You're supposed to be outside." She nudged the dog with her foot, but he only cast her a resentful look and didn't budge. *Strange.* Spud was normally bursting to go outside and hunt for foxes. Ivy shrugged and dragged the table around the lethargic terrier into the kitchen.

There were the crates, still open and empty as she'd left them. The Imps had already abandoned their post. But where had all the cakes and things gone? There was nothing but clean crockery on the big wooden table. Then she noticed the kitchen door to the garden was wide open;

she could hear Kenny's whoops and Esme's giggles just beyond.

"Kenny!" She had to shout several times before her brother, pretending to be a red Indian on roller skates trying to capture a princess played by Esme, noticed her. "Where are all the puddings?"

Kenny looked at her like she'd lost her marbles. "There on the table!" He shouted back. "We were taking a break before we started working!"

Ivy ignored the nonsense of that statement and called out, "They're not there!"

Kenny skated to the open door with the princess scurrying behind him and peered in. He shrugged. "I dunno."

Ivy bit her lip, trying to sort out what could have happened. No one else was at home to have moved them. There was not a single soul in the Briscoe house except…

"Oh no."

Just as the dreadful thought entered her mind, as if on cue, Spud staggered like a drunken sailor into the kitchen, stopped right in front of the children, and spewed up an enormous pile of vomit. Ivy stared at it. There in the mess was something that looked distinctly like chunks of cherries, and it smelled strangely of rum.

"Poor Spuddy!" Esme ran and threw her arms around the dog.

"Eeeew!" Kenny shouted. Then he caught the look in Ivy's eyes, which were still fixed on the pile of dog's vomit. "Errr, don't worry. I'll clean it up!" He ran and came back double time with a mop and pail, as if that one good deed would mop out his criminal offence of letting the dog eat her bake sale.

Ivy felt the temperature rising up her neck and knew an eruption of volcanic proportion was imminent. There was only one thing to do. With her jaw tightly clenched to hold back all the things she wanted to say to Kenny, she stomped out the door, under the rose trellis, past the privy, through the garden gate that led into the paddock, and all the way to the stable. She needed to ride.

6

NEW ARRIVALS

The wonderful thing about riding was that Ivy didn't think. Whatever her troubles, they seemed to fly off her shoulders with the wind as it washed over her. She had taken Napoleon out this time—Ernie would be glad to know his horse was getting exercise—and she and the steed had galloped across three meadows at top speed, letting bits of Ivy's anger and frustration trail behind them. Finally, she slowed the horse to a canter, ready to face home and the ruins of her glorious idea.

She steered Napoleon around the edge of Emmett's sheep pasture, out into the dirt lane that ran along the other side of the farmhouse. The sheep lifted their heads as they chewed last year's sugar beets; then, unimpressed, lowered them again. A second later, they all lifted their heads with an agitated jolt as a low hum grew out of the distance. When it had grown quite loud enough for the poor beasts' fragile nerves, they bounded away from the road in unison, bleating their complaints in their retreat.

Even Napoleon started up, but Ivy managed to rein him in just in time before a very expensive-looking dark green motorcar zoomed past them. There were two people in the back seat; one of them, a boy, turned his head to look at her out the back window before disappearing the next second.

"Whoa, Napoleon." She spoke calmly to the horse, but she felt annoyed all over again. Who did those people think they were, zipping up a farm road like they were on a race track?

Probably somebody too important for their own good going off to a soirée at Ashbury Park.

She tapped Napoleon's side with her heel, and they trotted on down the lane through the muddy ruts the car had left behind.

Mrs. Briscoe was waiting for her at the door, fists poised on her hips. "Ivy Elisabeth Briscoe."

What had she done now to make Mother use her full name? *Surely, if anyone, it ought to be Kenny getting the full-name treatment.*

"You went riding without your coat? Don't you know it's below freezing out there?"

She honestly hadn't felt cold at all. "I had to go right away," she said flatly, sinking into a chair and staring blindly at the table in front of her. "If I hadn't, I'd have murdered Kenny."

Mrs. Briscoe gave her a look, but didn't scold. "Yes, I heard about that rather unfortunate turn of events." She sighed. "But you know he didn't mean it. He was only trying to help you."

Ivy opened her mouth to argue, but Mrs. Briscoe was too quick. "The Emmetts have some evacuees come to stay.

Lorna just phoned to ask if you children would go over for tea to make them feel more at home. It's a boy and a girl—about your age, I think."

How could she face Mrs. Emmett after what had happened to her baked goods? "Can't we go tomorrow?" she pleaded.

"No. You can go now. Never put off 'til tomorrow what you can do—"

"I know, I know," Ivy grumbled.

"Oh, and here you are." Mrs. Briscoe handed Ivy a large round tin. "At least Spud didn't get my jammy biscuits. You can take them over as a welcome present."

Mrs. Briscoe made Ivy wear a dress and brush her hair, which only succeeded in giving it the appearance of brown candyfloss. She attempted to scratch at her torturous woolly stockings through her coat as the three children stood outside in the cold and knocked at the farmhouse door.

"Not a *word* about *the incident*!" she hissed at the two little ones with as threatening a look as she could muster.

The door opened, and there was Mrs. Emmett, her rosy round face beaming at them. "And how did the cakes do?" she asked.

Ivy winced, but quickly transformed it into a forced smile. "Your cakes were very popular. They went down splendidly!"

"Yes!" Kenny echoed. "They got eaten right up!" Ivy jabbed him in the back to shut him up. At least they hadn't lied… not exactly.

Mrs. Emmett ushered the Briscoe children into the front parlour, which was noticeably finer than the other rooms in the farmhouse. It was homey, with comfy tartan sofas, warm lamplight, and a cabinet of little china figurine.

Esme tugged on Ivy's skirt. "We've never been in here before!"

Mrs. Emmett overheard and blushed. "We don't use it much, but it's warm if you sit close to the fire. I'll just go and tell the children you've come. They're upstairs, freshening up from their journey. All the way from London!" The way she said it, Ivy wondered if Mrs. Emmett thought London was on the moon.

The three Briscoes sat down on the sofa facing the door and waited. Ivy felt as fidgety as the two little ones. She hadn't forgotten that these newcomers were relatives of the Ashbury sisters. She was determined to act naturally, but suddenly, she couldn't remember what acting naturally looked like. Without thinking, she opened the lid of the tin she was cradling and stuffed a whole jammy biscuit into her mouth.

Just at that moment, the parlour door opened. Mrs. Emmett came through first, followed by a girl around Ivy's age and a tall, gangly boy who looked a bit older. She recognised him as the boy who had looked back at her from the car.

Panic-stricken, Ivy tried to chew the jammy biscuit quickly and swallow it before anyone could notice. But her mouth was dry, and jam and mashed biscuit stuck her tongue to the roof of her mouth like wet mortar. And now it was too late! The newcomers were crossing the room…

"Well now, why don't you make your own introductions while I go and fetch the tea. Oh, and have you brought something to share around, Ivy?"

Desperate, Ivy nodded and tried once again to gulp down the mercilessly sticky substance, but to no avail.

"How kind." Mrs. Emmett looked lovingly at all the children, smiled, and left the room.

The tall boy took a step closer and cleared his throat as if to make a speech. "Well, shall I commence the introductions, then? May I introduce my baby sister—"

The girl impatiently pushed past him and, holding her nose in the air, said, "Flora Arabella Marguerite Woodall." She made a miniature curtsey. "And my brother, Theodore Reginald Henry Woodall." Once she'd spit out that mouthful, she propped herself on the edge of a settee and primly smoothed the pleats of her skirt over her knees.

Meanwhile, Ivy—still struggling with her own mouthful—was mortified to discover that her turn had come to introduce the Briscoes. Thankfully, the boy was not done. He shook his head and said, "But never mind all of that rot. She's Flora, and you can just call me Teddy." He reached out a friendly hand.

And now Ivy's time really was up. She took the hand and made one last desperate attempt to swallow the biscuit, which was still only half-chewed. A chunk lodged itself in her throat, and she gagged. Then she doubled right over in a coughing fit, still gripping the older boy's hand!

"I say, are you alright? You there—" He signalled to Kenny. "How 'bout giving your sister a good, solid pound on the back. That's a lad. Ah, here's the tea now. Bravo, Mrs. Emmett! Just what was needed."

Through watery eyes, Ivy watched Teddy pour milk and tea into a cup and put it in her hands. "Steady on. No sugar, I'm afraid." He was gripping her elbow, helping her sit.

She sipped and sipped until the biscuit mortar at last melted away. But even when she could breathe again, Ivy did not look up from her cup. She could feel all eyes in the room boring into her... could feel rather than see a look of shocked disdain coming from the girl on the settee.

"Well, that was an eventful introduction!" Teddy's chirpy voice broke the pained silence. "But I dare say, I didn't quite catch your names."

"Alright, Ivy?" Mrs. Emmett leaned over the girl and stroked her head, disheveling the heap of curls even more.

Ivy nodded, eyes still fixed on the tea cup.

"I'll leave you all to it, then."

"Ivy, is it?" Teddy persisted.

Kenny took charge. "She's Ivy Elisabeth Briscoe, I'm Kenneth Michael Briscoe, and that's Esmerelda Grace Briscoe. But you can just call us Ivy, Kenny, and Esme. We've got another sister and brother too, but they've gone off to the war. Our brother Ernie's going to be a pilot in the RAF!"

"You don't say?" Teddy began pouring the others cups of tea and passing them around. "Ah, I love things with jam in!" he exclaimed, spotting the open tin beside Ivy. "May I?" He took a large bite out of one and plopped himself down on the settee beside his sister, jolting her momentarily out of her perfectly poised position. "Lucky chap, your older brother. Gosh, I wish the war would've had the decency to wait until I was eighteen. What's he going to fly? Fighter? Bomber?"

And now, as Kenny and Teddy jabbered on about aircraft, Ivy had the chance to really take in the newcomers.

The girl, Flora, had perfect white-blonde sausage roll

curls which spiralled down to her shoulders from beneath a little sailor's cap. Her face, complete with a pinched nose, a little strawberry of a mouth, and absurdly large blue eyes, wore a constant look of agonised boredom. She looked every bit like a porcelain doll. Ivy wondered if she broke as easily as one.

Teddy was a different story altogether. His sandy blond hair was combed into a neat quiff. His face... *well, it's not exactly handsome,* Ivy told herself. Not like Father, who everybody thought looked just like the actor Cary Grant. Teddy's ears stuck out a bit, and his nose was peppered with freckles.

But perhaps he was a *little* dashing, the way he combed his hair to one side and left his top collar buttons undone in a carefree, holiday fashion. Or maybe it was his lopsided smile, or the easy readiness in his eyes. He looked like the sort of boy who could sprint a mile with the same effort he might use to lounge with a book. True, his pleated trousers and tasseled shoes looked expensive, but at least he didn't look tight and pinched and dissatisfied with everything like his sister. Ivy had recently read the word *winsome* in a book. Something about Teddy brought it to mind.

As she tried on this thought, the boy unexpectedly caught her eye and winked at her!

"Finally come back from the dead, have you?" he teased.

Ivy suddenly became aware of her awkwardly long legs, her wild hair, her chubby cheeks, and—*O spite!*—the fact that she was blushing. How she hated to blush! "I'm fine now, thanks. It was really just a crumb gone down the wrong pipe." She hadn't meant to sound so testy, but embarrassment had made her words come out that way.

But Teddy seemed not one bit put off. "Say, here's a thought. How would you local yokels feel about showing us city kids a thing or two about life on the farm? I'm green as grass about livestock and crops, but I'm an eager student. How's about it? Shall we go now?"

Flora gave him an aghast look. "What, and leave me here all alone with these simple people?"

Now it was Ivy's turn to be shocked and Teddy's turn to blush at his sister's rudeness.

"No, nitwit. We wouldn't inflict you upon the Emmetts like that. You're coming too, so put your coat on."

Flora obstinately crossed her arms over her chest and pouted like a grumpy baby.

"She doesn't have to come if she doesn't want to," Ivy said, feeling the sooner she could be out of Flora's disdainful view, the better.

"That's right," Flora told her brother in a cringingly high voice. "And anyway, mother told us strictly not to mix with the local riff-raff, Theodore, or don't you recall?"

Ivy's temperature skyrocketed, but before she could speak, Teddy made the comeback.

"Come off your high horse, Flor. Honestly, you're as sheltered as mother's hothouse geraniums. I mix with all sorts up at school, and this lot is hardly what she meant by riff-raff."

"Oh? Let's see then." She shifted her upturned nose so she was looking right down it at Ivy. "And where do you go to school?"

Ivy's blood was already at boiling point, but she was determined Flora wouldn't have the satisfaction of tipping it over. "To St Wilfrid's. It's the village school," she answered with forced calmness.

Flora raised a disdainful eyebrow and turned triumphantly to her brother. "There, you see? *Local riff-raff.*"

Ivy pretended she hadn't heard it. "Yes, we all went to the village school, and it didn't stop my brother Ernie from getting a university place at Cambridge, or Vera from getting a scholarship to the grammar. And my father went to the local school in his day, and it didn't stop him from going to Oxford and becoming a doctor."

"Oh!" Flora squeaked. "So you're the village doctor's daughter. How quaint."

Ivy's restraint was hanging by a thread. She felt that her fist might fly out and strike Flora's snub-nosed, pinched little face at any second. Luckily, Teddy stood up right between them in the nick of time. "Oh shut it, Flora. You're a right beast. It's no wonder you haven't any friends."

Flora turned her face away with a "Humph!"

Esme, who hated upset of any kind, tugged on Ivy's sleeve and asked, "Why is Flora unhappy? Is it because she misses her mother so dreadfully?"

If Flora was touched at all by the little girl's compassion, she didn't show it; but it did seem to cool Teddy's temper a bit. With a smile at Esme, he said, "Alright, gang. Let's get a move on before the cows come home!"

They all stood up—except Flora.

"Cows?" she whimpered with a horrified look.

"It's just an expression, you old ninny," Teddy sighed.

"Then again, in this place, maybe it's not." He winked at Ivy again. She looked down quickly, pretending to struggle with one of Esme's coat buttons.

By the time they all got bundled up and out the door, the winter sky had turned a pale rose colour, and the first few stars were blinking through the boughs of the cedars and beeches. Esme ran home to her bath while the other four trudged through the crystallised grass, breathing in the icy air and puffing it out again. Nobody paid much attention to Flora, who trailed behind, squeaking and groaning with each step as if she were being made to tread over hot coals. They came to the sheep pasture fence and climbed one-by-one over a stile, but when it came Flora's turn, she stopped on the top rung and clung to the gate post.

"Oh! Look at all that mud! I'm not stepping in that!"

"Haven't you brought any boots with you?" Ivy noticed for the first time that the silly girl had come out in dainty little slippers.

"Boots? Why would I bring boots? How was I to know I'd wind up living on this miserable farm? I was *supposed* to be lodged at a manor house!"

She straddled the top rung of the stile, clinging to the fence post like it was the mast of a sinking ship, while Ivy sent Kenny to run home for her spare pair of boots. Flora grimaced as she put them on, as if they'd belonged to a leper. As they stood about, shivering and waiting for her, Teddy struck up the conversation again.

"So, Kenny tells me you're thirteen. That makes you the jam to our sandwich!"

Ivy frowned. "Beg your pardon?"

"The jam! You see, I'm fourteen—*nearly* fifteen—and Flora here's twelve, so you're squashed right in the middle, just like jam."

Flora pulled on the second boot. "Oh Teddy, how perfectly vulgar! Then again, perhaps jam suits *this lot* perfectly."

"Never mind Flora," Teddy said, giving his sister a yank on the elbow to hurry her up. "She doesn't mix much in society. Mother keeps her coddled up at home like the fragile thing she is."

"That's not true." Flora yanked her arm out of her brother's grasp.

But Teddy's remark had struck Kenny's curiosity. "But don't *you* go to school?" he asked, looking at Flora.

She shook out her curls. "*I* have a governess."

"But do people really still keep governesses?" Ivy asked, trying not to sound particularly rude. "I thought that was only in the olden days!"

"Lots of people in *our* society do. *We* like to maintain the olden ways, for if we didn't, England would go to the dogs. That's what my mother says."

"I love dogs!" Kenny shouted. "We've got a smashing dog called Spud. He can stand on his front paws. Oh Ivy, can't we take them back to The Beeches so they can meet Spud?"

"No thank you," Flora butted in curtly.

Teddy rounded on his sister. "Oh, pish-posh. Why don't you go? No need to stick around and make yourself a nuisance, after all. You'll tire your poor delicate self right out."

Flora opened her pouty lips as if to retort; then clenched

them tightly closed, twirled on the spot, and stomped off towards the farmhouse, her golden ringlets springing after her with every step.

Ivy's eyes followed Flora as she struggled over the stile and marched across the lawn. As they resumed their trek into the sheep pasture, she turned to Teddy. "Is she *always* like that?"

"What, that? Oh no, she's rarely *that* charming. She's just especially prickly today because, well, it was true what she said. We weren't actually expecting to stay here—with the Emmetts, I mean. Our mother had arranged for us to stay with our aunts up at Ashbury Park, but then the Royal Air Force turned up there, so we got the boot and landed here on the farm. Personally, I couldn't be more chuffed! Who wouldn't want to stay on a real farm? You know, get the whole evacuee experience? It's the next best thing to actually being in the war, I suppose."

Ivy smiled. However horrid and insulting Flora had been, Teddy made up for it with his eagerness to be pleased with everything and everyone he met. Ivy looked at the lanky boy happily breathing in the country air and thought how surprising it was that she should have something in common with an Ashbury. Teddy was the only other person her own age she'd met who wanted to *do* something for the war—something big.

"Do you really want to go off and fight?" she asked, fascinated.

"Do I ever!" he answered without a second thought. "I plan on joining up with the Army the day I turn eighteen. I'm already a cadet sergeant with the Eton College Officers Training Corps."

"Eton? Is that where you go to school?" Ivy knew about Eton. It was where important people sent their boys so that they too would become important people when they grew up.

"That's right."

"But couldn't you have stayed at school? I mean, Eton's safe enough from the bombs, isn't it?"

"Sure I could've. But with loads of our tutors joining up to the war, education's on a bit of a hold, you see. And now they're billeting *girls* from the grammar…" He trailed off, clearing his throat before continuing. "Not that there's anything wrong with girls. Only, one gets used to his school being all lads after a spell and doesn't like to see it change so. But I suppose the tides of the world are changing now, and we all must ride them out."

Ivy, not quite following Teddy's poetical speech, asked, "So, your parents sent you here because of girls at your school?"

"Heavens, no!" He laughed heartily. "That's nothing to do with it really. Mother and Father sent me to look after *that* piece of work mostly." He gestured over his shoulder in the direction in which Flora had stomped off. "Mum's gone on tour with our father to North Africa—he's a general, you see. And she didn't want Flora staying on her own here. As you've seen, she is as delicate as a spider's web. Sticky as one, too."

"So where will you go to school now?"

"He can come to St. Wilfrid's with us!" Kenny, who had been occupied with sneaking up behind sleeping sheep, rejoined the conversation.

"Well yes, that is the idea. The priest… what's it? Oh

yes, Father Bertram. He's going to oversee my independent studies. And Flora... well, what she doesn't know yet won't hurt her."

"What doesn't she know?" Kenny asked.

"She's going to the village school with you lot."

7
ENEMIES AND ALLIES

In the days following the Woodalls' arrival in Ferny Hill, Ivy didn't forget about her fundraising scheme for the war, though the pair of them did prove a distraction in their different ways. Ivy found herself at war with Flora, but at least she had gained an ally in Teddy.

It was the fifteenth of January, the first day Teddy and Flora were to come to St. Wilfrid's School. Teddy, used as he was to the pomp of Eton, could hardly wait to experience 'quaint' village school life. But Ivy was bracing herself for the certain drama that would unfold if Flora refused to come. In fact, she was half-expecting the telephone call when it did come that morning as the Briscoe children sat eating their breakfast.

"Why good morning, Lorna," Mrs. Briscoe answered. "Oh dear, how perfectly dreadful. The poor lamb. Yes, of course. I'll send him right over. Not at all."

Ivy, still finishing her slice of toast and marmalade, looked up to hear what her mother had to say about the 'poor lamb' next door.

"Noel!"

Dr. Briscoe, having his coffee as usual in his armchair in the sitting room, set down his paper. "My dear?"

"You'll have to go right over to the Emmetts'. Lorna says the little Woodall girl is in a terrible way. I'll send Ivy with you to cheer her up."

Ivy rolled her eyes. It would be easier to cheer up a viper whose nest had just been robbed.

Flora lay groaning in the Emmetts' best guest room bed under fresh chintz linens, a hot water bottle on her forehead. Dr. Briscoe pulled up a chair beside her and took her wrist between his fingers and thumb, checking her pulse. Mrs. Emmett stood in the doorway, wringing her hands. Ivy and Teddy observed from the foot of the bed, passing unimpressed looks back and forth with each of Flora's sensational groans.

"Is it mumps? Measles? The black death?" Flora asked shrilly and with a great show of head-tossing and eyelash-batting. "If I should die, Teddy, tell Mother it was all because of these awful, contaminated living conditions. She should never have sent me here! In fact, someone should contact her now, before it's too late!"

To Ivy's relief, Dr. Briscoe jabbed a thermometer in the girl's mouth, shutting her up for a minute at least. After checking the result and performing several other little checks, the doctor clipped his bag shut and stood up. "I see nothing wrong with you, Miss Woodall. You're as healthy as a horse."

The next-to-dead act fell off at once. Sitting upright, Flora shouted, "What do you mean, nothing wrong? Why, I —" She caught herself and slouched back down, letting her head roll back against the pillow. "I'm as good as in the grave, I tell you."

Ivy and Teddy exchanged another look.

"What I suggest," Dr. Briscoe continued, unmoved, "is a good breakfast and a brisk walk to school. That should cure you of any lingering fatigue."

Flora scowled but said nothing.

"I don't suffer malingerers, Miss Woodall. It would do you no good being shut up like an invalid when you're not one."

"Fine, then," the girl snapped. She wasn't giving up so easily. "I have religious reasons for not going. I'm not Catholic. It would be against my principles to go to a school run by nuns."

"I'm not a Catholic either," Dr. Briscoe responded cheerfully. "My wife is Irish Catholic. I'm Anglican. My children attend a Catholic school and an Anglican church on Sundays. I think you'll find it'll do no harm to your principles. It may even strengthen them."

Teddy looked from Dr. Briscoe to Ivy, astounded. "To think! Centuries of Britain's religious wars brought to harmony under the Briscoe family roof." He thrust his hand out to Dr. Briscoe. "You really are a marvel, Doctor." Ivy could see her father holding back a laugh as he shook the boy's hand.

From downstairs in the sitting room, they could all hear Flora stomping across the floor above. At least she was getting ready, even if she insisted on doing so like an angry rhinoceros.

"You were right to call, Lorna," Dr. Briscoe assured the farmer's wife. "The girl is in a bit of shock being so far from home, that's all. What I prescribe is patience and a good dose of friendship." Ivy looked down at her hands, but she knew her father was looking at her. She felt it. He had a way of making her feel the need to better herself. If that meant trying to befriend a spitting cobra like Flora, she would do her best.

And she did try, *all the way to school*. She offered Flora her bicycle. Flora wanted to walk, thank you. She tried to get Teddy to hang back when Flora dawdled behind them down the lane. Flora stuck her nose up and crossed to the other side, and Ivy couldn't help laughing just a little to herself when Flora's dainty foot sunk into a mud puddle just as two handsome young officers turned into the lane to see it happen. Ivy even tried to take the girl under her wing at school when Teddy left them alone to go off to his Greek and Latin tutorials with Father Bertram.

Ivy's friend Sharon Watson bounded over to greet them.

"This is Flora Arabel... erm, Flora Woodall," Ivy explained. "She's staying next door at the Emmetts'."

"How d'ya do," Sharon said with perfect politeness. "We've lots of new evacuees this week, so I'm sure you'll fit right in."

Her warm welcome was returned with a critical look up and down at her simple frock, followed by a falsely sweet reply. "Oh, I'm not an evacuee. I'm a special guest at Ashbury Park, but I don't suppose you'd know the difference."

Sharon looked at Ivy with the taken-aback expression of an unsuspecting victim of a slap.

The worst came when it was time for the girls to go to

the church hall for Irish dance class while the boys went out into the frosty meadow for gymnastics.

"Don't worry if you've never done jigs before," Ivy tried genuinely to encourage Flora when she saw her frightened face. "It's quite easy."

"Easy? Well of course it's easy. It's positively savage!" Flora snapped, crossing her arms over her chest.

She stood thus while all the other girls followed Sister Ursula. The twiggy nun picked up her habit, kicked up her legs, and skipped about the room; but she stopped abruptly when she noticed Flora standing like a haughty statue amidst the whirlwind of jigging girls.

"Would you like us to start again, Miss Woodall, so you can join in?" she asked meekly.

Flora batted her baby doll eyes at the nun. "I'm sorry, but I don't *do country* dances. They're only for the ordinary classes. I shall wait and join in when you teach a *real* dance. A foxtrot, for instance. Or a waltz."

Poor Sister Ursula looked so stricken, Ivy thought she would burst into tears. After that, the nun kept forgetting the next step in the jig and having to go back to the beginning.

"Well!" Sharon whispered as the girls changed out of their gymslips before going to dinner. "That Flora thinks she's a right peach, doesn't she?"

"A rotten peach, perhaps."

That made Sharon giggle, but Ivy felt a tiny tinge of remorse for having said it when she looked around and saw Flora sitting on a bench alone, clutching her bundle of clothes to her chest. Ivy wanted to please her father and be a friend to Flora, truly. But some things just weren't possible, even for someone as determined as one Ivy Briscoe.

At last the grey winter days grew longer and milder, the first daffodils peeked up through the muddy ground, and the ice on Leg O'Lamb pond began to melt. Flora's icy behaviour, however, did not. She remained as prickly and impenetrable as a sea urchin.

Ivy gradually learned just to ignore her. After all, she had bigger fish to fry with the war charging on. And there was much more fun to be had with Teddy. Though it often irked her, she couldn't help admiring how much Teddy knew about the world, and especially about all things war-related. When they passed troops in the village, he could tell Ivy their exact rank and position, just from the stripes on their sleeves! He knew every airplane that droned overhead—sometimes without even seeing it, just from the sound the motor made.

The Briscoes and Teddy made a game of this talent. After school, they would lie back in Moony's Meadow behind the church. Teddy would close his eyes and wait for the hum to begin. Then, without opening them, he'd describe the aircraft to Ivy, who would tell him if he had got it right or not.

They were all enjoying this very game one especially balmy day at the start of May. While Esme chased butterflies, Ivy and Kenny tested Teddy's skills.

He had just successfully *heard* a Lancaster bomber and two Hurricanes when he sat up with a restless look in his eyes. "All these planes and bombers. They're getting ready for something big over there behind those stone walls at Ashbury Park. Personally, I think the military is bracing itself for an invasion."

"You really think so?" Ivy asked with a squirm of her stomach. She wasn't sure if it was due to fear or excitement at the thought of an invasion. Maybe a bit of both.

"Yes, I do think so. After all, we're already evacuating all the children from the Channel Islands before the Huns take them over, and it's only a matter of time 'til Hitler presses in on the mainland." He squinted into the distance as if he could perceive the far-off thoughts of the enemy. "I reckon the military is cooking up a counter attack, and probably planning to launch it from right here in Ferny Hill, right under our noses. If only we could get a good look inside Ashbury Park to see what sort of larks the RAF are getting up to." He picked a stem of sweet grass and chewed it wistfully. "Those chaps aren't sparing any measures in guarding that place, and you know what that means?"

Ivy squinted in thought. "They must be hiding something in there... something top secret."

"I'll bet my best breeches on it," Teddy exclaimed. "Why else wouldn't I be permitted to pay a visit to my dear old aunts in our own family home, eh?"

It was Kenny who sat up next, his eyes wide as parachutes with an idea. "I know how we can see inside!"

"Go on, old bean. Spit it out," Teddy urged.

"Marshwood Forest! It's where us Scouts practice our survival skills. Mr. Blackwood takes us fishing there in Fishpond's Bottom, and it goes right up next to the walls of

Ashbury Park. There's even a water drainage pipe that goes right under it!"

"But Kenny," Ivy countered, slightly annoyed he had come up with an idea before she had, "we can't just trespass on Mr. Blackwood's private property. We'll have to ask permission, and then he might feel he should tag along to supervise us."

Kenny shook his head with a smug grin. "He said we Scouts could use the pond any time we liked. Being in his patrol comes with special privet-ledges."

"I think you mean *privileges*?" Teddy interjected.

"Yes, those. Anyway, I'm sure he won't mind if I bring you tenderfoots along."

Ivy made a face. "Tenderfoot? Why I..."

But Teddy cut her off by bouncing to his feet and clasping his hands together. "Well then, chaps," he said, weaving his long fingers together and stretching them out in front of himself until they cracked. "Looks like we're going fishing!"

8

MR. BLACKWOOD'S SECRET

Kenny insisted on dressing in his full Scout regalia—including garters, staff, whistle, and binoculars—before they set out on their mission through Marshwood Forest. He took his role as sortie leader very seriously; often, as the children blazed their way through the mud and underbrush, he would hold up his hand to silence them and use his binoculars to scope out their surroundings before giving them the signal to carry on.

"You do know you don't need binoculars to fish?" Ivy chided him as she tugged her foot out of the mud with a squelch. There was a reason the wood behind Mr. Blackwood's cottage was called Marshwood Forest.

Kenny raised an eloquent finger and replied, with dignity, "Always be prepared."

Teddy, who was bringing up the rear with Esme on his shoulders and his lanky arms loaded with tackle, chuckled. "He's right, you know. And the one thing we won't be prepared to do is run if we get caught. I dare say I'm beginning to sink!"

"Here." Ivy squished and squelched her way back to him and helped Esme transfer over to her own shoulders. "No man gets left behind," she grunted as Esme's tailbone dug into her shoulder.

"I most appreciate your team spirit," Teddy replied with a salute.

At last, they emerged from the dark thicket of cedars and bramble into a clearing. Kenny turned and made a low bow. "Ladies and gentlemen, I present to you Fishpond's Bottom!"

"First-class work, Private Briscoe," Teddy lauded Kenny, who beamed with self-satisfaction. "Now, I see what you mean about the pond sidling right up to the wall. Look, Ivy. Once we get around this pond, we could hoist you up on my shoulders. Reckon you could see over it then?"

"Or better yet," Ivy offered, not feeling entirely enthusiastic about standing on Teddy's skinny shoulders, "We could climb that pine tree that's growing right up next to the wall. Then you can see in as well as me."

Teddy rubbed his hands together. "Well spotted." Then to Kenny: "Lead onward, Private Briscoe!"

They trudged single-file around the rim of the pond, their rubber-clad feet sinking knee-deep in the mire, then finally climbed up the bank onto higher, more solid ground on the other side. Once they'd reached the gnarly old pine tree, Ivy wasted no time in trying to disembark Esme from her aching shoulders.

"Don't put me down in the stinking nettles, Ivy!" Esme shrieked, clinging like a baby baboon to her sister's hair.

"Shhh! Ow!" Ivy winced as a strand of her hair caught in one of Esme's buttons when Teddy helped her down. "They're *stinging* nettles, and we won't put you down in them, silly. Look. Stand on the roots of this big pine tree."

"That's curious," Kenny said, peering up through the boughs of the tree with his binoculars.

Teddy dumped his load of tackle down beside the tree's roots and cocked his head back to try and see what Kenny had found. "Is it?" He squinted. "What is?"

Kenny lowered his binoculars and looked at Teddy as Columbus might have looked upon first spotting the New World. "This Scots pine is flat on top. And you know what that means?"

Teddy scratched his chin in reply, so Kenny continued. "I'm certain there's an owl's nest up there. Oh, do let me have a look!"

The older two children looked at one another and sighed in a way that meant, *Better let him have his look or he'll never be satisfied*. Kenny *had* led them all the way to Fish-pond's Bottom, after all.

"Alright then," Ivy said. "Step up on my back. That should get you up to the first branch." She knelt over to make a table top while Kenny scrambled up her back and launched himself at the lowest limb. In a minute's time, he had reached the top of the tree. Watching from the ground, they could all see him gaping at something.

"Well? Is there an owl's nest up there or what?" Ivy hissed, impatient for her turn to climb the tree and carry on with their mission, now that they had come within a hair of the RAF training ground.

"It's hollow!" Kenny shouted down.

Ivy placed a finger over her lips and glared up at Kenny, warning him to pipe down.

"What do you mean?" Teddy called up in a hoarse whisper.

Unable to mimic Teddy's whispered shout, Kenny scrambled down the tree and dropped to the ground. "I mean it's a *hollow tree*. Right down to the bottom, I think. And there's wires coming out the top... and a sort of metal stick thing."

Teddy looked at Ivy with a flicker in his eye. "Wires. Why, that metal stick must be an antenna for transmission! Bully me if those wires don't lead to some sort of secret radio transmission station."

She gave him a look like he'd gone away with the fairies; but before she knew it, Teddy was down on all fours, feeling around in the mulch like a squirrel in search of a lost acorn. In a few seconds' time, he sat back on his heels. "Well, what are you waiting for, gang? Get digging. If we find the wire at ground level, it's bound to lead us straight to its source. Dig for victory, chums!"

Under Teddy's command, they all dropped to their knees and dug with their bare hands through the forest debris, pine needles, and clods of soil.

After several minutes, feeling sweaty and a bit silly, Ivy sat back on her heels and wiped the hair out of her eyes with the back of her hand. "But what if there aren't any wires on the ground? I mean, maybe there *was* a radio station once, but there's not anymore."

Just at that moment, Esme screamed, "Ouch!"

"Shhhh! Ezzy, *be quiet*. What is it, a wasp?"

"No." Esme pouted and rubbed her backside. "I sat on

something very very hard. Look." She pointed to a metal rod with an eye hook sticking out of the ground between the tree's roots.

"Why Esme, you're a hero!" Teddy bounded over like a long-legged tree frog and bent down to examine the rod. "Well, it's not like any radio transmitter I've ever seen." He shrugged and gave the rod a firm twist.

There was a slight groan from the ground in front of Ivy. She fell back and gasped. Right under the spot where she'd been digging a moment before, a trapdoor rose and—as if by magic—swung open on a hinge.

All four children scrambled on hands and knees around the hole, peering down into the darkness in speechless wonder as the musty smell of earth filled their nostrils. What they beheld was a brick shaft with a ladder going straight down and disappearing—who could say how far?—below the ground.

Finally, Teddy sat up. "Right. Who's going down, and who's keeping watch?"

"You and me'll go down," Ivy replied. "Imps keep watch."

"But that's not fair! I found it!" Kenny moaned.

"Shhh! Fine. Ezzy can keep watch, and the three of us can go down."

Now Esme crossed her arms over her chest and pouted. "I don't want to stay up here all by myself. There could be grey men!" *Grey men* was what she called the Germans because of pictures of them in their grey uniforms.

"No, there couldn't," Ivy said impatiently.

Teddy raised a finger. "How about we all go down, but

we two lead the way—just in case of snakes or booby traps."

Ivy agreed. Teddy—the oldest, after all—went down first. Ivy heard his feet meet the grimy floor as she came down after him. She heard him click the switch of Kenny's torch then exclaim, "Holy mackerel!"

"What is it?" she asked as her own feet met the floor. But as her eyes adjusted to the torch light, she could see for herself.

The subterranean chamber before her eyes was far bigger than she'd ever have guessed. She ducked down and stepped from the ladder shaft into the main room, then stood up straight again. It was a long, domed bunker with wood plank floors and two bunk beds folded up against the wall on either side. The wavy metal walls and ceiling looked the inside of a tin can. There was a wooden table in the furthest corner with several candles and other bits on it. But Teddy had his eyes glued on a dozen or so crates stacked against the left wall. Ivy came to see what could have stunned him so and read the letters printed on the tops and sides of each crate: 'TNT'.

"Ivy, I'm scared. What if spiders is down here?" whimpered Esme's lisping voice from behind.

Ivy twirled around, suddenly aware of the potential danger they'd walked into by trespassing in an underground bunker filled with dynamite. "Go back up! Go back up!" She shooed the Imps back towards the ladder.

"But I want to see!" Kenny shoved past her. "Heavens! is that *real* dynamite?"

Teddy barred the way before Kenny could get close enough to tear the top off one of the crates. "Steady on, chummy. I wouldn't touch anything, though we should be safe enough from explosion so long as we don't light up any matches."

Ivy breathed a sigh of relief and told herself that, of course, she had known as much. But she still held tight to Esme's hand as they stepped deeper into the bunker and continued exploring. She wiped a finger across a tea pot perched on a shelf and held it up to the beam of light. "There's no dust."

"Beg your pardon?" Teddy said.

"Everything is clean," she explained. "I think someone's used this place quite recently."

Teddy wasn't listening. His attention was, once again, drawn away by some long object he had just pulled out from under a wooden bench. "I don't believe my eyes! They've got Big Bertha down here!"

"Big Bertha?" Ivy scrunched up her nose, well and truly confused. "Who's she?"

Teddy held up the object and turned around to face Ivy, his grey eyes shining in the darkness. "Do you know what this is?"

"Of course," she answered with an affronted air. "It's a… a gun." She had the sinking feeling Teddy was about to educate her.

"Not just any! This is a .22. A sniper's rifle! You can only get one through government issue. Not even the Army uses these."

Brushing aside how a boy of fifteen knew so very much about these things, Ivy shrugged her shoulders. "So you think the government built this place? But why would they stash a load of dynamite here in Marshwood Forest? The war is out there, on the Continent. Not here in Ferny Hill."

Teddy grimaced. "Not yet."

Ivy eyed him sidewise. "What's *that* supposed to mean?"

"It means that I was right. The British government is preparing for an invasion. That's what's going on behind the walls of Ashbury Park. The RAF is planning its defence. Just look at this place. It's absolutely loaded with fuse bombs, hand grenades, every kind of booby trap in the book. If this isn't some sort of resistance armoury to use against the Huns when they show up, then my name isn't Theodore Reginald Henry Woodall."

Just then, Kenny, whose attention had been given fully to inspecting a ration pack in an alcove under the hatch, came galloping over with his own theory about the bunker to share. "They've got dried sausages. This place *must* belong to German spies. And to think, they might be planning to blow up Ferny Hill any day now! Why, they could be sacking the town right this very minute!" He mimed throwing a hand grenade and mimicked an explosion sound.

Ivy glanced at Teddy, who turned back to the table to hide his smirk. He picked up a booklet he hadn't noticed before and thumbed through it.

"Look at this." He held it up so that Ivy could read the words across its cover: 'Farmer's Calendar'.

"What about it?"

"Ever seen a farmer's calendar like this?" He handed it to her, and she likewise flipped through its pages. Each one was full of instructions for stealth manoeuvres and sabotage.

"Who exactly did you say this property belongs to?" Teddy asked Kenny, who was in the middle of a charade gun attack.

"Mr. Blackwood, our Scoutmaster."

"What sort of chap is he? What does he do for a living?"

Ivy answered. "He's a retired old sergeant major. Doesn't talk about it much, though. He came here from South Africa after he fought in the Boer War."

"*And* the Great War," Kenny added smugly. "*And* Father told me that Mr. Blackwood knows Mr. Churchill personally because he helped rescue him from prison when he was in Africa."

"Well, well." Teddy rubbed his chin. "That partly makes sense of things."

Ivy once again had the prickling feeling of being left out in the dark from Teddy's ingenious thought process. "What's Mr. Blackwood got to do with it?"

"Well, it's obvious, isn't it?"

Did he have to rub it in? She raised one eyebrow, waiting for him to say what was so obvious.

Teddy continued: "I think your Scoutmaster is involved in some sort of guerrilla warfare. The question is whether he's working for the right side, or some renegade group of militants."

Kenny looked dumbstruck for a moment, then slapped his knee and guffawed. "Mr. Blackwood isn't a gorilla! And he can't be on the wrong side. He's friends with Mr. Churchill!"

Teddy shrugged. "Let's hope you're right, chum.

Looks like there's a tunnel passage from this bunker that goes right under the wall into Ashbury Park. A lot of damage he could do to the Royal Air Force if he had a mind to."

Before another word could be uttered, they all froze. The soft thud of footsteps on mulch approached the open hatch, then stopped.

The children shot anxious eyes at one another, each one's breath puffing out in heavy, humid clouds. But no one dared speak. Esme whimpered and clung with both hands to Ivy's arm.

"Wait here," Teddy mouthed. Ivy nodded as he picked up 'Big Bertha' and crept to the hatch.

Crouching down, Ivy put an arm around Esme's shoulder.

"Do you think it's a grey man? Or a gorilla? Oh, I hope it's a gorilla!" Esme whispered in her sister's ear.

Teddy signalled for them to hush. At the same moment, a deep, gruff voice from above shouted, *"Achtung!"*

"I told you it was Germans!" Kenny hissed from his hiding place behind Ivy's back.

Ivy felt icy fingers of terror crawl up her spine. Had Kenny been right? Had they actually got themselves cornered in a German spy's bunker?

Teddy pressed himself flat against the stone wall and raised the rifle as the steps thudded closer and closer until…

A face appeared in the hatch opening. They all screamed, though Teddy quickly turned it into a sort of throat-clearing noise. There, blinking in the torch light, was a big, bearded, ruddy face which, in the dark, might easily have been mistaken for a German's—or an ogre's, for that matter. But in fact, it was neither.

"Mr. Blackwood? But… it can't be." Kenny came out of his hiding place and approached the man now descending the ladder. "*You're* a German spy?"

Ivy stepped up beside her brother as Mr. Blackwood reached the ground and took the rifle out of Teddy's hands. "He's not a German spy, silly," she chided. "He's just got a bunker full of TNT because… because… Why have you got all this stuff, Mr. Blackwood?"

The old Scoutmaster didn't hurry to answer, but rather pushed passed them into the long, domed cave to inspect for anything out of place. The children watched him in silence.

Mr. Blackwood was a barrel-bellied man with arms and legs the size of young trees and a greying red beard that could have housed a family of squirrels. His bare forearms bore the scars of countless adventures in the African bush, not to mention two wars. Each one had a story behind it, many of which Ivy and Kenny had heard around the campfire on Scouting expeditions. But the Briscoe children knew Mr. Blackwood's bark was infinitely worse than his bite. They weren't afraid as he lumbered up to them in the darkness like some Viking chieftain, thumping the butt of the rifle against the hard floor like a walking stick. Ivy was, however, perplexed. Mr. Blackwood was a man with many secrets, but a bunker full of dynamite…?

"What is all this for?" she repeated.

"This…" He finally began, patting one of the crates of TNT like it was an old dog. "This is my old collection. Leftovers from the Great War." He nodded, satisfied with his answer, then quickly furrowed his bushy brow. "And it's nothing that concerns you lot, and you'd best forget everything you've seen and not breathe a word to a single soul, or else…" He hesitated.

"Or else what, Mr. Blackwood?" Teddy asked—not as a challenge, but with genuine curiosity.

Mr. Blackwood took in Teddy properly for the first time. "And just who might you be, young buck?"

"Teddy Woodall, sir. Eton Corps, Cadet Sergeant and Master Marksman." Ivy watched with wonder as Teddy automatically stood at attention, straight as a board with long arms glued to his sides. "You may have heard of my father, General Woodall. He served in Africa as well, in his early days. I know military weapons when I see them, sir. That firearm there, the .22—it's government issued. A rare specimen, if I may say so."

"Ya. Well, you know, having the Prime Minister in your debt has its perks. These things are just… gifts." Mr. Blackwood nodded as if convincing himself. "That's right. A few gifts from Churchill's toyshop."

"Forgive me, sir, but I thought you said they were your old collection…"

Mr. Blackwood realised he had met his match in Teddy and, like the bear he was, gathered himself up to his full height. "Just what are you sniffing at, lad? You're a clever one, I see. Just hope you're clever enough to keep your lips sealed."

Teddy had hit on something serious, that was clear. Ivy had never seen the Scoutmaster look quite so dangerous.

Timidly, she asked, "You mean you really are some sort of spy, Mr. Blackwood?"

Mr. Blackwood didn't take his gaze off Teddy, and Teddy held it, even as he answered, "He's a spy, alright. But a spy on the right side. You're Resistance, aren't you, Mr. Blackwood? All these weapons and dynamite... they're meant for the Huns, should they try and take over."

Mr. Blackwood lumbered slowly up to Teddy until they were nearly nose-to-nose. Teddy didn't flinch but kept his board-like posture.

"Listen to me, boy. This is serious. Who told you about the Resistance?"

"Nobody told us, Mr. Blackwood," Ivy broke in before Teddy could dig them into any deeper trouble. "We were just coming here to... to fish. And we found your bunker by accident when Kenny climbed up the pine tree."

Kenny pushed passed her eagerly, a superior look on his freckled face. "You see, Mr. Blackwood, I reckoned on finding an owl habitat up in that tree, like the one you showed us on the spring expedition, so I climbed up to see. Well, that and we wanted to have look over into Ashbury Park... what? Well, we did, didn't we?" Kenny shrank back from the murderous glare Ivy was aiming at him.

Mr. Blackwood took out a spotted handkerchief and wiped the sweat off his brow. His face had gone as red as his beard, and he looked uncharacteristically flustered. "Don't you know you might've been shot?"

When the children looked down at their feet, Mr. Blackwood cleared his throat and continued. "Listen. All of you. I want you to get on home and forget everything you've seen here, ya? Not a word of it to anybody."

"You mean you're not going to tell our father?" Kenny asked hopefully.

"I'm not going to tell a soul, and neither are you if you ever want to grow up to see the other side of youth. You're just children—remember that. And this is no business for children. Understand?"

"Mr. Blackwood." Teddy stood at ease, plunging his hands into his pockets. "Perhaps we can come to... an arrangement. You see, it might be difficult for us simply to forget what we've seen here, as we're only children. And, as we're only children, you can't arrest us or kill us."

"What do you suggest I do with you, then, lad?"

Like a panther ready to pounce on its prey, Teddy made his move. "If there's a Resistance movement happening, then we want to help. You could talk to your superiors and ask them to make our silence worth our while by giving us a job to do."

Ivy couldn't believe Teddy's boldness. But more than that, she couldn't believe that Mr. Blackwood actually appeared to be considering his proposal. *This could be it!* she thought. *A way to do something important.*

"We're not afraid, Mr. Blackwood," she put in. "Honest." She heard Kenny gulp loudly as she said it.

After a long minute studying the the two of them, the Scoutmaster finally spoke. "No. You're too young. Clever and courageous," he added, looking from Teddy to Ivy. "But you don't know what you're asking. If the Germans invade, it'll be dangerous enough for you as it is. Get involved, and you won't last a day."

Ivy felt the hopeful breath she'd held in her chest deflate like a day-old balloon. She could see Teddy's jaw twitching with agitation.

"But I'll tell you what you can do." They both looked up

eagerly. "Those Huns would love to find out what's going on behind those walls." He gestured over his shoulder in the direction of Ashbury Park. "Keep a close eye out for suspicious behaviour. If you suspect a spy in Ferny Hill, you let me know."

Teddy resumed attention and saluted. "Yes sir, Sergeant Major Blackwood. I've always felt I've got all the makings of a downright smashing special agent."

9

VERA'S NEW BEAU

The early days of May brought in a balmy breeze that promised summer was on its way, yet a sinister chill was creeping its way into Ferny Hill. Teddy's suspicions, as always, proved correct. *Invasion* was the hushed word on everybody's lips, the primary topic of every radio broadcast. Within a fortnight, air raid sirens howled like moaning ghosts almost every night.

At first, the Briscoes stayed in their beds, though Kenny and Esme scrambled into Dr. and Mrs. Briscoe's bed each time the howling kicked off. Ivy was big enough to stay in her own bed. She didn't need her mother's soothing words or her father's calm assurances. But each time the sirens woke her, she would lie awake long after the others had gone back to sleep, listening for planes.

The next week brought more dreadful news of the enemy's attacks on the homefront. A bomb had dropped on Hillside Farm, just ten miles away, and had killed the entire household. Dr. Briscoe decided from then on that the family would take refuge in the Anderson shelter whenever the sirens sounded.

Then June brought even worse news. The British Expeditionary Force over in France was being driven back all the way to Dunkirk. The Germans were taking France chunk-by-chunk, right up to the English Channel. And Hitler would never stop there. The new Prime Minister, Winston Churchill, was ordering the whole country to prepare for the worst, for now nothing stood between the Enemy and England but the narrow Channel. Ivy pictured it each night while lying awake: the horrible man with the stupid moustache—just as Ernie had described him—standing on the French shore like Napoleon, peering across at the white cliffs of Dover, greedily drumming his fingers together like a thief regarding an unlocked house.

And each night she'd clench her fingers into fists under the covers and repeat Ernie's words under her breath: *This is our hour. We have to stand and fight. This is our hour...*

Ivy, Teddy, and Kenny discussed Mr. Blackwood's warning about spies every spare moment they could steal. It helped that Flora still kept a wide berth of the other children when they walked to and from school each day, so they could talk freely without worries of a spy in their own midst.

"Thing is, it could be anyone," Teddy mused one afternoon as they walked home down the leafy green lane towards The Beeches.

"I know who!" Kenny's hand shot up. "I'll bet Sister Tabitha's a spy."

Ivy snorted in spite of herself when she pictured the nun hiding a Nazi uniform beneath her habit.

When they reached the gate at The Beeches, nobody wanted to go inside. It was one of those perfect, balmy, early summer afternoons when one wants to do nothing but bask in the warm breeze, as if floating in a jungle pool. Ivy invited the Woodalls to stay for lemonade on the terrace, to which Teddy exclaimed, "Smashing idea!" Flora looked bored, but didn't outright object.

Ivy had just set her hand on the kitchen doorknob when it opened to reveal Mrs. Briscoe, all aglow and smiling so widely that her pretty dimples appeared on each cheek.

"Oh Ivy, there you are. Come inside, all of you!" She beckoned to the group of them hanging about the garden. "Yes, you too, Teddy, Flora. You're most welcome. Ivy's sister Vera has surprised us with a visit!" Then she added, in a lower voice so only Ivy could hear, "She's brought a young man back with her, so do be on your best behaviour."

Ivy's first reaction was a disgusted grimace. Vera had always had a talent for catching boys and reeling them in only to throw them back into the pond with a heartless 'plop'. Ivy found this sport revolting.

"Ivy..." Her mother gave her a warning look.

"It's not me you ought to worry about. It's Mr. Kenny Chatterbox back there. And how come Vera's home?"

"She got permission to come on leave! Only for the day, though. She's back to Oxford after dinner. Esme! Kenny! Leave that dog alone and come say hello to your sister."

Ivy slid past her mother's scolds and walked softly into the sitting room. Dr. Briscoe was leaning against the mantelpiece, talking with his pipe clenched between his teeth as he always did. There on the settee sat Vera in a very grown-up, V-neck polka dot number. Her honey-coloured hair formed an elegant, cresting wave over her forehead. Snuggled up beside her with an arm around the back of the sofa sat a clean-cut, nice-looking man of at least twenty-five, though he looked older in his military uniform. He had jet black hair, eyebrows to match, and a deep cleft in his chin. In the hand not embracing Vera's shoulder, he held a glass of wine, and raised it up and down with animation as he spoke to Dr. Biscoe.

"It's a marvel, Doctor, an absolute marvel to be in your presence... in your home even! Why, don't think for a minute I only took an interest in Vera because she was your daughter. I'd marked her out the moment I saw her, but when she told me who her father was, well… it all added up, shall we say!"

Dr. Briscoe looked relieved when he noticed Ivy loitering in the doorway. "Ah! Mr. Larson, may I introduce you to another one of my lovely daughters? This is Ivy. Ivy, Vera's friend, Lieutenant Barney Larson."

"How do you do, miss?" He stood up and gallantly crossed over to Ivy to extend a handshake. Ivy smiled and tried not to wrinkle her nose at the whiff of aftershave that accompanied him.

"Why Vera, this can't be the *baby* sister you talked about? This girl's practically a lady!"

Vera twittered, and Ivy faked a smile. She knew when she was being patronised, and she hated it. Besides, the last thing she wanted to appear to be was 'a lady'.

It got even worse when Vera minced and came over to hug her. "Why, it's true, Ivy. How you've grown!"

And then the Imps stampeded in, rendering the room into a state of chaos.

"Vera! Vera! Have you brought us any presents?"

"Golly! Are you a real soldier? We never had a real soldier in our house before... except for Father, but he's retired. What's it like? Have you shot anyone?"

In the hubbub that followed, Ivy looked around to see what had happened to Teddy and Flora. Both Woodalls hung back in the entryway, each one behaving rather strangely. Flora's usually rosy cheeks had gone fuchsia, and she staggered like one hypnotised into the sitting room to plunge into a chair, her blue eyes transfixed on Barney.

Ivy rolled her eyes and didn't think much of it. Then Teddy sidled up beside her, and she noticed that he, too, was pinker than usual, his eyes strangely dreamy. Ivy followed his gaze and—to her repulsion—discovered it was Vera who had captivated him.

"That's your sister?" he muttered in a slightly raised voice.

"Yes. So what?"

"Er, oh! Nothing. Just, well, you're not very alike, are you?"

Ivy didn't answer. She wished she could be alone in her own room, away from her pretty sister to whom everyone always compared her. Not that she usually minded one jot. Not that she, Ivy, had any interest in catching boys like tadpoles, or in spending hours curling her hair. But Teddy... Teddy was supposed to be *her* friend. Couldn't just *one* person prefer *her* to Vera?

To make matters worse, the Woodalls stayed for dinner that night. Ivy spent the rest of the evening trying her hardest to ignore Teddy, although she couldn't help noticing how he gawked at Vera and guffawed at every little thing she said like a giddy idiot. He was as bad as Flora, batting her bovine eyelashes at Barney like she was trying to keep the flies out!

Mrs. Briscoe had cooked up a splendid dinner: meat and macaroni pie, butter bean soup, and even fig charlotte with cream for pudding. It was the best meal they'd had since rationing began. Ivy couldn't enjoy a single bite.

Barney, on the other hand, showered the cook with compliments between answering the questions Kenny peppered him with about the war on 'the Western Front'.

This, at least, was interesting to Ivy, and she tried her best to tune out the rest of the circus around her so she could capture every word. Finally, someone in Ferny Hill with *real* information about the war! So what if he wore too much aftershave and minced at Vera like a blithering idiot? Ivy could even forgive him for calling her a 'lady'. Here sat a *real* soldier who had fought *real* Germans!

Ivy's only complaint was that Barney didn't give away much—only that he had fought in the terrible battle at Dunkirk and only just, by some miracle, returned safely to England. Now he was on leave until the Army called him back to the fighting. How Ivy wished he would answer more of Kenny's quick-fire questions about battles and bombs and sinking ships! But she could hardly fault him for being humble.

A modest hero, just like Father or Ernie, she thought, her heart warming to the newcomer in light of the comparison.

"And that's the other reason I'm here," Barney was explaining. "Of course I wanted to meet you all, and you especially, Dr. Briscoe. You are, after all, a model to us young soldiers."

Dr. Briscoe gave a modest nod and allowed Barney to continue.

"But besides that, I'm looking for a little peace and quiet—a chance to find my feet again. I thought perhaps Ferny Hill might be just the place. Why, I already know the prettiest girls come from here." He took Vera's hand and pressed it ever so tenderly to his lips while she bashfully batted her eyelashes at him. This was too much even for the adoring Kenny, who turned cherry red, leaned right over, and made pretend sick noises under the table. Everyone laughed—even Mrs. Briscoe, though she scolded him for his 'dreadful manners'. Everyone but Ivy—and, as an accidental glance his way informed her, Teddy. His face was no longer stupidly spellbound, but serious, his brows knitting together some new string of thoughts.

Hmph. Probably just feeling jealous of Barney, Ivy thought, and reminded herself how much she *didn't care.*

"I know just the place!" Mrs. Briscoe chirped, helping Barney to another serving of fig charlotte. "The Emmetts have a little room fixed up in their barn. Don't you remember, Noel dear? I'm sure they'd hire it to you for a fair price. It's a little rustic, mind you; but then, if a stable was good enough for our Lord..."

"Why, a barn is just the sort of thing I'm looking for, Mrs. Briscoe. Could you introduce me to these friends of yours?"

"Oh, they're just next door! Teddy and Flora here are

lodging with them as well. I'm sure they'd be happy to escort you over and introduce you, wouldn't you, children?"

Flora looked happier than Ivy had ever seen her.

Teddy wiggled his nose before smiling and answering curtly, "Of course."

Barney took Vera to the station to see her off. After they'd all said goodbye to Vera at the door, Teddy tried repeatedly to catch Ivy's eye. She pretended each time not to notice. At last, despite her best efforts to give him the cold shoulder, he outwitted her, sneaking out the back door after her when she'd gone out to water Nelson and Napoleon.

"Wait up, will you!"

She didn't, but with a few of his long-legged strides, he caught up anyway. "So. What do you think of him?"

"Who?" She trudged on.

"Of Lieutenant Larson. What's your impression?"

"Why?"

"Because I don't trust him. His accounts of his training and of Dunkirk were very patchy. Didn't you notice?"

In a sudden urge to wound him, she stopped and turned so they were shoulder to shoulder. "No, I didn't. I think he's grand, and you're just jealous. It's no wonder Vera likes him so much. He's a *real* soldier, a hero. Not just some schoolboy cadet know-it-all."

Teddy said nothing. He stood over her, so close she could feel the breath coming from his nostrils. He held her eye-to-eye, and Ivy could see from the look in his eyes that her well-aimed shot had hit home. She hated that look. It *almost* made her want to break the silence, to take back what she'd said. But before she got the chance, Teddy nodded to her, turned on his heels, and walked slowly back towards the house through the gathering dusk, his hands deep in his pockets. She watched him go—heard him whistle to himself and kick the occasional stone. Then she turned, flung open the stable door, and slammed it shut, startling both the horses into a stamping frenzy.

Why couldn't she get anything right?

"Whoa, Napoleon." She grabbed the stallion's bridle, stroking his neck to calm him. He'd been especially fidgety ever since Ernie had gone. And he was getting thinner.

"I know," she whispered, a gust of loneliness taking her breath away like a rush of cold water. "I wish he'd come home, too."

10

TO THOSE WHO WAIT

The next morning, Teddy and Flora were waiting for the Briscoe children outside the kitchen door as usual. But when Ivy piled out with the Imps into the misty morning sunlight, she ran smack into a wall of coldness. Teddy, usually ready with a gung-ho greeting and some piece of fascinating information he'd just learned from a book, turned his back on her and started off down the lane with Kenny skipping to keep up. Ivy and Esme were left to walk with Flora—who was in a suspiciously pleasant mood, for a sea urchin.

"I couldn't sleep a wink with those awful sirens going off last night, could you?" Flora asked whilst dumping her satchel onto Esme's shoulder so she could fix a loose strand of hair.

"Slept right through them, actually." Ivy took the bag from her little sister's slouching shoulder and handed it back to Flora. Even that didn't provoke her usual haughtiness.

"Fascinating man, that Lieutenant Larson. Oh. I mean

Barney. That's what he told me to call him when we were all sitting up chatting last night. All except Teddy, that is. He went straight to his room like a bad-tempered child. He can be so brooding sometimes."

You're one to talk, Ivy wanted to say. But at the same time, she felt a guilty twist in her stomach. If she'd only known how much Teddy would take her words to heart... it was too late now to take them back.

The iciness remained between the two of them all that day, whenever their paths crossed. Ivy told herself half-heartedly that it didn't matter. So what if Teddy knew an awful lot about weapons and aircraft and could deduce problems with the ease of Sherlock Holmes? She could do just fine without him, thank you. And she would prove it, too.

She reminded herself of the time Kenny had told Teddy about the disastrous bake sale. Teddy had replied sarcastically, "You mean you actually intended to raise enough money for a Spitfire with a bunch of cakes? You *do* know how much just one of those engines costs, don't you? Ha! A bake sale! Now that's a lark!" Ivy remembered with a pang how foolish she had felt. She let the feeling simmer a bit, hoping it might overcome the guilt she was feeling for having wounded Teddy's pride. *He thinks he's so clever,* she told herself. *But what is he doing to help the war?*

She was still simmering after school; but, out of habit, she joined the others to wait outside the vicarage for Teddy to come out from his tutorials. Eventually, Father Bertram emerged in his gardening coveralls. He saw them and called out, "If you're waiting for Mr. Woodall, I'm afraid he's already gone. About half an hour ago."

The others walked home in a sullen silence. They said a short goodbye to Flora at the gate just before Ivy kicked it open.

"I didn't know we were getting new furniture!" Kenny exclaimed out of the blue.

"What are you on about?" Ivy grumbled.

"Well, why else would there be a furniture truck in the drive?"

Ivy lifted her eyes. Sure enough, there in the drive was a large white truck with *Bunter's Fine Home Furnishings* printed on the side. A clanking, clattering cacophony lured them around to the back garden. What they saw there made Kenny's eyes grow as big as Mrs. Emmett's prized bramble-berry pies.

The furniture truck must have been a cover-up, because there was no sign of new furnishings. Instead, between the rose trellis and the old abandoned henhouse, there were six men in army uniform, entrenched in a freshly dug pit as long as a small swimming pool and deep enough to hide a grown man standing. An enormous heap of sandy soil rose up on one side of it like a giant ant hill. Half hidden behind the mound, Dr. Briscoe stood talking to a tall, important-looking officer with a bushy moustache. At first sight of his father, Kenny shot off at top speed. Ivy and Esme ran behind him, careful to avoid the shovels-full of sand flying out of the pit.

Kenny, oblivious to the furrowed brow of the tall officer, tugged at his father's sleeve. "Are those *real* sappers, Father? In *our* garden?"

"What's sappers?" Esme lisped, peeking around Ivy to eye the formidable stranger.

"Colin, these are my children: Ivy, Kenneth, and Esme."

"A pleasure." The man spoke in a voice as deep as he was tall. He looked less frightening, though, when he removed his hat to reveal a balding head. He gave them a grandfatherly smile. "Fine, healthy-looking youngsters you've got here, Captain."

No one ever called their father 'Captain' these days. It was always just 'Doctor'.

"You lot, this is Colonel Gubbins. He is a friend of mine. We know each other from the last war. He's come to ask us to do something—something important."

Ivy's ears perked. She looked at the tall older man; he caught her eye and gave her a nod.

"Children." Dr. Briscoe crouched down and pulled the two younger Briscoes close to him. "Listen very carefully to what I'm about to say. You know about the invasion, don't you, Ezzy darling?"

"You mean about the grey men wanting to come and boss us all about?" she replied matter-of-factly.

"Precisely. Well, the new prime minister wants us all to be ready in case that should happen. He has asked us to keep an eye on things here in Ferny Hill and report back to him about what's going on. That way, *if* the Nazis invade, we'll have practised and got ourselves ready to make as much trouble for them as possible."

"You mean like spies?" Kenny asked hopefully.

"Exactly like spies," Father answered. "Now. We're all in this together. Here is what I want each of you to do. You must promise me and Colonel Gubbins here to keep this"—he gestured at the sandy pit—"and everything that goes on here a secret. You must not tell your playmates, our neighbours, even your school teachers."

"What about the Vicar?" Kenny asked.

"As it so happens, the Vicar is in on our secret. But best not to mention it all the same. Idle talk costs lives, you know."

Kenny's eyes grew wide again with the weight of this new responsibility. He solemnly raised three fingers and recited, "A Scout's word is his honour."

A sound very much like suppressed laughter erupted from the colonel standing behind Father, but he quickly cleared his throat and looked serious again.

"But Father, you haven't quite told us what *this* is going to be." Ivy nodded towards the ever-deepening hole, though she felt she had a pretty good idea already that it would be some sort of bunker, like Mr. Blackwood's... *though, surely, this bunker would have another purpose than storing barrels of explosives,* she hoped.

"Ah, quite right, my dear. Let me show you." He led them around to the front of the old henhouse, through its wooden-framed, wire door, and right to its back wall, where a new privy had been fitted in. All three children looked at him, bemused. Dr. Briscoe was enjoying the joke.

"It's a trapdoor. Watch." With the turn of a hooked rod like the one that had opened the hatch in Marshwood Forest, the toilet bench seat lifted up, and Dr. Briscoe hoisted it right above their heads. They all now looked directly down into a deep square shaft. "This will be the door, you see."

One of the sappers down in the pit stuck his head into the shaft and called up to them. "Clever, ain't it? That way, should any Huns comes sniffing 'round here, they'll think it's nothing more than an ordinary old henhouse and leave the place well alone, none the wiser."

When they'd come out into the bright daylight again, Esme cocked her curly head thoughtfully to one side, then tugged on her father's jacket.

"Yes, Ezzy?"

"But Father, if the grey men do come here, won't they wonder where all the chickens have gone?"

Her father took her chin in his hand. "Why Esme, my lamb, you're absolutely right. Colonel, might we get a few hens in here to make the ruse more believable? I could ask Farmer Emmett next door if he could spare a few."

"That's a fine idea." The colonel winked at Esme, who was happily basking in her moment of genius.

When Dr. Briscoe sent the children inside for their tea, Ivy lingered out of the way behind the rose trellis, listening to the two men talk.

"You know the locals better than anyone, Noel," the colonel said presently. I'd value your recommendation as to who we can trust as a message runner. It won't be an easy job, mind you. Whoever it is must understand the high costs involved."

This is our hour.

Ivy didn't stop to think as she stepped out from behind the rose trellis and cleared her throat.

"I could do it."

The colonel turned with a look of surprise. "Why Miss Briscoe, I thought you children had all gone inside."

She took an unabashed step closer. "I want to help," she pressed. "I could be your message runner."

The colonel turned to Dr. Briscoe, who was observing his daughter with a thoughtful eye and just a hint of a smile.

The older man turned from her father back to Ivy. "How old are you, my dear?"

"Thirteen." As an afterthought, she added, "Sir."

"Thirteen, you say? It is mighty young to be taking on so big a task. You see, the message runner will have to travel far distances by day *and* night to collect the messages from dead letter drops scattered all about the area. I admire your willing spirit"—he bestowed another grandfatherly smile—"but I'm just not sure how you'd go about it."

Ivy had her answer ready. She'd pictured it from the moment she heard the words *message runner*. "That won't be a problem, sir. I'm a proficient rider. I could use Nelly, my chestnut mare, to deliver messages by day, and Napoleon—he's black, you see—by night. I take them out riding every day, so nobody would get suspicious." She hoped she hadn't sounded too desperate or childish, like Kenny pleading with Farmer Emmett to let him operate the tractor.

In the pause that followed, Dr. Briscoe finally spoke up. "It *is* a big task, Ivy. It may cost you a good deal of free time, sleep, and even your studies. Are you prepared to do that?"

She nodded.

Colonel Gubbins cleared his throat. "I don't wish to frighten the girl, but I must be very clear. Leisure time will be the least of your sacrifices should the Germans succeed in invading. If you are found out, they will not hesitate to line you up against a wall and shoot you, parents and children alike."

Ivy clenched her fists at her side and took a deep breath. "I'm ready, sir."

"Well, Colonel, you have a willing volunteer here." Dr. Briscoe stood beside Ivy and placed a supportive hand on her shoulder. "Ivy has a good, cool head on her shoulders, and you'll not find a finer rider in these parts."

"That's all fine, Captain Briscoe, but—begging your pardon, young lady—do you think she'll run at first sight of a Nazi?"

Dr. Briscoe looked down at Ivy with an appraising look. "My Ivy doesn't frighten easily. No, I've never known her to fold at anything. Not bucking horses, bulls... not even schoolmistresses."

Ivy caught the sly look in his eye. Father did have a way of always finding out her secrets.

"Well, then." The colonel gave Ivy an approving nod. "I suppose no one would expect a country brat on a horse of being a government spy. I'll draw up the recruitment papers. Oh, and you'll have to agree to the Official Secrets Act. You won't be able to tell your schoolmates anything about it. No glory for spies, I fear. Still want to take it on?"

Ivy nodded emphatically. "Yes, Colonel. I can keep a secret."

"Good. When it comes to delicate operations such as these, secrecy is everything. Now, let's get you briefed and trained, Private."

11
SPECIAL DUTIES IN ACTION

The next morning, Ivy woke up with the rooster's crow from next door. She peeked behind the heavy black wool curtain. A few pale stars still straggled behind their companions to greet the dawn. All the same, like Spud when he spotted a jack rabbit, she sprang out of bed and pulled on a vest, a pullover sweater, and her riding slacks. No time to attempt tackling the wild nest of her bedhead hair. She was out the door, tiptoeing past the bedrooms where her brother, sister, and parents still slept, then down the stairs. She pulled on her riding boots at the kitchen door, then trudged across the dewy lawn to the stable to saddle up Nelly.

Today was the day she would prove her worth as a Special Duties message runner. Today, she was a real spy-in-training. Today—*at last!*—she had her own part to play in this war, and she was going to give it everything she had.

Setting out on that first message collecting run gave Ivy a sense of complete satisfaction. She filled her lungs with an exhilarating breath of a new morning ripe with purpose.

How she loved watching the sunrise from the back of a horse, hearing nothing but the early robins and the pounding of hooves on earth. The world belonged to her and Nelly alone, theirs to enjoy while everybody else still lay in bed.

The village high street was quiet except for a few early signs of human activity. The baker's shop windows were open, a lady's smooth singing voice from the wireless and the smell of fresh bread wafting out into the street. A few Tommies left over from the night's watch hung about the clock monument in the village square, having a cigarette and a laugh. They tipped their heads to Ivy as she trotted past. *They'd never guess I'm on duty too,* she thought, smiling to herself.

A short hour later, she and Nelly were greeted by the smell of sizzling bacon as they cantered up the drive to The Beeches, their first mission complete. All had gone to plan, just as Colonel Gubbins had briefed her, and she'd found every message in its respective dead letter drop. She'd first collected a rolled-up slip of paper from a hollow door knocker in a quiet alley in the village. Next, she'd ridden cross country to the neighbouring village of Babbington and taken another scrolled paper from a metal pipe fixed into the ground beneath a steppingstone in the churchyard. Then, she had to ride up the hill to Ravensbrook Farm, where another hidden message waited for her in yet a different sort of dead letter drop.

This one had been slightly harder to find, though the colonel had shown her a diagram and explained in detail how to extract it. Fixed into a gate hinge of a fence was a hollowed-out bolt, which, when twisted clockwise, could be pulled out. She had tried all the bolts twice without success before the right one finally slipped out into her hand so that she could extract the scroll.

Her final run brought her to the crossroads just up the lane from The Beeches. The road signs had been taken down to confuse the Germans should they invade and come looking for directions, but on the ground beside the old signpost was a little metal plate. She wedged her fingers under the plate's lip and pried it up. Once she'd removed the concealed scroll of paper, she turned the plate around before laying it over the hole again.

This dead letter drop was special—the message inside it contained the key for coding the messages before sending them on to HQ. The key, Colonel Gubbins had explained, would change every fortnight, and Ivy would find the new one at the crossroads. He had stressed the utter importance of turning the metal plate upside down once she extracted the key. That would inform the agent who came along after her that it had been found by the right person and had not fallen into enemy hands. If it appeared that someone *had* tampered with the plate and possibly stolen the code key, the incident must be reported to HQ immediately before vital information could be leaked.

Thankfully, no disasters had clouded that perfect morning, and Ivy sat down, happy and hungry, at the breakfast table to devour her eggs and bacon.

"Have a nice ride, did you?" her mother asked with a wink. Mrs. Briscoe knew what Ivy had been up to, but her parents and she had agreed on keeping her missions a secret from the Imps. The less they knew, the easier for them to keep mum.

"Mmhmm," Ivy answered, her mouth full of hot, runny eggs and bacon.

"Good. I'll help you with that wee bit of homework you mentioned right after breakfast."

"That wee bit of homework' really meant 'the code'. Ivy and Mrs. Briscoe had to translate the messages before Dr. Briscoe could send them on through the wireless, hidden in the fresh new substation under the henhouse.

Once the table was cleared and the Imps sent upstairs to wash their faces, Ivy and her mother laid out the messages on Dr. Briscoe's desk, along with the key. It had seemed a tricky business when Colonel Gubbins first showed them how to decipher coded messages; the words looked like gobbledygook. One had to sort out what number in the alphabet matched each letter in the message, then subtract from that number another number in the key that went along with the same letter, then match up the number that was the difference of the two with *its* corresponding letter in the key. It all seemed terribly mathematical at first, but Ivy found that, after completing the first message step-by-step, she got the hang of it and even quite enjoyed the mental exercise. They zipped through the remaining messages as if solving puzzles, without a single hitch.

There was nothing particularly exciting in what the messages had to say—just things about the local surroundings and suspicious persons raising curtains after blackout, etcetera. But, as the colonel had taken pains to explain, these messages must be treated as highly important and confidential information. After all, this was all practice in case of invasion. If they did the job well now, they'd be much more prepared to spy on German military officials right under their noses, should it come to that.

Ivy's next job was to scroll up the messages, stick them inside a tennis ball with a slit cut in one side of it, then drop them down a pipe beside the rose trellis that fed right into a little basket down below in the substation wireless room. And that dispatched her duties for the morning. It was up to Dr. Briscoe down below to communicate the messages through the wireless to Special Duties headquarters. But Ivy didn't want to miss a single step of the operation, so she pretended to "feed the hens" so she might sneak down into the substation and watch him at his work.

That night, the whole process had to be repeated—only, this time, Ivy rode Napoleon, his sleek black coat rendering them almost invisible under cover of darkness.

By the fourth day of this routine, Ivy stopped feeling quite so tenderly towards the rooster next door when it woke her in the predawn hour. At school, she fell asleep on her slate and lay dreaming of coded letters floating in the air and rearranging themselves… the *tap tap tapping* of Morse code sounded in her ear… until she opened her eyes to discover the tapping was actually coming from the tip of Sister Tabitha's pointer stick as she tapped it against Ivy's desk. Ivy spent the rest of the day writing out from Proverbs, "Slothfulness casteth into a deep sleep; and an idle soul shall suffer hunger."

When night fell, Ivy began *almost* to envy her younger siblings when they went upstairs to bed for a long, carefree night's sleep. But before such feelings could take hold of her, she pushed them out of her mind. She wasn't a child anymore. She was a soldier. If Ernie and Vera could work hard and make a difference, so could she. *This is our hour.* The words beat in her weary brain like a war drum. *This is my chance to do something important.*

So why didn't it feel as important—as glorious—as she had dreamed it would?

When she came in from her morning ride on the fifth day, everyone was gathered around her father at the breakfast table, fidgeting to get a look at a leaf of paper in his hand.

"Ivy, my dear. Come. Sit," Dr. Briscoe invited her. "We were waiting for you to read it."

"It's a letter from Ernie!" Kenny said, hopping from foot to foot.

"What's it say? Has he got his wings yet?" Ivy slid into her seat, as eager as any of them to hear Ernie's news.

Dr. Briscoe cleared his throat, perched his reading glasses on his nose, and began to read.

Ernie, with his usual thoughtfulness, asked after all of the family first. Then he described his living quarters on the training base, told Mother he was getting good, square meals, and said a bit about his new friends among the fellow pilots-in-training.

Ivy hung onto every word, and especially the last bit, so full of Ernie's strength and sense of duty:

> *... Training's been a real challenge for all us lads, but it's paying off at last. I'm to go on my first sortie over France any day now and can hardly wait.*
>
> *The boys in Dunkirk have been hit hard, and a lot of our aircraft went down too. They reckon it'll be Britain's turn next,*

only the battles will be fought mainly in the sky. Keep one eye out for me, and I'll wave down to you lot below!

And most of all, be brave and keep good faith. Like Mr. Churchill says, God is on our side. May He watch over you all until we're together again at The Beeches.

Your loving,

Ernie

That night, as Napoleon galloped across Badger Croft Meadow, Ivy heard the now familiar growl of a motor growing louder from behind her. A plane passed overhead —*a Spitfire,* she thought, *like Ernie's.* Teddy would've known for sure.

She pulled Napoleon to a halt to watch its course until it disappeared behind a giant purple cloud. At the same time, a heavy cloud of loneliness passed over her. She closed her eyes and imagined again what it must be like to sit alone in the cramped cockpit of a Spitfire, scouting the skies for an enemy who was likely scouting the skies for *you.* That didn't sound like freedom to her. Knowing you might be shot down at any moment, knowing your last seconds before burning or meeting the ground would be spent alone in that cockpit… unless, of course, you managed to bail out.

Oh please watch over Ernie, Ivy prayed, her fists clenched tight around the reins. But how many other mothers and fathers and sisters prayed the same thing for their boys and brothers off fighting the war; and yet reports of the fallen came over the wireless every day. Colonel Gubbins had warned her: 'You must know the cost…'

Suddenly, her own *important* work didn't feel so important anymore. *Her* life wasn't at risk… not yet, anyway.

Ernie and the other young pilots were keeping that risk at bay by patrolling the British skies. How was riding her horse all over the countryside, picking up messages about pubs operating after hours and where such-and-such RAF officer had been seen having afternoon tea, *really* going to help win the war? How she wished she could be a pilot. If Ernie was going to face the enemy all alone up in the air, she wanted to do it with him.

Ivy delivered that night's messages to Dr. Briscoe by hand rather than through the tennis ball shoot. She plopped down on a stool beside him in the wireless room, her eyes absently watching the gaslight throw shapes on the concrete walls. He silently scanned the messages, waiting for the designated moment to tune in to headquarters. After a silent moment, Ivy suddenly realised he was watching her.

He smiled softly. "You look weary, my dear. Why not go up to bed?"

Ivy picked at the dirt under her thumbnail before answering. "If there really is going to be an invasion over here, shouldn't we be learning to fight the Germans, like our soldiers are doing right now on the Continent? After all, they'll be busy fighting over there, so shouldn't *we* be ready to do the same here?"

Her father put an arm around her shoulders and smiled down at her. "My brave girl, just now we need to fight the war on our knees. If the Nazis make it onto British soil, we will have to outwit them. That's what we're planning for here, with all of this." He gestured at the wireless and messages on the table. "But for now, let us pray it never comes to that."

For the first time, Ivy noticed the deep circles under her father's eyes as they smiled wearily back at her. Never had she stopped to think how much her parents were sacrificing, or how exhausted her father must be—carrying on his doctor's rounds with hardly getting a wink of sleep—or how sick with worry her mother must be. Still, she managed to stay busy and cheerful *and* run the ambulance.

Ivy lay awake for what felt like hours that night. "What a pig I've been," she confessed to the darkness.

Without permission, her mind wandered to Teddy and the hurt look in his eyes when she'd lost her temper—all because she had been jealous of Vera. She thought about how, in her heart, she had crowed over Teddy when she got her duties from the colonel. *How utterly stupid,* she reprimanded herself. Teddy had been a real friend, someone who understood the frustration of being too young to be allowed to make a difference. Yet the truth was that if anyone so young could make a difference, it was Teddy Woodall.

If only I hadn't ruined it with him, Ivy fumed at herself. *If only we were in this thing together.*

12

FOUND OUT

The next morning, Ivy winced her eyes open. Her head felt as though it had been locked in a vice all night long; her jaw ached from clenching her teeth. There was only one thing to do: she forced her thoughts to Ernie and his tireless training… for all she knew, he might be up in the sky at that very moment. That thought was enough. She sat up with fresh resolve to do her duty without complaining.

Returning from the morning's mission, she opened the kitchen door and did a double take. Her mother was always there to greet her with a hot plate of eggs or a bowl of porridge. This morning, though, it wasn't her mother standing over the range, but Father. He wore Mother's frilly apron and was having a go at a pan with a spatula as if digging up dirt with a spade.

"Where's Mother?" Ivy asked, pulling her second boot off and walking across the kitchen in her socks to see what in heaven's name he was up to.

"Ah, welcome back! I'm afraid your mother"—he

grunted as he tried to pry a blackened egg from the frying pan with a salad prong—"is frightfully unwell this—*grrr*—morning." At last, the egg prised free and went soaring through the air, landing gracefully beside the dog's bed. Spud leapt out, licked it up, and returned, contented, to his cushion. "Ah, just as well. I don't think it was edible by human standards anyway."

It was astounding to think that a man renowned for his ability to perform surgery under pressure of gunfire was so utterly lost when it came to frying an egg.

"But what's wrong with her?" Ivy asked, taking the butter rations down from the larder and spooning a small lump of it onto the pan.

Dr. Briscoe cracked another egg just as the two sleepy-eyed Imps shuffled into the kitchen. "It has all the signs of an allergic reaction, though I can't think what can have caused it. The only thing she's allergic to is cats."

A little squeak from Esme made Ivy look around.

"Bless you, Ezzy. I hope you're not coming down with it too?" Dr. Briscoe left Ivy with the prongs at the range and felt Esme's forehead. "Nope. As cool as a cucumber."

But Ivy couldn't help noticing that Esme was one cool cucumber with a guilty look on her face.

Ivy had to code the messages by herself after breakfast. She was dizzy with sleepiness, but managed all right. Then, as it was Sunday, she cleaned herself up from the morning's ride and helped her little sister dress for church while Dr. Briscoe forwarded on the messages.

"Is Mother *very* ill?" Esme asked as Ivy pulled her gingham dress down over her pillowy head.

"I suppose so. She'd have to be quite ill to let Father

have a go in the kitchen." The dress popped down to reveal the little girl's eyes wide with fright and her chin quivering ever so slightly. "She'll be alright, Ez," Ivy tried to comfort her. "I'm sure of it. Anyway, it's not *your* fault."

Esme burst into tears. "But what if it *is* my fault!"

"Don't be silly! How could it possibly be—"

Before Ivy could finish the sentence, Spud streaked past them into the room and skidded to a halt in front of the wardrobe. Spud yelped and stood up on his back legs, pawing frantically at the wardrobe doors. His yelps were answered from within by angry screeching and clawing.

"Ezzy, you haven't!"

Ivy got up from her knees and marched to the wardrobe. She scooped up Spud—wriggling and whining with all his stocky little body—and carried him out into the corridor, leaving him to whimper on the other side of the closed door. When she turned around to face the mystery creature in the wardrobe, Esme had blockaded it with her outstretched arms.

"Ezzy, move over."

"Oh no, oh no, oh no!" The little girl shook her curly head side to side. "Please don't take Billy away. He *needs* me!"

"And just what *is* Billy?"

Esme sniffled. Slowly, she pulled open the wardrobe door. The clawing tabby that came bolting out of the wardrobe was the least of Ivy's worries.

"Eurgh! That smell! Ezzy, how long has that cat been *in* there?"

Esme cornered the cat, who had surged towards the window and a chance of freedom, and scooped him up in her arms. "Only since yesterday… around lunch time. He's a stray, and he's been coming by the garden looking for scraps all week, and… and… it's not right that he shouldn't have a home of his own!"

Ivy took a deep breath to control herself from shouting the words that came easily to mind. Instead, she knelt down and took the shivering cat out of her sister's grasp. "You know Billy can't live in the house. It's not fair on Mother, really, is it?"

Esme's chin started to quiver again.

"But…" Esme looked up hopefully as Ivy continued, "*maybe,* he could be our new barn cat, and we could bring him scraps there."

Esme looked intently at the cat, much like her father inspecting a patient. "I don't know if Billy *wants* to be a barn cat."

"Well that's the best we can offer Billy if he wants to take up residence at The Beeches."

Esme thought a little longer. "Could I take him out there now? I want to explain everything to him, about Mother and why he can't stay with me like he wants."

Ivy took another deep breath (which she quickly regretted when her nostrils filled with the aroma of day-old cat urine), and gingerly handed the animal back to her sister. "Alright then. You show Billy his new lodgings. I'll clean up this *ghastly* mess before Father comes in." *How did she get into these things?*

"But don't dawdle," she added over her shoulder as Esme crept out the door like a bandit. "We're leaving for church in fifteen minutes!"

It took the full fifteen minutes for Ivy to dispose of the

soaked, reeking towels and to air out all the clothes in the wardrobe, not to mention scrubbing her hands and arms with lye soap. *Still* she fancied she could smell a faint whiff of cat's wee on her hands. So, she sent her family to church ahead of her, claiming she would rather cycle. The last thing she wanted was for any of them to catch her in the act of applying scent from Vera's vanity to her arms.

Ivy abandoned her bike at the side of the church and shuffled into a pew with the other Briscoes just as the bells tolled their final call to worship. She felt fine for the first few hymns. Then the reading began, the vicar's voice ebbed and flowed like a lullaby, and Ivy's head grew heavier and heavier until...

"Pssst!"

Her head jerked up, and the world spun around her: a blur of tweed coats, ladies' hats, and stained glass. Everyone else was standing up, singing again. Her eyes finally focused on Kenny's freckled face staring back at her.

"You were *snoring*!" he whispered. "During the Lord's prayer!"

Red-faced, she got to her feet. A prickling sensation—the sense of someone's eyes on her back—made her take a furtive look over her shoulder.

Two rows back sat the Emmetts, and on the pew beside them were Flora and Teddy. He wasn't looking at her, but his lips were curled unmistakably into a big, cheeky grin.

Ivy joined in the hymn with a hot-headed vengeance.

After the service, she rounded the corner of the church to fetch her bike and found Teddy leaning against the wall beside it. The sight of him brought all the humiliation back in a rush: the perfect kindling for a temper flare-up.

"Long time no see, chum!" He *sounded* friendly enough, but no doubt he was only there to have another laugh at her. She said nothing.

"Whoa there. I've been wanting to have a word with you all week, only… well, I s'pose I've just not found the right time." He paused.

Ivy bit her nail. If he was waiting for *her* to apologise, he had another thing coming.

Teddy blew air from his lips like a horse. "Can't we come off it, all this quarrelling nonsense? Why, what is it we're even quarrelling about?"

Ivy fidgeted as he waited for her answer. "I dunno," she mumbled. "I just didn't think you were like that."

"Like what, pray tell?"

"Oh, you know. The way you were all goo-goo-eyed over Vera. It was… disgusting."

He reddened. "Look, I'm sorry about that. Honest, I am. I don't know what got into me. To own the truth, she's not even my type, as girls go."

Ivy wondered what *was* his type. *Not that it matters.*

"But I still think she could do better than that creep Larson."

"And *I* still don't see what you've got against him. So what if he's a bit of a mush? He's still a *real* soldier."

"Let's agree to disagree about him for the time being. I'll grant you that he's innocent until proven guilty. How's that for a fair fellow? But please, let's have no more cold shoulders and all that. After all, that's Flora's game, not mine and yours."

That made her bite her tongue. The last thing Ivy wanted

was to be compared to Flora, who held a gold medal in grudge-holding. She heaved a heavy, relenting sigh. "Alright then." Stiffly, she added, "Is that all you wanted to talk to me about?"

"No. There's something else." Teddy scratched his nose thoughtfully. "Well, I'll just come out with it then. There's no use beating about the bush." He took a step closer, so he was just on the other side of the handlebars, and leaned in. Ivy instinctively leaned away, causing Teddy to shake his head. "Would you hold still so I can speak without being overheard?"

"Oh. Sorry." She straightened up again, feeling a despicable blush on her cheeks.

"I want to know what you're up to. Why you keep riding off on a white horse in the wee hours of the morning, and go out again at the same time every night on a black one."

At first, Ivy was taken aback. Had he been watching her all week long? She quickly got ahold of herself and put on a careless smirk. "That's a stupid question. I love riding. It's what I do best!"

Teddy gave her a dubious look. "I wasn't born yesterday, Ivy Briscoe. I'm a man of nearly fifteen years, remember? And I know you've not been going on mere joyrides. You're on a mission. Ten to one it's something to do with the Resistance operation, isn't it?"

Ivy clenched her teeth. Under her slowly cooling temper and hurt pride, she ached to tell Teddy the truth. But she just couldn't. She'd sworn an oath of secrecy with her hand on a Bible. "You're wrong," she answered, looking down at her Sunday shoes.

Teddy ignored her. "I could help you, Ivy, if you'd just let me."

She scowled. "Who says I need help?"

"It doesn't take a genius to see you're worn out. Falling asleep in school, at church... why, you're no fun anymore! But you needn't shoulder it all by yourself. We could work together. Let me help."

The thought of sharing the secret with Teddy was so very tempting; and yet, the way he said it pricked at her pride again. Who did he think he was, offering her help? As if she couldn't handle the task on her own! He didn't know the half of what she was doing. And no fun? That really was the last straw.

"What I do is none of your business, Teddy Woodall." With that, she swung herself onto her bike and peddled off, leaving a gangly, solitary boy behind in a cloud of dust. When she turned around at the top of the church walkway, he was gone.

Well done, Ivy Briscoe. A right mess you made of that.

13
FRIENDLY FIRE

"You've been staring at that book for an hour, yet I'm not convinced you've read a word."

Ivy snapped out of her sulky stupor and blinked up at her father, who leant back to appraise her through narrowed eyes, fingers stroking his chin thoughtfully. She returned her eyes to the open page. As usual, her father was right; *The Sword in the Stone* had lain open across her lap on the same page since she had first sat on the settee to read it an hour ago. She shrugged, idly thumbing through the pages.

"How's Mother?" she asked, hoping to redirect his attention.

"Much better, as a matter of fact," he answered, picking up a folded newspaper from the coffee table and sitting down in his armchair. "Her symptoms are almost entirely cleared up. It's the strangest thing."

Ivy nodded. The diversion had worked.

"But it's you I'm concerned about just now." Dr. Briscoe peered over the top of his paper.

Ivy bit her lip. The diversion hadn't worked.

"Why don't you go outside with your brother and sister? Get some sunshine. Unless of course you want to talk about what's on your mind?"

Ivy blindly scanned the page. "It's nothing. Just tired is all." She slid further down into the settee cushions, knowing perfectly well she had just told her father a half-truth; and, what was more, she was certain he knew it.

He smiled his knowing smile. "Well, I suppose you have a right to be tired. You've worked hard these past days, my girl, and I'm proud of you." He flicked his paper and cleared his throat, then added from behind the wall of news columns, "Just be sure you're taking some time out for your friendships; that's all." He said no more, only left her to sit and wonder how on earth he always knew what she was thinking, and what she should do next.

She didn't have to battle too long with herself—she was perfectly sick and tired of being at odds with Teddy. Something had to be done, and she would have to bite the bullet and do it. She slammed the book shut and sat upright. She would go right over to the Emmetts' and explain that she was sorry for riding off in such a huff; that she wished she could tell him why she had been behaving so oddly, but that it was a matter of gravest importance and security that she keep quiet. *Wasn't that how Colonel Gubbins had put it?* Teddy would have to understand *that.* Then, at least they could be friends again.

Once she was resolved, wild horses couldn't drag Ivy Briscoe from her task. She got to her feet and, tossing her book on the cushion, ran right out the kitchen door, around the house, and through the passage in the shared hedge between The Beeches and Emmett's Farm.

It was such a fine day. The sky was full of wooly white clouds, and a gentle breeze rustled through the copper beech leaves. Teddy was sure to be out of doors. She ran around the back of the house, where he sometimes sat on the terrace to read, but he wasn't there; nor on the old bench under the copse of cherry trees (another favourite reading spot). Next she tried the barn, where she found, *not* Teddy, but Barney Larson. He was sitting on an old milking bench, his elbows propped on his knees as he applied polish to a shoe.

"Why hello there, Miss Briscoe!" He set down the shoe and wiped his hands on a rag. "I hoped you would pay me a visit soon. Your delightful little brother and sister are the only Briscoes I've seen all week!"

"We've all been rather busy lately," was her rather weak explanation; though, in truth, she wondered why she hadn't thought to pay Barney a visit earlier. She had been so preoccupied with her work and worrying about Teddy, she hadn't even realised Kenny and Esme had been around to see him.

"To be sure." He sat up with his hands on his knees. "Your father is a very busy man, isn't he?"

Ivy shrugged. "Yes, well... he *is* a doctor."

"Mmm, quite. And, I imagine, he's deeply interested in the war effort. I bet the Army has got him doing some job or other?"

Ivy opened her mouth without a clue of how she should answer Barney's question. But as her eyes meandered around the barn, looking for inspiration, she could feel Barney's watching her.

"I... erm... don't think so. No. He just listens to the radio... you know. To hear the news abroad."

Barney nodded as he threaded his fingers around the back of his head and leaned against the post. "Ah yes, what with your brother flying back and forth across the Channel, I'm sure your parents are very eager for any little bit of news. Naturally."

Ivy perked. *Was Ernie flying back and forth across the Channel?* His letter hadn't said so. Perhaps Barney knew more... perhaps he could tell her what the other adults were hiding.

"Look here, Ivy, I've been meaning to say..." Barney leaned in so they were on eye level with one another. "If you need somebody to talk to sometime... well, you can always count on me."

Once again, Ivy didn't quite know what to say. She swallowed a little too audibly and blushed.

Barney grinned and pressed on. "What I mean to say is, it can't be easy for you—being the oldest left at home while your brother and sister are off fighting a war. Vera told me just how close you and Ernie are."

Ivy looked up in surprise. Had Vera really spoken to Barney about her? She didn't think Vera ever had a thought to spare for her 'baby' sister while she was off flirting with officers and attending dances.

Ivy suddenly became aware of the earnest way Barney was looking at her, as if trying to peer into her thoughts.

"I can bet you're worried about him; and—as much as your parents care for you—well, they're awfully busy people. They've got important tasks to perform, and maybe they just don't see how hard it is for you to sit on the sidelines. You're not a kid, after all. You're a bright young lady."

Ivy was surprised to find that, for once, she didn't retch at being called a 'lady'. She met Barney's warm gaze and felt that he really understood: she wasn't just a kid playing around while the adults did the important work. This was her war too.

Barney laughed casually and reached out to pat Ivy's shoulder. "What I'm really trying to say is, you've got a friend in me. I've been out there in the thick of battle. I know how hard, how lonely it can be. If ever you need a listening ear, you've got one right here. And mum's the word, you can count on it." He mimed locking his lips and throwing an imaginary key over his shoulder.

Ivy took a deep breath and nodded. Truth was, she *did* want someone to talk to. She *ached* to share her heavy load with someone who could understand. Maybe she *could* talk to him, the way she could always talk to Ernie. She wouldn't have to tell him any particulars about her mission or the substation...

"Oh, Barney. There you are!"

Ivy saw her golden moment for talking disappear as Flora skipped into the barn to nuzzle up beside Barney on the milking bench. "You said you'd teach me to play Rummy, remember?"

Ivy couldn't keep from grimacing at the disgusting way Flora pouted and batted her eyelashes. Her baby-doll eyes suddenly turned catlike and narrowed on Ivy. "What are *you* doing here?"

Ivy had almost forgotten why she'd come in the first

place. "I was looking for Teddy. D'you know where I might find him?"

"Pff. How should I know?" Flora tossed her hair.

Barney scratched his head. "Teddy, Teddy, Teddy… where did I see him? That's it. He was sniffing around here earlier when I came downstairs about half an hour ago. Think he had a bag of corn husks over his shoulder… might try the pigpen. I must say, he looked a little down in the mouth, like he didn't want to be disturbed."

"Thanks." With a twinge of guilt, Ivy took off at a jog around the barn and across the little lane that separated the barnyard from the animal pens. She slowed down a few yards from the pigpen, feeling a little doubtful. Suppose Teddy didn't want to see her or hear what she had to say after the way she had treated him at church…

She pursed her lips, determined. *There's only one way to find out, Ivy Briscoe. Stop being such a ninny.*

Passing the pigpen, she heard laughter—ridiculous, hysterical female laughter.

"Oh stop!" a girl squealed. "Did you really say that to Lord Halifax? You cheeky thing!"

Then Ivy thought her ear caught the sound of a familiar voice… a boy's voice. She followed the voices around the corner of the barn and soon found their source. There, leaning nonchalantly against a fence post, was Teddy, and he was chatting up two Land Girls: one a redhead, and the other a brunette who was batting her big cow eyes at him.

Ivy turned on her heel to march off in the direction she'd come, but before she could take three steps, she heard her name.

"Ivy Briscoe! What gives?"

Her face burned red hot, but she turned around with a careless air. "Oh, nothing. I just came over to see if Farmer Emmett could spare some eggs... Mother wants them."

"Eggs, you say? Aren't your own hens laying any?" he asked slyly.

She eyed him with a momentary suspicion. How could he know about the henhouse? Did he know what it was hidden below, too?

He must have read the confusion on her face, because he quickly added, "Esme showed me the hens yesterday while you were out riding. There were plenty of eggs then."

"Yes, well... Mother needs more."

The redheaded Land Girl spoke up, her voice as flouncy as a lace blouse. "Well honey, I'm afraid we already gathered up all the eggs this morning. Took them over to the farmhouse and left them in the kitchen for Mrs. Emmett."

"Thanks." Ivy faked a smile. Without another word, she stalked off before Teddy could try to stop her again and make her feel like an idiot in front of his audience of adoring female fans.

She had reached the hedge when she heard the pound of running feet behind her.

Teddy. Again.

"Whatcha! Aren't you forgetting your eggs? Here, I'll help you carry them."

Why was he being so annoyingly helpful? She almost growled something like *mind your own business,* but managed to bite her tongue just in time. She followed him to the Emmetts' kitchen door, wondering how she'd got herself into this stupid situation, for heaven's sake! She'd come to make amends with Teddy and get the apology she'd prepared off her chest; now she'd be going home burdened down with even more anger and a lot of useless eggs she'd have to explain somehow to her mother.

"Right-o." Teddy opened the door a crack and thrust in his head, peering this way and that before strolling in and crossing over to the larder. "No Mrs. Emmett, but eggs aplenty!" He found the basket of fresh brown eggs in the larder in efficient time. "How many shall I bag up for you, madam? I'll add them to your tab, shall I?"

Ivy didn't answer. In fact, she had barely heard a word. She was leaning against Mrs. Emmett's work counter, straining her ears at a strange sound coming through the door of the sitting room—a sound like muffled sobs.

"What the devil…?" Teddy circled around the table and stood beside her, listening.

As if a tiny voice had called to them from the countertop, their eyes fell in unison on a rectangular piece of paper lying in front of them. A telegram. Teddy snatched it up and mouthed the words as Ivy read them silently:

It is with great sorrow that I inform you that on the 4th of June 1940, your son, Private John Frederick Emmett, died in combat with the enemy in Dunkirk…

They read no more. Teddy's hand fell as if weighted down by a mill, and they looked at one another in silence. Ivy's heart felt like it had stopped beating. Everything was still and quiet—everything except the sound of Mrs. Emmett's stifled sobs in the next room.

14
UNEXPECTED GUESTS

How deceptive was that lovely, gentle Sunday afternoon. Bluebells nodded in the breeze and robins chirruped; yet Johnny Emmett—good old friendly, hard-working Johnny, Ernie's schoolmate and his parents' pride and joy—would never come home to Ferny Hill.

The news sent shock waves rippling throughout the whole village. Even the ladies of Ashbury Park paid a visit to their faithful overseer and his wife, bringing a wreath of red poppies. The Emmetts weren't the sort of people who liked a lot of notice, so Mrs. Briscoe—believing, quite rightly, that they would rather mourn in privacy—invited Teddy and Flora to come and stay the week at The Beeches.

Though the Woodalls had visited The Beeches countless times since their arrival in Ferny Hill, somehow, their coming as house guests with bags in tow made it all feel a little awkward. A stiff formality unknown to the Briscoe house followed the little party up the stairs as Mrs. Briscoe showed the children to their rooms.

"Flora, you'll have Vera's bed. It'll be nice for Ivy to have someone to share with again." Mrs. Briscoe gave Ivy a sidewise glare, daring her to make a protest.

Ivy wanted to speak her mind—that she'd rather sleep in the stable and share with the horses than with Flora. Then she remembered the Emmetts' troubles and decided she could suffer for their sake.

At first, Flora turned her nose up at her room. She was more than usually put out with the world due her separation from Barney for a whole week.

"Oh, I do so hate this war. It's positively ruining my life!" She plopped down with a defeated air onto Vera's floral comforter. Then she spotted Vera's vanity table and quickly forgot her troubles at the sight of her own reflection in the little oval mirror.

Ivy wanted to slap her. Never again would she complain about having to share a room with her sister. She'd rather share her room with Farmer Emmett's hog than Flora. Why, she'd even prefer Vera, whose gagging cologne smelled at least as bad as the hog.

Closing the door and leaving Flora to take comfort in her own reflection, Mrs. Briscoe ordered Ivy to show Teddy to his room while she went back down to the kitchen to start tea.

"Come on," Ivy muttered. "Ernie's room is up in the attic." She led the way with Teddy behind; the Imps, overcome with the excitement of having house guests, took up the rear.

In Ivy's opinion, Ernie's room was the best in the house, as well as the highest. She pushed the door open and walked straight to the window to take in the view, letting Teddy and the Imps pile in after her.

"I say!" Teddy looked around happily. "I know we've never met, but I get the sense your brother is my kind of chap." Without wasting a minute, he plonked his leather duffle on the bed and picked up a stack of books from the desk, all about history and war tactics. He lay them down again and put his fists on his waist. "I consider it a privilege to occupy his quarters while he occupies the sky."

Though nothing had been said about it, the ice between them had all but melted away since the shock of the telegram. The raging beast of Ivy's hurt pride had shrunk into a mere trifle in light of such a tragedy. Somehow, it had made them friends again.

But there was still one thing standing in the way of their old friendship, and that was Ivy's secret. She knew the question was coming when Teddy had the bright idea to send the Imps down to give Flora a tour of her new room. He waited until he heard them at the bottom of the stairs, then closed the door and flopped down on the bed with his hands behind his head.

"Alright then. Let's have it out. We both know that *I know* you're involved in *something*. I can either figure it out on my own—especially now we're living under the same roof—or you can spill it here and now. I'd opt for the latter. Don't get me wrong, I'm a terribly good sleuth. But the way I see it, why waste time?"

Ivy perched on the window ledge and turned her face to look out. She could see over the rose trellis from up there, with a clear view of the henhouse that concealed the secret substation. Supposing she *did* tell him… Truth was, she could use the help. She was supposed to be keeping a careful eye out for suspicious circumstances, military personnel, vehicles… all sorts of things Teddy knew more about than she did when it came right down to it. Surely it couldn't hurt to break her oath of secrecy *just* this once for a good cause. And anyway, who would know?

The answer descended like a lead weight. *Father would know. I would know.* She could never live with herself if she broke her oath. Lonely and trying as it was, it was her duty.

"Sorry, Ted. I can't." She turned to face him and saw him looking back at her intently, eyes squinted like he was trying to read her mind. "Please don't ask me again." There was no irritation or temper in her voice this time. It was a genuine plea.

Teddy seemed to understand. He sighed. "Fine. I see you're under sworn secrecy." He sat up and, running a hand through his sandy hair, said, "I'll not ask again. But I can't promise I won't figure it out. And when I do, you won't need to tell me a thing."

"Ha! *When* you figure it out," Ivy chided, the old mischief returning to her voice. "How about *if* you do, which I highly doubt?"

With that parting challenge, she scampered out the door, leaving him to puzzle. Teddy Woodall *was* a good sleuth, but even he couldn't outsmart Colonel Gubbins, the local commanding officer of the British Resistance. Still, so long as she didn't drop any hints, she half-hoped he would do it.

That night, Ivy lay awake for what felt like hours, listening to Flora snore through her pinched little pug-nose.

Just as sleep mercifully began to pull her under its spell, an air raid siren started wailing. Both girls sat up, Flora screaming uncontrollably.

"Shush!" Ivy growled. Then, attempting a more calming tone, like her mother used to reassure Ezzy when the air raids frightened her, she said, "Don't worry. We've got plenty of time to get to the shelter."

Flora didn't budge. She just gripped the quilt up to her chin and shook like an autumn leaf. Ivy had to physically help her out of bed, bring her slippers, and lead her to the door and down the stairs, where everyone else was waiting at the meeting point.

"There you are, girls." Mrs. Briscoe took the shivering Flora under her wing. "Here, Flora dear, wrap this blanket over your shoulders."

"How is anyone supposed to sleep a wink with all these sirens going off all the time?" Flora cried. "I hate them! I hate this whole wretched war."

"There there, we all do," Dr. Briscoe replied, with what Ivy thought astonishing patience.

Ivy shot a glance at Teddy in his striped pyjamas, his hair standing out in all directions like hedgehog spines. She nearly laughed out loud until she remembered she was wearing Vera's old nightgown that, on Ivy, looked like a potato sack with a lace collar.

"Kenny, got the torches?" Dr. Briscoe asked.

"Yup!"

"Ivy, take this jug of water, would you?"

She did.

"Ezzy, is Spud all ready to go?"

Everyone looked down at Esme when she didn't answer. She held the dog's lead in both hands and looked as petrified as Flora, her eyes wide and glowing in the torchlight.

"Why, Ezzy darling." Dr. Briscoe squatted down and pulled the little girl close to him. "We're all going to be fine. That's why we've built our shelter especially."

"But couldn't we just stay inside like we did before?" she squeaked.

"No, I'm afraid we can't, my angel," Mrs. Briscoe joined in. "But it's going to be snug as anything in our little shelter. You'll see. I've even got a tin of biscuits for a special treat."

Esme didn't say another word, but her face remained terror-stricken.

Kenny blazed the way across the garden with his torch, but Spud darted past him, pulling Esme behind him so fast that the two of them reached the Anderson before anyone else.

"What's got into that dog?" Mrs. Briscoe marvelled.

Spud barked and scratched at the shelter door, then dug furiously at the ground like he meant to burrow his way in.

"Take hold of him, Noel. That dog's clearly out of his mind. Poor little Esme can't control him when he's like that."

Dr. Briscoe gripped the lead with one hand and pulled open the shelter door with the other. All at once, Spud started howling. This was greeted from inside the shelter with a chorus of hissing and mewing. Dr. Briscoe stopped dead in his tracks and peered into the darkness.

"What in heaven's—? Quiet down, Spud. Kenny, shine the light in here, son."

Everyone crowded around the door to see what Kenny's torchlight would reveal. It fell on a pair of glowing green eyes in the far left corner of the shelter. In a crate filled with spare blankets, lay Billy the cat, sprawled out on one side and nursing five little squirming hairballs.

"Billy?" Esme stepped down into the shelter and took two steps towards the cat before turning around with a confounded look. "I thought Billy could live in here instead of the barn since we don't use it much, but I don't know where all these other cats came from."

Only Ivy had the slightest idea what Esme was on about. But the others (including Mrs. Briscoe, who had started to sneeze) were bursting with laughter right through the sirens, the howling, the hissing—the whole chaotic show. Even Flora stopped scowling at first sight of the kittens and made a little cooing sound.

Ivy crouched through the entrance to stand beside her little sister, who looked dazed and a bit offended by the sudden outburst. "I think Billy is a *she*, Ez. She's had kittens."

"You might consider renaming her Willamena, eh?" Teddy offered through the tears of laughter streaming down his cheeks.

Thankfully, the 'all clear' sounded just minutes after the discovery of the cats. But by then, everyone was wide awake with all the hysterics and in no mood to go back to bed; so Mrs. Briscoe offered to put on hot chocolate and serve her tin of biscuits in the sitting room. Though it was nearly June, Dr. Briscoe lit a little fire in the hearth, and the children (excepting Flora, who perched on the settee) sat cross-legged on the hearth rug, enjoying their midnight feast.

"I know what!" Kenny shouted through a mouthful of shortbread. "We can sell the kittens for the Spitfire Fund! That's loads better than a bake sale."

Ivy flushed at the reminder of her failed endeavours. "Don't be stupid, Kenny. Spitfires cost a fortune, so there's no way that—"

"Actually," Teddy butted in, "I think it's a bully idea! After all, every little bit helps. I can just see it now." He waved his hand across his face at an invisible sign: "'Kittens for Spitfires'. Brilliant! I only wish I were half so enterprising."

Ivy gave him a look that meant *you big liar.* Kenny gave *her* one that meant *told you so.*

Meanwhile, Esme sipped her cocoa dolefully. "But I don't want to sell the kittens. It will break Billy's… I mean Willamena's heart. Couldn't we just keep them in the Anderson?"

Before Ivy could explain why that wasn't a good idea, Kenny—on a roll of good ideas of his own—blurted, "We could, actually, because *we* can use our other big shelter under the henhouse during air raids, and then the cats can live in the Anderson!"

Nobody spoke. Kenny looked about for approval and found his parents and Ivy glaring at him instead. As it slowly dawned on him that he had said too much, he added, with a guilty smile, "I meant *if* we had another shelter under the henhouse…"

"Kenny, I believe it's time to get back to bed," Mrs. Briscoe said sternly. "Same goes for all of us."

As the little ones sulkily finished their cocoa and began to lumber back to their beds, Ivy dared a glance at Teddy. He caught her eye and winked the way he had when she first met him. Now she knew what that wink meant: the gears in Teddy's mind were turning fast.

15
NEW DUTIES

The very next morning following the 'Anderson incident' (as it was affectionately called ever after), Ivy woke extra early—despite the eventful night—to Flora's gorilla-like snores. She got dressed and crept downstairs, taking extra care to avoid the stairs she knew to be squeaky. The last thing she wanted was to wake Teddy (along with his inner Sherlock Holmes).

Now the Woodalls had come to stay and school had broken up for the summer holidays, it was going to take a great deal more effort to hide her secret missions. The Beeches suddenly felt very full of eyes.

She made it through the sitting room, stepped over Spud without disturbing him, and tiptoed into the kitchen.

She nearly choked. There was Teddy, sitting at the kitchen table with a cup of coffee and an open newspaper in front of his face. He peered around his paper with a phony look of surprise, as if he owned the place and hadn't expected any visitors.

"You're shameless," Ivy said, shaking her head.

"What? Can't a man enjoy his paper before the daily bustle begins? I've always said: early to bed, early to rise, etcetera."

"*Early* to bed? We went back to bed at three o'clock in the morning!"

"Yes, well, I see *you're* still up with the birds—*and* in your riding attire, no less?"

Rats. She had no comeback for that.

Teddy kept the ball in his court. "I know I mightn't look like a jockey, but I'm actually quite an accomplished equestrian myself. How's about I join you for your little morning joyride?"

She gave him a withering look, but replied with half a smile: "Don't flatter yourself. You'd never be able to keep up." Swiping an apple from the fruit bowl on the counter, she took a loud bite and waved the rest of it at him as she slipped out the door.

For the next two days, Teddy kept up an admirable act of *not noticing* when Dr. Briscoe disappeared and reappeared at the same time morning and night, or when Mrs. Briscoe invited Ivy to "look at that bit of work in the office" twice daily. But Ivy knew he observed every detail and stashed away every clue in his mind. Soon enough he was certain to deduce what it all meant. But she wasn't doing anything to help… nor to hinder him.

What mattered most was that Flora should remain absolutely oblivious; she couldn't be counted on not to blab. But Ivy felt confident that there was no danger in Flora's case.

The only thing Flora could deduce was her own misery. Not only that, but Flora was scarcely to be seen. She kept disappearing through the hedge for hours on end.

"Where have you been?" Teddy asked in his most big-brotherly voice when she reappeared in the Briscoes' garden, late for dinner. Teddy and Ivy had been sent out as a rescue party.

"Just next door," came the sugar-coated answer. "I have every right to go over there. The Emmetts are our hosts and therefore have a responsibility to us."

"The Emmetts?" He heaved a derisive laugh. "You never wanted to set foot in the Emmetts' house until now. And in case you forgot, the whole reason we're staying *here* is to give the Emmetts a bit of space to grieve the death of their son!"

"Yes, I know." She said it without even a hint of an apology. "Barney says they've treated him like a king ever since it happened, just because he was in Dunkirk too."

"Barney." Teddy's eyes narrowed. "*That's* where you've been? To see Barney?" Ivy could never have imagined Teddy, Mr. Friendly, looking dangerous until that moment. The vein in his forehead pulsed with anger.

"Oh yes. Poor Barney, stuck all alone over there with nobody civilised to talk to! Honestly, not a one of those Land Girls has any breeding."

Teddy's time bomb ticked its last. "You listen to me, you little monster. I forbid you to go back over to that farmhouse until… until I say."

Flora just turned up her nose and stomped all the way to the dinner table.

By the next afternoon, Ivy almost wished Flora would disappear through the hedge again. She was making herself as much a nuisance as possible to get back at Teddy.

"It's so unbearably hot!" she moaned, snatching the book Kenny was reading right out of his hand and using it to fan herself.

It was a remarkably warm day, and they had all brought books out into the garden to enjoy the cool, purple shade of the copper beeches.

Only Flora was miserable. "If Mother *had* to send us away, why couldn't she at least have sent us to the seaside?"

"Because, you ninny," Teddy grumbled without taking his eyes off his book, "the first place the Huns will land their invasion will be the seaside."

Flora pursed her lips. "Well, I don't see that the Germans are all that bad, really. Why should we have to go to all this trouble to have a war with them?"

"Do you know," Kenny butted in, "my friend Geoffrey says he's got a cousin in Jersey where the Krauts have already invaded, and *she* said in a letter that German soldiers don't smell of sauerkraut at all! They smell of tobacco and aftershave, same as our soldiers!"

Flora ignored that piece of information and carried on with her own thought. "In fact, some of the papers that Barney reads say the Germans are in the right and it's us that's in the wrong."

Teddy and Ivy put their books down in unison. Everybody's ears—and mouths—were wide open.

"Just what sort of papers *does* Barney read?" Teddy demanded.

"Heavens, I don't remember what they're called. I only had a look at the page he was reading yesterday. You'll have to ask him yourself. Oh look!" She sat up and waved her hand at someone behind them. "There he is now! Oh Barney!"

The tall, dark man strolled over to where they sat. Now in a pair of smart trousers and a jersey, he looked more like a movie star than a soldier. With a casual grin, he called out, "Don't suppose you lot have any interest in these?" and pulled two handfuls of colourfully-wrapped sweets from his pockets.

"Pineapple creams? Yippee!" Kenny hooted, as he snatched the sweet Barney tossed him out of the air, unwrapped it, and plonked it into his mouth with record speed. Through a mouthful of pineapple cream, he asked, "But how'd you get them? Mr. Sidwell's been clean out for weeks. Sweets's practically gone extinct!"

Barney chuckled. "Well, let's just say being a soldier comes with its special privileges. And there's more where those came from, whenever you fancy a visit to old Uncle Barney."

Teddy snorted behind his book. Ivy gave him a sour look, which had nothing to do with the lemon drop she was sucking on.

"Say—" Barney clapped his hands together. "What a fine day it is! How about a tour of the grounds here at The Beeches? I hear your mother's quite the gardener."

Kenny shot up into the air like a loose balloon. "I'll show you around!"

"No, you won't, Kenny." Everyone turned to look at Teddy, still lounging on his side. He'd picked up a military magazine and was casually flipping through its pages, as if the world answered to his command. Ivy felt the urge to smack him upside the head, just to knock him out of his regal pose.

"Don't you remember?" Teddy raised a cautionary eyebrow. "Your mother warned us about a wasps' nest in the begonia bed." He gave his magazine a flick. "I certainly wouldn't like to be the one to disturb them."

Kenny's balloon of enthusiasm popped, and he withered back down to the ground.

"Ah, never you mind, Kenny." Barney gave him an encouraging wink. "There will be more fine days to come, you can bet your breeches." Scratching his chin, he glanced at Teddy, who was taking great care *not* to raise his eyes from the magazine.

"Say, Ted, I wondered if you'd fancy going shooting with me some afternoon. I should be keeping sharp while I'm on leave, and I hear you're one heck of a marksmen. What d'ya say? Give me a few pointers?"

Teddy lazily folded back the page before answering. "I'll have to consult my diary. Awfully busy."

Ivy's mouth fell open. Teddy had really crossed a line this time, and by the look on Barney's still-smiling-but-taken-aback expression, he thought so too. How could Teddy behave so childishly?

Before Ivy could react, Barney broke the tension with a stiff laugh. "Well, I'd best be on my way and leave you lot to your leisure." He dipped his head and, raising it, looked right at Ivy and gave her a wink. She returned it with a wincing smile that she hoped would convey an apology for Teddy's behaviour. At the same moment, Flora flung herself on the unsuspecting man's arm.

"I'll go with you, Barney."

"No, no," he said good-naturedly while trying to pry Flora's fingers from his forearm. "You enjoy the day with your friends. I've got boring old business to tend to."

"Oh never mind about *them*." She tossed a degrading look at the others sprawled on the grass. "They've never anything interesting to say. I'd much rather help you with your business."

With another good-humoured chuckle, Barney finally managed to pull his arm free and make a hasty retreat for the hedge, calling a friendly "'Bye for now!" over his shoulder as Flora watched him go, her shoulders sagging with bitter disappointment.

"Bit of a dandy, don't you think?"

Ivy turned her eyes back on Teddy, who was still gazing listlessly at his magazine.

"Especially for a clever girl like Vera," he added, off-handedly.

Ivy's gut gave a little wrench. Before she could stop herself, she snapped, "Dandy? Huh. You're one to talk. You've got a top hat in your wardrobe. I've seen it."

"That's different," he answered indignantly. "It's part of my school uniform, and it's all in perfectly good taste. But look here, what I want to know is when that flakey fellow and his pockets of sweets are getting shipped back to war. I'm beginning to wonder if he's on leave at all. Supposing he's really a deserter… though he'd have to be an even bigger fool than *he* looks to play at desertion right under your father's nose."

Before Ivy could respond, Flora gasped. "Why Theodore Woodall, you take that back! What a horrible, nasty, unfair thing to say. Barney is a war hero, not a deserter!"

Teddy laughed dryly. "If he proves to be a 'war hero', I'll eat my top hat!"

Ivy was just about to say that maybe he *should* eat his hat, if it would shut him up saying stupid things about Barney; but she was prevented from delivering the sting by a loud motor rumbling up the drive at the front of the house.

"Expecting more company?" Teddy asked.

She glared at him and strained to listen. The sound of a single car door shutting was followed by steps on the gravel, then a knock on the door. A second later, Ivy heard her mother's clear voice welcoming the mystery visitor: "Why, Colonel Gubbins! What an unexpected honour. Do come in."

There was a moment's pause in which Ivy and Teddy held each other's eye; then, as quick as if they were drawing a duel, they both shut their books, shot to their feet, and sprinted for the house. Ivy was fast, but Teddy—with his long, froggy legs—got there several strides ahead. He waited, with a gentlemanly gesture towards the door, to let her be the first to intrude upon the colonel.

The distinguished old man sat in Dr. Briscoe's high back chair in the sitting room, already sipping a cup of tea through his well-kept moustache.

"That may be Noel now," Mrs. Briscoe said, peering around the partition as they came in. "Oh no. It's just the children. Colonel Gubbins, this is a guest of ours, Teddy Woodall."

Ivy jumped when, out of nowhere, Teddy suddenly clicked his heels together and stiffened into a salute. "Colonel."

"At ease, Private," the older man answered, a little bemusedly.

Teddy relaxed his arm, but remained stiff as a plank. "If I may, sir, it's Cadet Sergeant, Eton College Officers Training Corps."

"An Eton lad, eh?" The colonel regarded him from beneath his bushy eyebrows. "And already a sergeant? What did you say your name was, son?"

"Woodall, sir. Theodore Reginald Henry Woodall."

This was a very different Teddy than Ivy had grown used to. He never stooped to using his whole name. He was after something, Ivy was sure of that.

A look of surprise caused one of the colonel's eyebrows to stand up. "You don't say? You mean to tell me you're General Woodall's son? Old Poker Face Reggie himself?"

"The very one, sir." Ivy wondered how Teddy managed to move nothing but his mouth when he spoke, especially considering he was normally so lanky and loose.

"Well, well. Teddy, was it? It's an honour."

"The honour is *certainly* all mine, sir."

"And you're a friend of Miss Briscoe here?"

"Indeed, sir."

The colonel observed them thoughtfully for some moments. Ivy felt a little squirmy, wondering if he suspected she'd told Teddy the secret.

Thankfully, her growing tension was broken when the

door burst open behind them and Kenny galloped in, leading Dr. Briscoe and shouting, "You see, Father! I *told* you the colonel was here. You thought it was all a jest, didn't you?"

"Well, son, I did half-believe you were jesting, but I'm glad to see you were in earnest! Colonel, good of you to pay my family this visit." Father crossed the room and exchanged a firm handshake with the older man.

"Unfortunately, Captain, business doesn't allow me to stay long. Er, do you mind if I have a private word with you?" Then, turning to Mrs. Briscoe, "And perhaps with you as well, ma'am, if it's not too much trouble for these young'ns."

With her usual energy, Mrs. Briscoe rounded up the Imps and drove them upstairs for a wash. Ivy and Teddy were left to clear out. As they turned to head back through the kitchen, the colonel cleared his throat.

"Er, actually, perhaps Miss Briscoe should stay."

Ivy's heart jumped a beat. Had she done something wrong? She swallowed and reminded herself that she hadn't broken her oath. She could look the colonel in the eye and tell him so.

"Alright, sir." She took a seat on the settee beside her father, glancing at Teddy as he made his way out of the room. He returned her glance over his shoulder just before going out.

When the kitchen door had closed and Mrs. Briscoe had rejoined them, the old officer began. "First, I'd like to thank you, on behalf of myself, the Prime Minister, and the Special Duties Branch, for your fine service to your country these past weeks." He looked at Ivy. "Miss Briscoe, I know you've worked especially hard and sacrificed time with your friends, and I thank you."

Ivy swallowed again and nodded. She never was much good at receiving praise.

He continued, "I hope this doesn't come as too much of a shock for any of you, but we must close the station. Captain Briscoe, with so many of our troops rallying to the Front, there's a great need for medically trained officers. Now, don't worry, Mrs. Briscoe; nobody is asking your husband to join the fighting. But we are asking you, Noel, as one of the finest army doctors in the field, to offer your talents to prepare our young medics."

Dr. Briscoe nodded immediately. "Of course, I would be honoured to be of service. Kathleen's as capable a physician as I am, if not more so. She can carry on looking after my patients here; can't you, dear?"

Mrs. Briscoe smiled and nodded, but Ivy could see she was putting on a brave face.

"Good." The colonel settled it all with that one word. "In that case, you'll report to base in Norfolk by the end of this week. And that brings me back to the matter of the substation. It does seem an awful shame to abandon it to rot when it's only just got up and running—especially as it's such a vital connection in the messaging network. Mrs. Briscoe, I feel you'll have more than enough on your hands with looking after patients as well as your own children. Captain, have you any trustworthy neighbours you might like to recommend to keep the place in operation while you're on duty?"

Ivy's heart thudded against her ribs. She wanted to speak, but she waited while her parents thought out loud about their various acquaintances, unable to think of anyone who could spare the time away from their own duties. Finally, the conversation dipped into a lull—a space just big enough for Ivy to jump into, if she was quick.

She cleared her throat. "I could look after it, Colonel Gubbins. I've had quite a lot of practice now, and it's school holidays, so it won't interfere with my studies."

Mrs. Briscoe spoke up first. "But Ivy, dear, think how much work it's been among the three of us. If it were just down to you alone…"

"My thoughts precisely," the colonel chimed in. "I wouldn't feel right laying such a heavy burden on your shoulders unless I knew you had someone to help you."

It was the perfect invitation to say what she'd been hoping to say all the while. "But I wouldn't have to work alone. I know somebody who'd be perfect for the job. In fact, he knows a lot more about military things than I do. I think he'd make an excellent lookout."

"I don't suppose you mean your friend, Sergeant Woodall?"

Ivy nodded. The colonel gave her an appraising look. "Invite him in here, Miss Briscoe."

Teddy, it turned out, had been waiting just outside the door. He resumed his stiff posture when Ivy told him the colonel wanted a word with him.

"Your friend Ivy has been working these past weeks for a special government programme as a spy and messenger." Ivy waited for a look of surprise or annoyance, but Teddy's face remained as stoic as stone. "We need another agent to replace Captain Briscoe," the colonel continued. "She has put you forward as possessing the qualities needed to undertake such a duty yourself. Does this interest you?"

"Yes, sir!" Though his face remained the same, Teddy's voice was eager as anything.

"Very well, then. Being no stranger to the military, you will understand the dangers involved, especially in the case of an enemy invasion."

"Yes, sir."

"Well, Captain Briscoe." He turned to Ivy's father. "I never thought I'd commission children, but this war seems to belong to the young ones as much as to us old bags, wouldn't you say?" Dr. Briscoe agreed, and the colonel turned back to Teddy. "Once you've signed the Official Secrets Act, I shall personally induct you into the Special Duties Branch."

Before Teddy could respond, there was a thundering on the stairs as Kenny, Esme, and Spud tumbled down, landing in a heap at the bottom.

"We want to be spies too!" Kenny called out whilst trying to disentangle himself from his little sister. "If Ivy and Teddy can do it, so can we."

"Kenneth Michael Briscoe," their mother fumed, "what have I told you about eavesdropping!"

But the colonel was laughing. "From what I've just witnessed, I'm not sure about your spying credentials!"

"Can't we help too?" Kenny persisted. "We've not told a single body about the substation or the wireless or anything! Have we, Ez?" She peeked around her brother's shoulder and shook her curly head.

"That *is* to be commended. But I'm afraid you're both too young to sign the Official Secrets Act."

"But that's alright. We can give you the Scout's Oath of Honour, and that's much better."

All the adults were snickering now. The colonel, who had risen to his feet while interviewing Teddy, crouched down to the younger boy's level. "I'll tell you what. I shall take your oath *if* you can promise to follow orders from your superiors, even when that includes your older sister there."

Kenny scrunched up his face and thought very seriously about it. "If she promises not to be *too* bossy, then... yes, sir!"

By the time they said goodbye to the colonel, Kenny was tearing around the house, making war cries and boasting about how he would single-handedly catch any Huns who tried to invade. But in a quiet corner of the sitting room, Teddy extended a grateful hand to Ivy, and she shook it.

"I owe you one, Major Briscoe."

"Major?" She gave him a look like he'd gone mad. "The only Briscoes with ranks are my father and Ernie."

Teddy cocked his head and grinned. "The way I see it, I'm a sergeant, and you're my superior. That makes you at least a company sergeant major."

Ivy flushed, but shook her head. "The way I see it, we're equals. We're in it together."

He nodded. "One for all, and all for one. I say a hearty *amen* to that!"

16

CHURCHILL'S S.O.C.K.S

It rained in fits the whole next week. Ominous clouds appeared out of clear blue skies to chuck bucketsful on the unsuspecting children, then disappeared again, leaving them in a hot haze of steam.

Ivy's emotions mimicked the weather patterns. One minute, her heart soared at finally being able to share her secret and have a partner in crime; the next minute, she'd remember it was all because her father was leaving for nobody knew how long, and all her excitement and confidence would shrivel up.

Teddy and Flora returned to Emmett's Farm after a week at The Beeches, but Teddy rallied Ivy's spirits whenever they met with his grand plans and ideas for taking their spy duties to the next level. After taking the training in his stride, he had enough excitement and confidence for the two of them.

Before Ivy knew it, the twenty-second of June rolled around, when Dr. Briscoe was to travel to Norfolk. That very morning, news came over the wireless that France had surrendered to Germany, which cast an even heavier gloom over The Beeches. Winston Churchill had rallied the nation, saying, "We will go on!" Ivy took his words to her heart and repeated them in her head when it came time to say goodbye.

There weren't many dry eyes as Dr. Briscoe kissed each of his three children. Ivy's eyes prickled, but she forced herself to keep a stiff upper lip. She wanted her father to see he could count on her... to be confident he was leaving things in good hands.

"Esme, my tender-heart; Kenny, my entertainer; and Ivy, my brave girl." Ivy lifted her head up to look her father in the eye. "I want you all to work together. Look after each other and your mother. And remember to always do your best for God and country. And Ivy, don't forget: if the worst should happen, or if there's any sort of emergency at all while your mother's away working, go to Mr. Blackwood. He's your point of emergency contact."

"Yes, Father." She tried to smile, but her lips refused to cooperate.

"That's my girl." He kissed her on the top of her head, then kissed Mrs. Briscoe for so long that the three children looked at each other in horror. Then, with a last farewell, he was gone.

That afternoon, Ivy called for the first meeting of the new Special Duties recruits. After the week of rain, drizzle, mist, and every other kind of English wetness, the sun at last broke through strong and free—which meant, of course, the substation was stickier and more humid than ever. Nevertheless, Teddy and Ivy agreed that the meeting should take place in their headquarters, away from the prying eyes and ears of Flora.

But somehow, despite the mugginess, the bunker was much cheerier now she had company. They gathered around a wooden table in the main room, with two flickering candles up-lighting their faces, as if they were telling ghost stories around a campfire. Ivy passed around glasses of lemonade, then Teddy called the troops to order.

"Welcome to the inaugural meeting of the Ferny Hill Special Duties Command, First Platoon."

Esme tapped Ivy's arm and whispered, "The what?"

"It *is* a bit long for the Imps to remember," Ivy admitted.

Teddy leaned down towards Esme. "Well, it just so happens that choosing an official name for ourselves is the first item on the agenda. Any suggestions, troops?"

As usual, Kenny was the first to pipe up. "How about let's call ourselves the Allies!"

"Hmm," Teddy rubbed his chin. "I think that one's already taken. Any other ideas?"

No one had any, so at last Teddy said, "I've got one. We could be the SDCC for Special Duties Command Cadets."

Ivy wrinkled her nose.

"Alright, so it's not exactly catchy," Teddy conceded. "Ah, now that's it! How's about Special *Operations* Cadets. S.O.C., or *SOCs* for short."

Kenny scratched his temple in thought for a moment. "But that's not how you spell 'socks'. It needs a 'k' on the end."

"No, no it doesn't," Teddy insisted. "It's S.O.C., as in the abbreviation for *society*—like Chess Soc, or Greek Soc. You know?"

Blank stares met Teddy all around.

Kenny raised a finger. "I know! It can be Special Operations Cadet *Kids*. That spells SOCK the right way."

Teddy smacked his forehead with his palm and made a groaning noise.

But Ivy thought that, for once, Kenny might've struck on something. "Actually, that's not such a bad idea, you know. We could call ourselves Churchill's S.O.C.K.s, and nobody would know what we were talking about!"

Once they'd all agreed upon the name, Ivy, acting as scribe, wrote out S.O.C.K.s in block letters on the case notebook Teddy had donated to hold all their observations and records. That was just the beginning. Within an hour, the children had devised an entire new secret code language which grew more complicated by the minute.

It started out with simple things like, 'Are you wearing socks tonight?', which meant simply, 'Are you on duty tonight?'

"And how's this?" Teddy offered. "'Have you darned all your socks?' could mean 'Have you successfully collected the messages?'."

"Yes, exactly that," Ivy agreed. "And you might ask, 'Have you seen the vicar's socks lately?' to mean 'Have you collected the message from the churchyard?'."

It went on like this until Ivy had filled two pages with code phrases and suggested it might be best to stop at that.

"But shouldn't we all have code names as well?" Kenny asked.

"What's yours gonna be? Dumbo?" She gave one of his ears a little tweak.

Kenny jerked his head away with an indignant look. "No. Mine's Captain Fearsome."

Ivy snorted.

Teddy reached over and placed a hand on Kenny's shoulder. "Hmmm. Not much of a code name, though, is it? More like a pirate's name. Anyway, you see, you can't be a captain before you've been an officer cadet."

"What about you?"

"Me? Well, I've already got a rank—cadet sergeant."

"That's not much of a code name either," Ivy contested. "Unless you make it Sergeant Long Legs. That's it! We'll call you *Daddy* Long Legs!"

The Imps laughed, and Teddy shook his finger at her. "Careful. We've not yet given you a name, missy!"

"Ivy's already got a nickname," Kenny blurted through giggles. "It's 'Freckles'!"

Teddy nearly fell over backwards, he was laughing so hard. Ivy gave Kenny a murderous look.

Teddy wiped his watering eyes. "'Freckles is wearing her riding socks this morning' can mean Ivy's out scouting on horseback!" he guffawed.

When he composed himself at last, Teddy thought up names for Kenny and Esme. "How about Tootles and Pip? That way, you see, all *we* two have to do to alert *you* two is call out 'Tootle, Pip!' and no one's the wiser."

Esme giggled, but Kenny took a bit of convincing. Ivy had to remind him that one of Peter Pan's lost boys was called Tootles before he at last gave in.

"Right then." Teddy glanced down at his spiral notepad and took the pencil out from behind his ear to tick the items they'd accomplished. "Next up, Assign Duties. Ivy… I mean *Freckles*, are we agreed that you'll continue with your message collecting rounds and I'll be the main radio operator?"

"Yes, and we'll share the coding duties."

"And the scouting duties," he added.

Kenny was on the edge of his seat, quivering with so much excitement that it all came bursting out. "Can't I have scouting duties? I'm almost a First Class Scout, after all. I can teach us how to tie knots and track animals and everything!"

"Ah, young master Scout, we will certainly take you up on some of your expert training. But I have a much more important job for you, and Esme too." Kenny and Esme were all ears and eyes. "The two of you will be Lookouts. Tootles, if an emergency should happen, you'll be our runner to Mr. Blackwood. Tie this red handkerchief to the rose trellis, hoot twice like a barn owl, then take off to his place for help."

"I can get there fast as anything on my roller skates!" Kenny bounced on his wooden seat.

"That's fine. And Pip—"

"That's you, Esme. Remember?" Ivy nudged her little sister back into attention.

"Pip, you'll alert us if anyone comes snooping around the henhouse. What you'll do is pretend to be collecting eggs, then knock four times on the floorboards, very loudly. Try it now."

Esme had to try three times before her knocks were loud enough for Teddy. She gave a deep sigh. "But will we have to stand around on guard *all* day long?"

"Not a bit. Only when one of us is down here and can't see who might be sniffing around."

"Good." Kenny wiped his brow. "'Cause me and Ez—I mean Pip—still gotta sell those kittens. We could be the official S.O.C.K.s fundraisers!"

"Certainly, so long as you make time for special training."

Ivy frowned. "What special training?"

"Well, for one thing, if you're going to be a scout, you've got to be able to identify lots of things quickly and without a cheat sheet. Aircraft for starters."

Ivy crossed her arms. Teddy was beginning to get a bit big for his breeches. After all, she'd been doing this job for weeks without him. "*Pff.* Who said anything about special training? I'm already trained, remember?"

"Alright then. There's only one way to test your skills as a scout." Teddy stood up suddenly. "Shall we?"

Ivy craned her neck to look up into his eager face and frowned. "What, now?"

"We're in a war, chum! Now's all we've got!"

"Fine." She stood, brushing her hands together. "Badger Croft Meadow."

They had only been wading in the long, hot grass of Badger Croft Meadow a few minutes when the familiar humming, like a giant wasp high up in the atmosphere, tickled their ears.

Teddy shaded his eyes with his hand. "Ready, Freckles? What's that plane there?"

Ivy squinted at the plane. It looked just like one of Kenny's little tin models. "Spitfire?" she said at last.

Teddy's hand dropped. "Lucky guess. Wait, here comes another one, I think."

It was another fighter, Ivy was sure of that. "Spitfire again?" she wagered.

"Guess again."

"It's a Hurricane!" Kenny shouted.

Ivy gritted her teeth and plopped down in the grass. Teddy plopped down beside her. "I'll spare you admitting I was right, and do one better still. I'll share my secret with you."

"What secret? Being brilliant?" Ivy mumbled grumpily.

"Who said anything about being brilliant? But thanks for the compliment." He winked just before jumping back to his feet and offering her a hand.

When they got back to the substation, Teddy reached into his haversack and pulled out a pack of playing cards.

"Your secret is a deck of cards?" Ivy asked.

"You'll see." As he began to lay them all out on the floor, she did see. Each one had a picture of different aircraft on it —British as well as German.

Teddy drilled Ivy on the flashcards until dinner time. Then, after dinner, they used the cards to play a round of Snap with the Imps until it was time for Ivy to saddle up for her evening message-gathering rounds.

As she and Napoleon rode through the dusk, each time a plane flew overhead, she'd look up and call out what she thought was its name. "Lancaster, Hurricane, Spitfire."

As she and Napoleon waded through the yellow sea of Farmer Emmett's cornfield, she was joined by yet another high-flying companion. "Yep. You're definitely a Spitfire," she said out loud, as if the plane could answer.

But before it could, another fighter plane appeared from the opposite direction. She heard it before she saw it—the sound was slower, more intense, and somehow angrier than the Spitfire's murmuring engine.

Then she saw it. It was flying on its side, approaching the Spitfire fast. The rays of the setting sun glinted off its wings, which bore black crosses. *German crosses.*

"Is that a... a..." She wracked her brain for the right card. She could just see it... "A Messerschmitt!" she shouted, but her words were eaten up by the sound of machine gun fire. The two fighters zoomed towards each other, bolts of light flashing from their guns. It looked like they would either shoot each other out of the sky or collide, but just at the last minute, the Spitfire pulled up. It flipped in the air, turned on its side, and came back at its opponent.

But the German plane was just as fast; it, too, had turned, ready for the next stage of the dogfight. This time, the Spitfire charged at a deadly downward angle, giving the pilot the advantage of firing down on his opponent.

"Come on. Come on. Shoot him down!" Ivy didn't even realise she was shouting until she accidentally jerked on Napoleon's reins, causing the horse to start up beneath her. She steadied the horse and quickly turned her eyes back to the sky.

What she saw was smoke. Great, black, billowing clouds of it chugged from the Messerschmitt's engine. The plane appeared to hover, almost suspended in air for a moment. Then its nose tilted, and the rest of the plane followed in a graceful downward spiral of smoke. Within a few seconds, the German fighter disappeared behind the tree line. Ivy squinted at what looked like a little white cloud trailing behind it, down towards the horizon. When she could see nothing more for the trees, she lifted her eyes to the victorious Spitfire gliding off into the sunset. For the first time since the dogfight began, she let out a long breath of relief and wiped the cold sweat from her brow.

17
THE SHE-BEAR

Back at The Beeches, Ivy spent an hour before bed in the substation, coding the day's messages and sending their humdrum news on to headquarters. Before clicking off the transmitter, she added her own message: *Dogfight over Fairbank Wood at sunset. Messerschmitt down. Spitfire victorious.* She sat back, replaying the sensational scene in her mind's eye.

Already the memory of it had gone hazy around the edges, like a vivid dream that frays over time; and yet, the sight of that enemy plane whirling towards the earth, its ugly black crosses all a blur… the pillar of smoke… the little white cloud swallowed up by the trees… No, she would never forget those images—her first sight of real war in action. Perhaps she alone had witnessed the dogfight—*at last, something real to report!* But it was Teddy she most wanted to tell.

The next morning, Ivy dropped a tennis ball with the new day's messages down the chute and hurried into the house to help her mother with breakfast. It took all her self-discipline *not* to pop down into the substation herself to tell Teddy about the dogfight; but Mrs. Briscoe had an early nursing call to make and had especially asked for Ivy's help. Telling Teddy would have to wait.

The Imps were already seated at the table, looking groggy and famished. Mrs. Briscoe was dressed in a smart suit with a hospital apron, her auburn hair tucked neatly into a nurse's cap. "Thank heavens!" she cried as Ivy came through door, and thrust a wooden spoon into her hand. "Stir that porridge for me, would you, dear? I'll just get the tea."

"Mother, you won't believe what I saw last night!"

"I'd love to hear all about it, wouldn't I, ducky, but I've got to go right this minute or Lord help me, old Miss Bell will give me such a talkin' to. Your father says she has a tongue like a fiery whip. That reminds me, I ought to warn… I mean *tell* you all…" She hesitated and bit her lip. "But it can wait until I get home." She set down the teapot and threw on her coat. "Ezzy, Kenny, mind your big sister while I'm out. And don't forget to do something with those cats!" She closed the door behind her, and Ivy ladled the porridge into bowls, wondering what her mother had wanted to warn them about that had to do with a fiery whip.

Teddy came through the door next, bright-eyed and gung-ho as always. "What's for brekkies, Mum?" he teased as he scooped up the newspaper from the doormat and plopped into a chair.

As if he were the one that rode cross country through the night, Ivy thought. But there was no time to argue. She answered matter-of-factly, "I saw a dogfight last night, out over the fields, between a Spitfire and a Messerschmitt, and the Spitfire won."

Teddy had helped himself to a cup of tea, peering dubiously over the rim of it as he sipped. Finally putting it down, he answered carelessly, "I doubt that. A lone German fighter, here in Ferny Hill? Not likely." He flipped open the paper. "But don't let it get you down, Freckles. You're still a novice. One could easily mistake a Hurricane for a—*good grief!*" His eyes bulged wide at something on the front page of the newspaper.

"What is it?" Ivy skirted around the table to look over his shoulder.

"I don't believe it! Says here a German Messerschmitt BF-109 was shot down over Fairbank at zero hundred hours last night. That's just the next village over, isn't it?"

Ivy allowed a wry smile to spread across her lips. "I'll spare you admitting I was right. And I'll do one better still." She plonked a bowl of porridge down on the table in front of him.

It was to be a busy day for the members of Churchill's S.O.C.K.s. Teddy had drawn up charts of insignia which they were to practice identifying, along with land vehicles—armoured cars, artillery pieces, and tanks. The three of them sat up in Ernie's room, studying the charts (Esme had been excused to go and play with her kittens), but the subject of the plane crash kept sidetracking their progress.

"The fact is," Teddy mused, a heap of elbows and knees sitting cross-legged on the floor, "these Huns are getting rather cocky, flying fighters over the English countryside in full view of... well... people who happen to be out riding their horses at night. It sounds to me like they're getting a feel for the lay of the land before they drop in."

Ivy thought about this. "But won't they invade from the coast? We're miles away from the sea here."

"True," Teddy conceded. "I reckon the brunt of the invasion will come from the sea. But what's to stop Jerry from parachuting into inland locations like this one? Especially if it's true what Mr. Blackwood says about important military secrets closeted away in Ashbury Park."

Ivy tried to conceal a shiver. "But the Germans don't know that… how could they?"

Teddy made a sound that was not entirely reassuring. "Describe it again, the white thing that you saw going down behind the plane."

Ivy did describe it again, for the fourth time. "It just looked like a little white cloud going down behind the plane; that's all I saw."

"I reckon it was either a parachute meant to slow down the plane, *or* it was the pilot himself bailing out."

"The pilot? You mean a real Hun might be invading Fairbank?" Kenny asked eagerly.

Teddy's mouth twitched. "I doubt he'd have the nerve to invade on his own. One German's no match for a bunch of angry villagers. They'd probably skewer him with a pitchfork before he got the chance to draw his pistol."

"But if the pilot *did* survive…" Ivy thought out loud, "if there *is* a German out there, near Ferny Hill, shouldn't somebody go looking for him?"

"What are you suggesting, Freckles?" Teddy eyed her warily. "I can't say I'm entirely at ease with that look in your eye."

"Well, it *is* part of our job, isn't it? If we don't do it, who will?" Teddy still look less than convinced, so Ivy changed tactics. "What, are you scared, Daddy Long Legs?" she teased.

"Not a bit of it. I just think we're not quite advanced enough in our training to take on a scouting expedition which may lead to an armed and dangerous enemy, that's all."

Kenny raised his finger. "Do you think we ought to tell Mr. Blackwood about it?"

The older two exchanged a look. Ivy could see that Teddy was thinking along the same lines as Kenny, but something in her desperately wanted to keep the secret within S.O.C.K.s rather than simply handing it over to the adults and going back to transferring messages. This was their chance to get a piece of the action, and she knew Teddy wanted that chance as much as she did.

Finally, she answered, "I don't think we should bother him with it. After all, it's not really an emergency... The police and the military already know about the crash. If the pilot did survive, I reckon they'll sort him out." Carefully ignoring the dubious look in Teddy's eye, she continued, "We should just carry on spotting planes and spying on the locals and leave important things like Nazi invaders to the *real* soldiers." Out the corner of her eye, she saw Teddy stiffen and knew she'd got him right where she wanted him.

After a short pause, he said in a bored manner—as if only to humour her, "I suppose we might go in search of the crash, just to gather clues. After all, if the pilot survived, he won't be anywhere near the scene by this time, so it can't be too dangerous for Tootles here… unless, of course, you find the notion of potentially encountering a dead body a little creepy for your liking, Tootles?"

"Hey, I'm no scare baby!" Kenny protested.

"No, you're a Scout. And I dare say, if we're going through with this, we're going to need those scouting skills of yours about now."

They were still upstairs charting maps and planning their first real manoeuvre—or as Teddy called it, Operation Bail Out—when Mrs. Briscoe came home that afternoon. Ivy had wanted to set out in search of the crash that very morning, but Teddy insisted they spend a couple of days preparing for the mission, so as to get it right. At length, they struck a compromise: they would wait for the following day, the eighth of July, after the morning's rounds. Ivy marked it in the official S.O.C.K.s notebook.

Teddy returned next door for lunch to see that Flora wasn't causing too much grief for poor Mrs. Emmett. Ivy was ravenous when she sat down at the kitchen table.

"My, you're eating like a couple of starved dogs!" Mrs. Briscoe marvelled as Ivy and Kenny wolfed down their spam sandwiches and milk. Esme, as usual, picked at hers like a little robin. "Busy morning?"

"Mmhmm." Ivy nudged Kenny under the table to keep him from squealing about their plans. She swallowed and quickly changed the subject. "What was it you wanted to tell us this morning, Mother? Remember, you said it could wait 'til later…"

"Oh yes, that!" Mrs. Briscoe smiled cheerfully, but something in her eye gave Ivy a foreboding feeling that she was about to drop a bomb on them. "I've had a call from Grandmammy Kennedy. She's offered to come up and help me keep an eye on things here while your father's away."

Ivy lowered her sandwich slowly. "And... you told her we were quite capable of keeping our eyes on things without her, right?"

Kenny, meanwhile, had gone a strange shade of pale blue, as if all the blood had rushed out of his face. "Grandmammy Kennedy." He repeated the name in a whisper, as if it bore a curse. Then louder, "But... but she's dangerous!"

"Now, Kenny," Mrs Briscoe scolded, "She isn't as bad as all that. You know as well as I, most of what she says is just empty threats."

Kenny gulped and shook his head. "Tell that to the poor old cockerel she strangled, just 'cause he disturbed her sleep one too many times!"

"Well I'm not afraid of her," Ivy put in, a bit snootily. "She's just a fat old woman."

"Ivy Elisabeth Briscoe! That's no way to be talking about your own grandmother. You'll hush up, or I'll let Grandmammy share your room. How would you like that, now?"

Ivy said no more. Though she would never have admitted it to her ten-year-old brother, in truth, she was every bit as petrified as he was. Grandmammy Kennedy was known far and wide as the fiercest old she-bear of a woman since Boudica. No one was safe from her scoldings, not even their distinguished doctor of a father! In fact, he often jested that should Grandmammy Kennedy ever meet the King himself, she wouldn't hesitate to give him a good dose of her 'what-for'.

"When is Grandmammy coming?" Esme asked, and the

other two realised they'd failed to ask that crucial question themselves.

"She left from County Wicklow yesterday and stayed the night in Dublin, so I expect she'll arrive in Ferny Hill on the ten o'clock train tonight."

Tonight? Ivy's shoulders slumped involuntarily. Only a few more fleeting hours of freedom, and just when they were really getting things going with S.O.C.K.s. She'd have to call a platoon meeting after lunch and put Teddy on his guard.

The troops were to meet again in Ernie's room (which Teddy had re-dubbed 'Training Command') at 1300 hours to review the insignia and land vehicle charts. Ivy decided that was the time to drop the bomb of Grandmammy Kennedy's imminent arrival.

"I don't see what all the fuss is about, frankly," Teddy responded, with his usual nonchalance, to the grave announcement. "She's only your grandmother, not the Nazi invasion!"

"Yes, but she's only slightly less dangerous. She's got special talents in meddling and scolding, which means doing our job—spying, running manoeuvres, everything—is going to be ten times harder now under her hawk eyes."

Teddy dismissed her fears with a wave of his hand. "As long as we're careful she's not looking when we *'feed the chickens'*, and if we use our code language, she'll never guess what we're up to. And if she does get suspicious we're up to something, we'll pretend it's all a great big childish lark."

"You mean like a meadowlark?" Kenny asked, confused.

"What? Oh. Not that kind of lark. It's like a game. But enough about that. We've got a scouting mission in a day's time. Seeing as you're both coming along with vehicle identification, I suggest we practice some stealth and camouflage in the hedgerows. Oh—" He looked at Kenny eagerly perched on the edge of the bed. "And tying knots, of course."

By the end of that sweltering afternoon, the three cadets were sticky with sweat and dirt, but they staggered home with a fine sense of readiness for the task ahead. They'd practiced camouflaging themselves by spitting in the dirt and wiping the muddy paste over their faces, then fixing twigs and sticks to their heads and bodies. Next, Teddy led them in an exercise that involved crawling on their bellies through hedges and thick underbrush. Their first experiment was to try out their stealth attacks on the sheep.

"Sheep," Teddy explained, "may be thick, but they're the first to respond to the slightest disruption to their tranquility. If you can sneak up on a sheep, you can sneak up on anything."

On the first attempt, Ivy snapped a twig with her knee, and several sheep bounded a yard backwards. But the second time, all three made it to the fence and practically stared an unsuspecting ewe in the face as she reached her head down to gobble up clover just inches away from their hiding spot.

It was then time to test their skills on humans, and the Land Girls at Emmett's Farm provided ready specimens. True to Teddy's theory, the girls proved much less astute than the sheep. Ivy watched, amazed, as Teddy got himself into the cab of a cart while the girls were loading it with hay. He managed to drive the mule a full three yards forward and park it again before the giggling, gabbing girls turned around with their pitchforks. It was all the three cadets-in-training could do to keep from laughing out loud as the girls stared in dumbfounded silence, then blamed each other for not hitching the mule as had been suggested, or not filling up his nosebag enough to keep him still, and the like. Only when the scouts made it safely back through the hedge did they allow themselves to fall over in the grass and laugh until tears streaked their mud-smeared faces.

The day's training so preoccupied Ivy's mind, she completely forgot about Grandmammy Kennedy until that night. Another message-collecting round complete, she and Teddy had coded the messages and sent them over the wireless to HQ. When Ivy turned in, the house was dark. Everyone was asleep, and Ivy's head felt as heavy as a watermelon. But as she climbed the stairs, lighting the way with her torch, she stopped halfway up. *What was that sound?* It was like thunder—or, worse still, like the low, threatening growl of a bear.

And then it dawned on her. It wasn't growling she heard. It was snoring coming from the nostrils of Grandmammy Kennedy.

Training Command was theirs no longer. It had been seized as the she-bear's den.

18

NAZI ON THE LOOSE

"That child hasn't a bit of your complexion, Kathleen."

Ivy yawned as she turned on the spot for Grandmammy's ritual inspection early the next morning. She always began her visits to the Briscoes this way, looming over each child in turn with her fists perched on her broad hips, her rage of white hair framing her scowling face like some saintly aura, her squinted hawk eyes scanning for any little flaw.

"And her hair! Just like a hornet's nest!" she continued in her lilting Irish manner. "Indeed, I wouldn't wonder if a few of them set up house in that mess."

As if Ivy had any choice over the matter of her wildly curly hair. She wanted to say as much, but she noticed her mother's nostrils flaring with exasperation, and so bit her lip for her sake.

"And she's as thin as a bean pole at that," Grandmammy persisted. "Are rations so exacting in this county that you can't afford to feed the child? Well, luckily, I've brought along a pound of good Irish butter. That should fatten her right up."

As unenthused as Ivy felt about being *fattened up,* she felt the sorrier for her mother; Grandmammy scolded Mrs. Briscoe worst of all, unsatisfied with every little detail of how she ran her home. At least her scrutiny of Mother would divert her notice away from the children and their top-secret activities… or so Ivy hoped.

They all agreed that they'd have to take extra care to act natural and avoid Grandmammy's notice that day—the day they were to execute Operation Bail Out. When Ivy came indoors for breakfast, her mother had already gone out on nursing calls. In her place was Grandmammy Kennedy, white hair billowing around her face like a storm and her sleeves rolled up around her muscular forearms. She stood over the cooking range wielding a carving knife as if it were a battle axe, hacking an unfortunate pork loin to shreds. Ivy slipped silently into her seat beside her younger siblings.

"Come in at last, have you, miss Ivy?" Grandmammy said over her shoulder, continuing to hack away at the loin. "Well, I'd have thought a girl of your age would make herself a bit"—*whack!*—"more useful around the house"—*whack!*—"while her mother's tending to the sick and dying."

Ivy, still catching her breath from her ride across the countryside that morning, felt stung by the comment. It took all her self-control to answer politely, "Sorry I wasn't here to help with breakfast, Grandmammy. I had to feed the horses and the chickens."

"Hmph" was, to Ivy's relief, the only reply.

She helped herself to two thick slices of toast, each

spread with a knob of Grandmammy's Irish butter. Whilst she didn't need fattening up particularly, she would need her energy for the day's expedition.

"Kenny, pass the gooseberry jam, would you?… Kenny." Twice more she said his name, but he never so much as flinched. His nose remained stuck deep in his book: *Scouting for Boys.*

Irritated by Grandmammy's scolding and Kenny's deafness to her simple request for the jam, Ivy reached over and snatched the book right out of his hands. Pulling a pencil out from one of her plaited pigtails, where she'd left it after coding messages, she scratched in large block letters beneath *Scouting for Boys,* 'AND GIRLS'.

Kenny scowled and stuck his tongue out at her.

"If you stick that tongue out again, I'll see it cut off," Grandmammy said sharply. The two siblings looked at her, then back at each other in amazement. How had she managed to see Kenny's tongue without so much as turning her head? Was it true Grandmammy had eyes in the back of her neck?

Ivy shrugged and carried on scribbling on the book's cover.

This time, Kenny reached out, grabbed her closest pigtail, and yanked it hard, like a bell pulley.

"Ow!" Ivy shouted at him, but Kenny didn't let go.

In a split second, Grandmammy had spun around with her right hand poised behind her head. With the aim of an Indian warrior, she let the carving knife loose. All three Briscoes gasped in chorus as the knife spun and whistled through the air straight for them. At the last moment, when it looked like the blade would pin Kenny between the eyes, it swung past his right ear and struck with a reverberating *plonnnng* into the wall just behind him.

Nobody dared say a word, or even to breathe, after that. The children swallowed down their breakfast whole and scrambled out of the house as fast as their legs would take them. Facing a Nazi in the forest would feel like child's play after facing the wrath of Grandmammy Kennedy.

"You chaps alright?" Teddy raised one concerned eyebrow when Ivy and Kenny found him at their rendezvous point behind the henhouse. "Look like you've just met with a monster."

"Fine." Ivy answered. Kenny had—for the first time in his life—been rendered speechless. "Let's just get going."

Once down the hatch, the three of them gathered around the table in the substation to chart out on their map where Ivy thought the plane must have gone down.

"It was due west, because the sun was setting in that direction. So, it probably went down in these woods, right about... here." She circled a forested spot on the map.

After going over the operation plan once more and camouflaging themselves with mud and leaves, it was time to ride. Ivy took Kenny with her in Nelson's saddle, and Teddy mounted Napoleon.

"Pip, don't forget—" Teddy looked down from his high perch on Napoleon at Esme's serious little face. "You're on lookout duty. Report anything suspicious when we get back, alright?"

"Yes, sir!" She saluted, then broke into a broad, snaggle-toothed grin as she waved them off.

Ivy led the sortie across the yellow cornfield where she'd watched the dogfight, then down the hill and into the forested valley. It was an old wood, and the trees grew wide enough apart that they could easily ride between them and see the sun through the treetops—which proved a good thing, as Kenny used the sun's position to help them keep their bearings. The wood sloped down to a little stream where they stopped to let the horses rest and drink.

Ivy jumped down with a soft thud on the springy bank.

"What's that?" Kenny, still in the saddle, was looking at something on the opposite bank.

"What's what?" Ivy asked, trying to look in the same direction.

"That white thing in that tree, just there. It is somebody's kite?"

She spotted what looked like a white canvas curtain tangled in the branches of an old oak tree.

"By jove!" Teddy exclaimed, then lowered his voice to a hoarse whisper. "That's no kite. That's a piece of parachute."

They all looked at each other, but no one needed to say anything. They all knew what it meant. The pilot had bailed out. If he had survived, he could be hiding anywhere… even behind a tree, watching them at that moment.

Ivy felt the urge to move—to do *something* other than just stand there. "Let's keep going… try to find the crash." She tried to sound casual, but even Teddy seemed jumpy compared to his usual lax and lanky self.

They left the horses at the stream and waded through it, their heads ducked low, following Teddy's lead. When they were level to the oak tree with the torn parachute, Teddy made a signal for the other two to wait while he went ahead. He crept up the bank, crouched low, and crawled along like some strange human amphibian, glancing through the trees in every direction. Ivy didn't take her eyes off him lest she lose his location when he disappeared behind a shrub. At last he waved to them to follow, and Ivy and Kenny scrambled up the bank on all fours, ducking this way and that just as Teddy had instructed them.

"No sign of the rest of the chute," Teddy whispered. "He must've destroyed it to hide the evidence, and you know what that means."

Ivy swallowed hard. "It means he lived."

Kenny, who was crouching down hugging his knees, suddenly pointed to a place on the ground. "Look!"

The other two scrambled over to see what he'd found. Left in the sandy dirt was a faded but unmistakable boot print.

"Looks like blood," Kenny whispered, making a face as he pointed at a series of faded red spots. "And here's more prints."

They followed the prints to a tangled mess of broken and charred tree limbs. It looked as if a storm had struck that one little patch of the forest, and it had. Ivy saw it first. There, in the middle of the debris, was all that remained of the Messerschmitt.

The front of the plane and the cockpit were hardly recognisable—just blackened shards of metal and shattered glass. But most of the tail was intact, and raised on it, like a banner hoisted out of the ashes of the wreckage, was the Nazi's hideous symbol: a big black swastika.

A trickle of sweat went down Ivy's back, and she shivered in spite of the mugginess of the forest. The charred plane, the footprints… it was all so real. Her nostrils tingled with the biting twang of burnt metal. It gave her the horrible, skin-prickling feeling of eyes watching them from behind a tree… terrible, inhuman, Nazi eyes. The thought was unbearable.

"We should go," she whispered.

To her relief, Teddy nodded. "If there was anything salvageable from the wreck, he's already taken it."

"And anyway, it's lunch time," Kenny added. "I'm hungry."

Ivy felt relieved that the others were as eager as she to get out of that wood.

As quietly as red Indians on the hunt, they made their way back to the stream and found the horses waiting patiently. As they saddled up, Ivy turned to look back once more at the hanging patch of parachute. Something else caught her eye a little further up the bank; something, she could almost swear, had moved. She held her breath and watched a minute longer. A woodpecker landed on a tree trunk and began to hammer away at it, but nothing else stirred.

She'd heard about soldiers getting jumpy and firing their weapons at the slightest rustle of leaves or a scampering squirrel. *It's just your imagination,* she reassured herself. But goose pimples dotted her skin for a long time after they'd ridden away from the crash.

19

SPIES AND RABBITS

The horses clip-clopped in and out of shady pools up the lane to The Beeches. Though none of them admitted it to the others, the three children all felt giddy with relief to be out of the forest and nearing the safety of home.

Kenny was in a particularly comical mood, and the other two were laughing at his impressions of Grand-mammy Kennedy. They were all so jolly, they didn't notice the petite curly-haired person walking in the same direction up the lane until they were nearly upon her.

"Whoa there!" Teddy pulled Napoleon to a stop. "Pip, what are you doing out here away from your station?"

"Ezzy!" Ivy pulled up beside him. "Where have you been? You're not allowed to walk to the village alone. You know that."

Esme's face was scrunched up tight from the weight of a big, lumpy, brown paper bag she was carrying. "I was keeping lookout, like you said, but then Flora said she really needed me to do an important job for her and she couldn't possibly do it herself because she had such a terrible tummy ache, and these would make her feel better."

"Why, that turkey." Teddy's lips curled in. "You know, you don't have to mind what she says. In fact, as a rule, I wouldn't."

"Whatever did she send you for?" Ivy asked.

Esme stretched out her arms and opened the bag so all could see. It was chock-full of every kind of sweet imaginable: barley sugars, naughts and crosses, pretty pollies, raspberry and pineapple creams—even mint victories, which cost a whole shilling each.

"I've never seen so many sweets!" Kenny said dreamily, mesmerised by the scrumptious prospect before him.

"She's a thief! A pirate! A scoundrel for involving an innocent child in her schemes!" Teddy fumed. "Flora's pocket allowance wouldn't buy a tenth of what's in that bag. She must've taken the money from the Emmetts. Those poor, good people..."

"But she didn't take it," Esme protested wearily, letting the bag drop with a thud to the ground. "Barney gave her lots and lots of ration coupons, and she told me to go and buy as many sweets as I could with them."

Ivy exchanged a look with Teddy. His patience had clearly reached the end of its fuse.

"Barney, eh?" he growled. "Well then, *he's* the crook. Those coupons must've been forged." He blew an angry puff of air out of his nostrils. "Mind if I take Napoleon over to the farm for a minute? I want to have a word with my *darling* sister."

Ivy nodded, not daring to object lest Teddy explode. As

he galloped off like a knight pursuing vengeance, she dismounted to help Esme, with her bag of sweets, up into the saddle in front of Kenny, then led Nelly by her reins the short distance back home.

She led the horse up the drive and around the outside of the garden so as not to trample her mother's vegetable patch on the way to the stable. Just as they were about to round the henhouse, Ivy stopped. Voices were coming from inside the henhouse. She put her finger to her lips to quiet the Imps and listened. One of the voices was deep and smooth like an oboe; the other, shrill as a broken violin.

"Would I lie to you, Barney?" the shrill voice said. "It was such a nasty trick they played. All four of them came in here, and when I peeked inside, all I saw were these filthy poultry. Can't we get out of here now?"

"Sure, in just a second," the deep voice answered. "And you say they've got some sort of club, eh?"

"It's some sort of silly spy society. Such a babyish way to spend one's time. They're probably off at it right now. Oh!" The violin broke a string. "This hen's trying to peck me! Get it away! I can't stand it!"

Flora came running out of the henhouse, kicking and flailing like she was fighting off a grizzly bear. Barney sauntered out behind her. As he blinked in the full sunlight, he suddenly spotted the horse and the three children. He gave a start, but quickly eased into his usual carefree manner.

"Ah, it's Ivy and her two sidekicks. You know, Flora's been telling me you kids have a secret spy club. Sounds like just the sort of thing I liked to do at Kenny's age." He winked. "And just what sort of information have you kids collected on these little expeditions of yours?"

Ivy had to think fast. "It's like Flora said." She shrugged. "Just a lot of silly kids' play. You know—spying on neighbours for sport, playing pranks… that sort of thing."

"Oh?" Barney took several steps closer so Ivy's eyes were level with the cleft in his chin. He began stroking Nelly's nose. "Doesn't sound silly to me. Sounds like jolly good fun!" He smiled up at Kenny.

Right on cue, Kenny blurted, "It *is* jolly good fun! Only, we can't tell you about it. It's top sec—"

Ivy doubled over in a coughing fit that drowned out the rest of Kenny's sentence.

"Alright there, Ivy?" Barney asked, taking her elbow.

"Fine. Just swallowed a midgie." She straightened up. "Well, we'd better get going. Grandmammy will be looking for us."

She gave the horse's reins a little tug, but Barney kept his grip on her elbow.

"Look here, Ivy," he said in a lowered, appeasing sort of voice that only she could hear. "Flora didn't mean any harm. She seemed lonesome, so I asked her to show me around. She thought I'd like to meet your hens, that's all. Don't be too cross with her."

Barney meant well. But far from smoothing things over, he'd just turned up the heat on Ivy's simmering temper. Too well she knew that Flora had no interest in putting herself in the company of hens. It was a blatant attempt to rat out S.O.C.K.s—to get them in trouble or spoil their fun. It was just like her too, sticking her nose in where it wasn't wanted.

The second Barney released her elbow and turned to go,

Ivy reached up and took the heavy sack from Esme's lap. She hoisted it over to where Flora stood scowling and dropped it right on top of her shiny little saddle shoes.

"From now on, do your own errands. My little sister's not your slave." Ignoring the shocked look on Flora's porcelain face, Ivy turned on her heels and marched back to her horse, feeling just a tad bit lighter in her step.

Ivy waited until she was sure Barney and Flora had disappeared through the hedge before she allowed the Imps out of hiding behind one of the giant copper beech trees. She felt sorry to let Barney down—whatever Teddy said, he had been nothing but kind to them—but as long as Flora stuck herself to his side like chewing gum to the bottom of a shoe, S.O.C.K.s had no choice but to keep a wide berth of them both. And they would have to keep a closer eye on that little snitch.

At the kitchen door, Ivy turned on the Imps, her eyebrows raised to show she meant no nonsense. "Tootle, Pip, you two watch out for Flora. If she asks you any questions, don't answer."

She felt cross enough to kick herself. Who knew how long Flora had watched them, or what she might have seen, without raising the least suspicion from Ivy? It seemed that little porcelain doll was a pretty decent spy, though Ivy felt sick to admit it.

She turned back to the door and gave it an angry shove. That's when she got her second shock in the span of ten minutes. Grandmammy sat facing them across the kitchen table, roaring with laughter, her head thrown back and her broad shoulders jumping up and down like a pair of rabbits. Ivy had never seen Grandmammy so much as chuckle, but there she sat laughing like a schoolgirl—and none other than Mr. Blackwood was the cause. He sat across from her, wiping his eyes. Ivy noted a half-drained whisky bottle and two shot glasses between them on the table.

"Ah, Koos. But those were the days," Grandmammy sighed, and she raised her glass to Mr. Blackwood before downing the lot. Only when she'd plonked the glass down on the table did she look up to see her three grandchildren standing dumbfounded in the doorway. Immediately, the smile vanished and the usual scowl took its old place.

"There you three are—about time, too. Ivy Briscoe!" Ivy braced herself. "I want to know who this young man is you're off gallivanting with all the livelong day? Is he Catholic? Well it doesn't really matter. You're much too young and too childish to be fillin' your head with boys when you ought to be learning to run a household."

Ivy's face went hot. This accusation was so outrageously unfair, it was only the memory of Grandmammy's flying knife that enabled her to bite her tongue.

Mr. Blackwood turned around in his chair. "Howzit, you three? I was just paying your Gran here a visit. We go quite a ways back, she and I."

Mr. Blackwood and Grandmammy, old friends? It was all too much.

Grandmammy's smile reappeared. "Do we ever, Koos! What year was it we went hunting wild boars in the African bush? Back when Carl was still with us, may the Lord rest his soul." Soberly she made the sign of the cross, then filled her glass for another swig of whisky.

"Ya, that it was." Mr. Blackwood nodded. "Well, Eireen, I should be getting on."

"Ay, ay. Was good of you to call, Koos, and to bring the rabbits as well!" Grandmammy gestured to a wooden crate beside the table.

"Not at all. I thought you could use them, what with the meat rationing getting tighter. What it is they put in them sausages down at the butcher's is a mystery."

Esme, who had become absorbed with the crate from the word *rabbits,* ran over and peered in. There was pure love in her big brown eyes when she looked up at Mr. Blackwood. "You mean we can keep them? Oh thank you, Mr. Blackwood!" She bent down and scooped up a bundle of tawny fur. "I'll call this one Charlie, and the white one Snowball, and the one with the very long ears can be... mmmm, Butterfly!"

"I wouldn't name them if I were you, lass," Mr. Blackwood mumbled through his beard.

Esme wrinkled her nose at that. "But they have to have names, Mr. Blackwood," she lisped. "They're Briscoes now."

The rotund man patted his bushy brow with his handkerchief. "Ya, well, Briscoes or no, they can't stay in the kitchen. How 'bout I just take them out to the stable for keeping in the meantime. You kids want to lend a hand?"

As the four of them trudged across the back garden, Esme hung on Mr. Blackwood's arm so as not to have to take her eyes off her new pets for a single moment. Teddy appeared, lolloping up from behind, and fell into step beside Ivy. Mr. Blackwood grumbled something unintelligible at him, and Teddy, in response, tipped his head and said, "Oh, hello again, sir." Then he lowered his voice so only Ivy could hear. "Can't find the little pest anywhere. Not even in her room pretending to be sick."

Ivy snorted. "That's because she was over here, showing Barney around the henhouse."

Teddy looked dumbly at her a moment, then shook his head as if to clear it. "How's that?"

"I'll tell you later," Ivy answered, with a sideways glance at Mr. Blackwood.

They were at the stable by then. The Imps were rounding up the kittens in an unused horse stall to make way for the rabbits. Mr. Blackwood suddenly turned to Ivy and Teddy with a look of urgency on his whiskery face. In a hushed tone, he began, "I was hoping to have a word with you two. There was an attempted break-in at Ashbury Park yesterday. The barbed wire was cut." He squinted at Teddy. "You wouldn't know anything about that, would you? Nothing to do with one of your training manoeuvres?"

Teddy's mouth dropped open. "Sir, I… we wouldn't dream of…"

"No," Ivy cut in. "Of course not."

"Right. I didn't think so, but had to ask, ya? Now that's out of the way, have you seen anything or anyone fishy poking around Ferny Hill on your rounds lately? Either of you?"

A look between them conveyed they were both thinking of the crashed plane in Fairbank Wood. Teddy turned back to Mr. Blackwood first, shaking his head. "Nothing that would explain the clipped barbed wire, sir." Then he folded his arms and squinted thoughtfully. "But sir, who do you suppose would be so eager to break into Ashbury Park?

There are hundreds of military bases dotted around Britain. Why target this one?"

Mr. Blackwood peered around, as if afraid someone might be listening, before answering, "The Germans have their beady eyes on Ferny Hill. I heard it on the wireless this morning from that traitor who broadcasts in English from Berlin, Lord Haw-Haw. He reported that strategic RAF plans for striking back at Germany were being made right here in our village."

"That explains the dogfight then," Ivy muttered.

Mr. Blackwood raised a bushy eyebrow. "Ah, you've heard about that, now have you?"

"In the morning paper." Ivy gave Teddy a sideways glance, then she hastily added, "But what's Ferny Hill got that's so interesting to the Germans anyway?

"Never you mind about—"

Mr. Blackwood's admonishment was cut short by a loud snap from Teddy's fingers. "Of course! *That's* what's going on in Ashbury Park. I'll bet my top hat they're mapping out bombing missions."

"Sshhhh!" Mr. Blackwood peered around again, then answered in a hushed but no less forbidding voice, "What's going on in Ashbury Park is none of your concern, understand?"

They both nodded.

"You've got enough on your hands minding what *is* your business. I want you kids to scout out the village for anyone behaving suspiciously... anyone with a foreign accent... anything out of place at all. Ya? Understood?"

"You're sending *us*?" Ivy felt her belly somersault with pride, then squirm with guilt for the lie she'd just told the man now entrusting her with a bona fide, important, and potentially dangerous mission.

"Ya, you," Mr. Blackwood said, nodding. "Nobody will be looking out for a couple of kids, see. An old soldier like me is more likely to raise suspicion."

"I quite agree with you, sir." Teddy nodded approvingly. "We shan't let you down."

"Mr. Blackwood..." Ivy spoke up tentatively. "About that German plane that went down. Well, just *suppose* the pilot survived. You don't think maybe *he* could be the one trying to break into Ashbury Park? I mean, just if, say, he got out of the plane alive and managed to walk off without getting captured..."

Mr. Blackwood's suspicious frown silenced Ivy, and she looked down at her boots.

"And what reason might you have for thinking the pilot could've survived?" Mr. Blackwood asked, his voice laced with suspicion. "I wouldn't like to think you lot have been snooping around Fairbank Wood..."

"I wouldn't exactly call it *snooping*, sir," Teddy piped up. "It was a highly organised mission, in fact, and executed with the utmost—"

"You two listen to me." Mr. Blackwood's baritone voice had dropped lower still until it rumbled. He pointed a thick, calloused finger at each of them in turn with a look that would've sobered a circus clown.

"Yes, sir," Teddy whispered and swallowed audibly.

"Your job is strictly to run your rounds about the village, send the messages to HQ, and report any unusual observations to me. You are *not* military personnel. You are civilians and children, and you will leave dangerous operations—

such as examining the scene of an enemy plane crash—to armed officers. Or do I need to inform Colonel Gubbins that the two of you are not capable of following orders?"

They shook their heads.

Mr. Blackwood grunted. "And that goes for this new mission, too. Should you discover a likely suspect, you *must not,* under any circumstances, try to be heroes and confront him yourselves. Don't you think for one minute those Krauts and their accomplices won't shoot you because you're children. You think they have scruples? I tell you, they'd as soon kill you as look at you. I know 'em. I fought 'em hand-to-hand in the war. I looked right into their eyes, and you know what I saw?"

Again, they shook their heads.

"Nothing. Nothing but pure malice. Not a trace of a human soul."

They waited until after Mr. Blackwood had taken his leave to discuss the new development.

Teddy broke the stiff silence with a whistle. "Well, how do you like that? You put your neck on the line for King and Country, and what do you get in return? A right smarting slap on the wrist." He overturned an empty barrel and plopped down on it. "I had a grim feeling he wouldn't be handing out medals for bravery if he learned we'd been down to the crash."

"Well, I had to tell him, didn't I?" Ivy grumbled defensively. "It *is* our duty to report back to him, or have you forgotten?"

Teddy crossed his arms and grimaced. "I've just been thoroughly reminded of our duties. Don't reckon I'm in need of another scolding, thanks very much."

Ivy pursed her lips and kicked at the hay on the stable floor.

"Look here," Teddy said more brightly. "Let's forget all about this pilot business. It's not worth losing S.O.C.K.s over. And anyway, we've a new pickle to solve. Didn't you hear? A spy in Ferny Hill!"

"I don't know that it's all *that* much of a pickle..." Ivy ventured.

Teddy looked at her sharply. "Go on, Freckles. Out with it."

"Well, we know there's a Nazi pilot out there, don't we? He might have seen what's going on in Ashbury Park from up in the air, and—"

"And what?" Teddy interrupted. "Reported it back to the Nazis whilst falling out of the sky?"

Ivy's hackles went up. "Or *before* he crashed... or after."

"And just how do you explain the barbed wire being cut? I suppose the pilot dropped a pair of shears as he flew over?"

Ivy shot him with a glare. "Don't be stupid. Maybe the barbed wire has nothing to do with the leaked information. Anyone could've done it... even children!"

"Know any children crazy enough to do a thing like that? *Other* than us, I mean."

Ivy crossed her arms, and Teddy scratched his head, making his hair as untidy as the hay-strewn floor. "I don't know, Freckles. I reckon if the pilot's out there, the Army'll apprehend him before we will."

"But what if he's in disguise... *as the spy*?" she persisted.

Teddy sighed. "I suppose you *could* be right—for argument's sake. Still, I wouldn't place my money on the pilot.

If you ask me, we should put him out of our minds—leave him to the experts, as old 'Major Blackmood' says—until we've made a fair search of the village for other, more likely suspects."

"Fine," Ivy conceded. "We'll search the village tomorrow. But for the record, I'm *still* putting my money on the pilot."

That night, Ivy fell quickly and deeply into sleep. She dreamt of men in grey uniforms with blank white eyes. They had tied her to a spit and were roasting her over a fire. She could feel the spit poking into her back… feel the heat of the fire… see those dead, white eyes fixed hungrily on her.

She woke with a start. The heat of the fire had been her own feverish temperature. She shivered, broken out in a cold sweat. Involuntarily, her eyes moved to the window. Somewhere out there, under the moonlight that streamed in and fell on her bed, a Nazi pilot was alive and biding his time.

At least, she hoped that was all he was doing.

20
UNDER COVER

That afternoon, four children went walking down a country lane, their hands full of kittens. No one passing would have suspected them of being undercover spies for the British government. Theirs was a secret mission, planned by candlelight in a military substation the night before.

The first stage of the plan was simple: they'd split up at the village square, and the older two would stop by Sidwell's to ask the shopkeeper if he'd encountered any unusual new customers lately. Next, they'd browse the village high street for suspicious characters, then finish their search in the village pub, The Rifleman. That's where most of the off-duty troops spent their time. Teddy had poo-pooed the idea of spying in the pub at first, insisting that a Nazi spy would stay clear out of the way of crowds of military personnel.

Ivy had considered this for a moment. She had learned never to contradict Teddy *too* quickly; chances were he already had a counter-argument aimed and ready. But this just didn't add up.

"If *I* were a Nazi spy," she countered, "and I wanted secret military information, I reckon a tavern full of drunken military personnel would be a pretty good place to start."

Teddy gave her an impressed look that made her blush. "I like your thinking, Freckles," he said, slapping her on the shoulder. "That's thinking like a bona fide spy, that is."

Ivy shrugged and quickly changed the subject by teasing Teddy about his clothing. He'd come out in his smartest pleated trousers, a sporty cable knit vest, tasseled brogues and golf cap. This 'get-up' served the purpose of making him look older, and therefore raising fewer eyebrows among the pub-goers when a couple of kids waltzed through the door.

Ivy hadn't thought of that, but there was no point in her dressing older than she really was. Everyone in the village knew her as the middle Briscoe child; and anyway, Clive Burnham, who ran The Rifleman, was a frequent patient of her father's. He'd never give her any trouble. The Imps, on the other hand, were too young to risk it. They'd have to be kept out of the way, and that's where the kittens came in. While Ivy and Teddy scoped out the pub, Kenny and Esme would scope out the village under cover of selling kittens.

Ferny Hill was small and quaint as villages go, but ever since the war had brought in a current of new blood, it was never quiet, except during Ivy's sunrise rides. That afternoon, the main street felt as busy as a town on market day. Mr. Hargrave the milkman greeted them as he passed in his delivery jaunt, his little pony's hooves clopping out a rhythm like a metronome that all the village seemed to move to. Tommy Childen, one of Farmer Emmett's farm hands, shepherded a flock of bleating sheep down the middle of the road. Two of Kenny's schoolmates were undertaking a challenge to see who could weave through the sheep whilst kicking a can the fastest, while fat old Mrs. Stuart waddled after them, shaking her handkerchief and scolding 'til her face turned beetroot red. Stalls of fresh flowers, lace curtains, animal feed, and other sundries lined the village green.

The children pushed their way through the shoppers with their basketsful and finally reached their home base—the monument in the middle of the grassy square. They'd chosen it as their meeting point for its direct view of the big-faced clock on the post office tower.

Ivy pried a kitten out of Esme's arms and placed it in the box with its squirming, mewing brothers and sisters. "We'll meet you back here in one hour. Got it?" She pointed to the clock. "That's two o'clock sharp." She knew almost every person in the streets, and they knew her. Why, then, did she feel so jumpy all of the sudden, like everyone suspected her of something?

Just then, a bicycle bell trilled, and Ivy swung around.

"What gives, you Briscoes?" It was Ivy's friend from school, Sharon Watson.

"Oh, hello," Ivy answered flatly. Normally she'd be glad to see Sharon, but this was not the time for chit-chat.

"Where on earth have you been, Ivy?" Sharon said, only half-crossly. "I thought you must've gone on holiday. Why, you've not called once all summer. I thought at least I'd run into you at Leg o' Lamb Pond, as I know how much you love to bathe, but you're never there either!"

Ivy hated to lie to her friend, but Sharon wasn't giving her much choice. "I'm awfully sorry, Sharon. I've been..." Before she could stop herself, Flora's old line came to mind: "... sick with the measles!"

Sharon gaped at her. "The measles? Thank heavens your parents are medical sorts, or you might still have them!" She took Ivy's hand in her own.

Ivy had an idea. She coughed slightly. "Oh, actually, I'm not at all sure I'm recovered. My mother says it may take weeks before I'm not... you know... infectious."

Sharon dropped Ivy's hand and took a big stride backwards. "Oh, you poor dear." She was wiping her hands on her skirt and looking around a little nervously. "There's my mother. Oh, I've just remembered. Mother wanted me to help her choose curtains for the parlour. I'd better run along."

Ivy breathed out a sigh of relief, then noticed Teddy smirking at her.

"Measles, eh? Never thought I'd hear you take a leaf out of Flora's book."

"Oh, hush up," Ivy growled. The clock struck the quarter hour and brought her back to her senses. "Look, S.O.C.K.s, we've got no time to lose. Tootles, Pip, move out and be back on the dot."

"But what if we've not sold all the kittens yet?" Kenny asked, squinting up at her through the midday sun. "We've got five, plus Billy... I mean, Willimena. It could take more than one hour."

Teddy buffeted Kenny's hair. "What, with salesmen

such as you two? I give it ten minutes… twenty, tops, and those kittens will be money in the bank!" He winked.

Esme gave him a half-smile, but she had taken two of the kittens from the box and clutched them a little closer to her chest.

"Buck up, Pip." He tapped her on the chin lightly with his knuckles. "They'll all go to smashing good homes, you'll see. Won't be long 'til you come back to town and find a line of cats parading after you, thanking you for setting them up so well in life."

Esme's smile filled out at that, and she nodded.

Once the two kittens were back in the milk crate, Ivy placed it in Kenny's arms. She and Teddy watched as he waddled off with it in the direction of the parish cottages.

When they were out of sight, Teddy and Ivy tried Sidwell's. They bought some liquorice, and Teddy asked casually, "Well, Mr. Sidwell, did you ever think you'd serve the world out of your shop?"

The wiry man waved a finger at them. "I was just sayin' to the missus last night, I said, 'Mrs. Sidwell, I never thought I'd see the day such exotic sorts'd come to Ferny Hill'. Why, just this very morning, an Irish woman came in to buy a pair of hose. I sold her the largest size I'd got, but I doubt as they'd fit her. As big as an ox, she was! Like one of them ancient Celts!"

"You don't say," Teddy answered as Ivy slunk away with the liquorices.

"Well, that was pointless," she groaned once they were back out on the pavement. Not only did she feel disheartened at being no closer to finding a Nazi spy, but now she had the image of her grandmother's enormous hosiery to blot out of her mind. "If the German pilot *is* in Ferny Hill, he might've gone to Sidwell's for supplies. It's the only food shop for miles... unless he's stealing from people's garden plots. Maybe he's staying hidden outside of the village. Maybe we should be looking for him in the woods near the plane wreckage."

Teddy shook his head and pulled her by the elbow into a quiet mews off the main road. "Don't start that again, Freckles. Remember, our spy could be anyone. It mightn't be the pilot at all," he whispered.

"Do you really think it's just a coincidence that a German pilot crashes his plane the very same week Lord Haw-Haw reports about Ferny Hill on Nazi radio?"

Teddy screwed up his mouth thoughtfully, then shrugged. "For all we know, it *might* be a coincidence. At any rate, we agreed to keep our minds open as well as our eyes and ears. We don't want to miss something right in front of us because we're dead set on this German pilot being our culprit."

Ivy picked at the dirt under her thumbnail. Part of her wanted to stomp her foot and call Teddy 'Mr. Know-it-all', but she'd made a pact to work together. This wasn't a game; it was a real mission with a real objective. She truly believed they were wasting their time not tracking the pilot, but she *had* agreed to search the village. So, doing her best to set a stiff upper lip, she looked Teddy square in the eye.

"Well then, Daddy Long Legs, are we going to The Rifleman or aren't we?"

The Rifleman had never wanted for business at any hour of the day since the RAF and Army had taken up residence in Ferny Hill. There were always soldiers and airmen aplenty making most of their few hours' leave, and Land Girls aplenty making the most of every chance to flirt with them. Teddy and Ivy stopped outside the door beside a sign that read 'Famous for our mutton stews, certain cure for Blackout Blues' and nodded to each other. Teddy removed his golf cap and ran his other hand through his hair. Putting on his careless smile, he transformed himself in the blink of an eye into a lackadaisical young lad without a care in the world. Thus disguised, he pushed open the door and stepped inside.

The heavy smell of hops and ale, mingled with a throng of merry voices and some jazzy music blaring from a gramophone, burst through the open door to meet them on the stoop. Ivy walked in behind Teddy, trying to look equally casual but finding the presence of her arms suddenly awkward.

"How 'bout that table over there?" Teddy nodded to a little table squashed against the wall to one side of the heaving bar. "Ginger beer?" he asked, then disappeared into the masses waiting for their drinks while Ivy propped herself onto a short stool in the corner and tried to arrange her tangle of legs under the ridiculously small table.

That's when she became aware of two officers leering at her through half-dazed eyes. She picked up an ashtray and spun it around, trying to ignore them, then remembered she was supposed to be observing people. She tried to listen, but her ears rang with hoots of laughter and slurred banter. She wondered what her father would say if he knew she was in a room full of stinko officers.

Then her ear caught a clear, smooth voice over the din, like a gull's cry against a boisterous storm. Ivy looked up.

Barney Larson was leaning against the bar with his back towards her, chatting to a couple of tipsy Tommies from Ashbury Park. She gritted her teeth, hoping Teddy wouldn't see him. Encounters with Barney always seemed to end in a row between the two cadets.

"How about another round, boys? I'm buying." Barney called out to the bartender and ordered two pints of ale.

"What'll *you* 'ave?" the bartender asked.

"Oh, just a cream soda for me. The kind of ale I like went out with the rationing."

One of the drunken soldiers slapped Barney on the back and said in slurred speech, "It's a cursed shame when an Englishman can't get his beer because of that blighter in Berlin."

"Don't I know it!" Barney replied, putting the fresh pint of ale into the man's hand. "Now, what were we talking of? Oh yes, you were just telling me about that bit of interesting business, over at Ashbury Park."

"Was I?" The soldier grimaced and rubbed his forehead. "Well, what d'ya want to know, Lieutenant?" He flung out his left hand that gripped the pint and made contact with somebody's face walking past the bar at that very moment, sloshing the contents of the pint all over the unsuspecting victim. Ivy jumped up when she realised the person whose front was now dripping with foamy ale was tall, gangly, and carrying two bottles of ginger beer.

Teddy mechanically set his bottles on the counter and pulled a handkerchief from his pocket. The drunken soldier stood back in trepidation as Teddy wiped his face, then rung out his kerchief in the man's now half-empty glass. The chap flinched as Teddy reached out his hand, as if he thought the boy would take a swing at him. But Teddy only patted him on the shoulder.

"Idle talk costs lives, Private," he said with a cheerful grin. Then, glancing down at his shoes swimming in a puddle of ale—"And in this case, a very fine pair of horse-hair loafers."

"Teddy, my boy!"

Teddy's eyes shifted for the first time to Barney and narrowed.

"I didn't think to see you here. Here, take my handkerchief." Barney slung an arm around Teddy's stiffened shoulders and turned him away from the speechless private so that they came face-to-face with Ivy. There was an awkward moment while Barney looked back and forth between the two of them, then at the two bottles in Teddy's hands, then gradually exposed his white teeth, as if something had dawned on him. He patted Teddy on the stomach. "Ah, I see, I see. Well, I don't want to interrupt your little date." He winked.

"It isn't... we aren't... it's definitely *not* a date." Ivy's words spilled out in a jumble. She was getting better at holding her tongue, but some things she simply could not let go un-contradicted.

"I see." Barney flashed his teeth again. "You two were just doing a bit of spying on the locals then..." Ivy shot a panicked glance at Teddy, but he didn't flinch. "Part of your little club, is that right?"

"We..." She was tongue-tied. *Why wouldn't Teddy say something?*

"Oh, that?" he said at last. "That's just something we do

to keep the younger Briscoes entertained. We were just after a soft drink ourselves."

Ivy glanced up at the wall clock over the bar and gasped. "Kenny and Esme! They'll be waiting for us in the square."

Barney took a long swig of his cream soda and clunked it down on the bar. "If you kids are heading back to the farm, how 'bout I walk with you?" He dropped his voice and added, "I've been meaning to have a word with you two, actually."

Ivy could see Teddy's jaw muscles clenching. She was sure the last thing he wanted was a walk-and-talk with Barney. But while it was an interruption to their mission, Ivy couldn't help feeling intrigued by Barney's confidential manner. For the first time, an idea occurred to her: *Could Barney be part of the Resistance, too?*

Barney didn't give away the matter as they crossed the street, but merely struck up a casual conversation. "I like to come down and have a few drinks with the lads. Keeps their morale up to hear from blokes like me—someone who's been on the front and made it back in one piece, see?"

They reached the square where the Imps sat waiting for them. They were leaning back against the monument, defeat written across their frowning faces. Esme was making a chain of daisies. And yet, there were no cats to be seen.

"Any luck?" Ivy asked.

Kenny shook his hanging head. "Nobody wanted to pay for a kitten, so we just had to give them away. We thought we might at least sell Willimena, since she's so good and tame, so we took her up to Susie Quinn's house, 'cause she likes cats."

"Well, what did she say?"

"She didn't. It was her mother." He turned his broad-brimmed Scout hat over in his hands. "Turns out the cat we were trying to sell her already belonged to her. Said shame on us for bootlegging and she'd have to speak to Mother about it."

Could the day get any worse?

"Buck up, crew!" Barney, with his usual poster-perfect positivity, pulled out a few sweets from his pockets' never-ending supply and offered them to the children. "So you want to raise a few bob, eh? Well I've got just the idea. Come on, I'll tell you all about it on the walk home."

Barney's grand idea turned out to be a variety show. "That barn at Emmett's has a platform. I'll bet he'd let you use that as your stage, and we could put folding chairs and blankets on the lawn for the audience. Why, you could invite the whole village! The Land Girls, all the guys and gals up at Ashbury Park... just imagine how it'd raise their spirits. It'd be a smash! And, of course, you could charge a shilling a head." He winked at Kenny.

Kenny, as usual, had already taken up the idea and was running full steam ahead with it. "I could do my Charlie Chaplin routine, and show knot-tying, and..."

Ivy squeezed his shoulder to make him quiet. "It's a nice idea, Barney, but I'm afraid we wouldn't have the time. You see, our mother's very busy, and we have ever so many chores to do around the house." So *this* was what Barney wanted to speak to them about? A variety show? The funny thing was, a few months earlier, Ivy might've felt as keen about the idea as Kenny. But things were different now. She had a real job to do, a real responsibility to her country. And anyway, she could just imagine how Teddy must be inwardly gagging at the idea of putting on a show with Barney's help.

She looked to him for reinforcement, expecting to see the sullen face he only wore in Barney's presence. To her surprise, he didn't look grumpy at all, only far-off in thought—until he caught her eye and snapped out of it.

"Heck, why not, Ivy? If we can bring a little joy to those brave men—so far away from home and waiting for their time to face the enemy—why, I'm all in!"

Ivy felt betrayed. What did Teddy mean by changing his tune towards Barney at the flip of a coin like that? Was she the only one who remembered about S.O.C.K.s? Had he completely forgotten there was an actual German spy on the loose?

"Come on, Ezzy." She dragged her sister past the others. She didn't feel like listening to their exuberant ideas bouncing back and forth.

"I'm tired, Ivy. You're walking too fast," Esme groaned. "I want to plan the show with Barney."

Ivy yanked her along. "Come on. Let's get home and play with your bunnies, shall we?"

Ivy managed to get to the house a good few strides ahead of the boys. She glanced up to see a porcelain white face peering out of the upstairs window of the farmhouse next door. With surprising quickness for one so delicate and prim, Flora was in the garden to meet them. Ivy pitied Barney for having to put up with a fawning little leech like Flora Woodall. She was all smiles and fluttering eyelashes when he walked up the drive, chatting away with a cigarette clenched between his teeth.

Within a minute, the whole idea of the variety show had been divulged to Flora.

"Oh, it's a dream!" she squealed.

Ivy rolled her eyes. Of course Flora would fall over backwards for any idea of Barney's.

"Come on, Ez. Bunnies, remember?" But even Esme had caught the fever and wouldn't be dragged away.

Ivy watched them all laughing and gabbing. Was there no one she could count on? She turned to the house alone, then remembered Grandmammy would be waiting inside, ready to barrage Ivy with her sayings and criticisms.

There was only one option. Ivy took off running to the stable. Whatever Teddy thought about it, somebody had to go. She wasn't Ivy Briscoe the kid anymore. She was Ivy Briscoe the scout, and she would find the enemy hiding in her village—alone, if she had to.

21

NEW TACTICS

"Just go away!" Ivy shouted over her shoulder, then nudged Nelly to pick up her speed. Still, Teddy—with Napoleon's help—gained on her, which annoyed her all the more.

Just before the edge of the forest, she pulled back on the reins, letting him catch up. There'd be no sneaking up on Germans with him trampling after her.

"As I recall, I never said you could ride my horse."

"Whoa now! There's no need to snap your cap. And as I recall, Napoleon is your brother's horse." He smiled a bit sheepishly.

Ivy returned his smile with a scowl and turned her head away.

"You are as temperamental as Farmer Emmett's mule, aren't you?"

She swung around and fixed him with an angry glare. "Me? I'm temperamental? I'm not the one who's suddenly so chummy with a man I couldn't stand only an hour ago.

I'm not the one ditching my task as Special Duties agent to go and join the circus."

She took up her reins, ready to take flight, but Teddy was too quick. He reached out and grabbed them in one fist, looking her intently in the eye. "Haven't you learned to trust me by now?"

Ivy stopped trying to free her reins from his grip and thought. The truth was, she did trust Teddy as much as she trusted anyone. He was an excellent cadet, and he had never let her down before. When they had squabbled, it had all been down to her own stubborn pride. Shame rushed over her, painting her cheeks hot red.

There you go again, Ivy Briscoe. You and your reckless temper. No wonder her mother's favourite saying for Ivy was 'a single thought saves a hundred foolish actions'.

Ivy heaved a defeated sigh and muttered, "I trust you."

"Good." Teddy relaxed his grip on her reins, but still eyed her as if she were a dog with its teeth bared for attack. "Because I've got an idea to wash out the spy, and I can't pull it off without you. Are you in?"

"'Course." The corner of her mouth raised slyly. "I just hope this idea doesn't involve you swimming in ale again. You smell like a drunkard!"

Teddy sniffed at his shirt collar and grimaced. "Fair show. No ale this time. Just pure showmanship."

"This'll do swimmingly," Teddy said later that afternoon, surveying Farmer Emmett's hay barn like a king surveys his castle. "Why, call me a turnip if you couldn't fit at least a hundred under this awning. And if we push back all the doors, the rest can sit outside if the weather holds up."

"A hundred?" Esme's eyes were wide with fright as she nestled her cheek against the white rabbit clutched against her shoulder. "Ivy, do I have to go up on the stage?"

"Don't worry, Ez. You'll have Spud with you. Everyone will be watching and cheering for him. They'll hardly notice you there."

"But what about the bunnies? They mustn't feel left out of the show."

Ivy sighed. "As long as they don't plan on sharing a dressing room with Spud."

"Bring Snowball up here, Ez. I know just what we can do with him." Kenny, right at home on the platform-cum-stage, was slinging his feet and arms about like a monkey in a wasps' nest. "Look at me! I'm Fred Upstairs!"

"I think you mean Fred Astaire, Ken!" Ivy shouted. "Come down off there! We're trying to think!"

Once Teddy had explained to Ivy that the variety show was just what they needed to flush the spy out of hiding, she had jumped all in. It was as good a plan as any. With the whole village there, along with the troops from Ashbury Park, the spy would most likely make a showing as well.

And S.O.C.K.s would be ready for him.

While Tootles and Pip performed their bits, Freckles and Daddy Long Legs would hand out popped corn and lemonade to the audience, giving the secret signal—removing their caps with their left hands—for Mr. Blackwood to see whenever they came across somebody unknown or suspicious. Even if they didn't have their spy by the end of the show, at least Mr. Blackwood would have a list of suspects, and he and S.O.C.K.s could take it from there.

Ivy felt a tap on her back. She stood up and leaned against the broom she'd been using to sweep up straggling bits of hay.

"Ivy, make him stop. Snowball doesn't like it." Esme, lower lip pouting out, pointed up to the platform where Kenny, with his toy wooden shotgun, was running circles around a petrified Snowball and half-singing, half-shouting, *"Run rabbit, run rabbit, run run run. Run rabbit, Run rabbit, run run run. Bang, bang, bang, bang goes the farmer's gun..."* at the top of his lungs.

"Kenny, I'm serious!" Ivy growled. "I can't think with you making that racket!"

"I just remembered!" Teddy dropped the hay bale he was carrying and bounded over to the rescue. "Tootles, Pip, how would you two cadets feel about trying out another fundraiser for the variety show? We're going to need a few bob for all the biscuits and fairy cakes and such."

"But we've nothing to sell," Kenny moaned. Esme scooped up her rabbit and hugged it tight, as if wary yet another one of her adopted pets might become the next item for fundraising.

"Don't worry!" Teddy said, swinging his arm and hoisting his chin into the air in his motivational manner. "You'll think of something. Just tell 'em it's for the war effort. Give 'em those irresistible puppy dog eyes. With adorable little faces like yours, you two will melt the money right off of 'em."

"Alright." Kenny shuffled begrudgingly off the stage, pulling Esme and her rabbit along behind him.

"That's an eager beaver. Knock 'em dead, Tootle Pip!"

Teddy winked at Ivy as the Imps scuttled off. "Now picture this, Freckles." He drew a window with his hands, boxing his view of the stage; but before he could cast his vision into it, he was interrupted by a cooing little cough from behind. They turned around in unison to see Flora standing in a golden spotlight of sun in the barn's open doorway. Her hands were clasped demurely behind her back and her eyes were cast down like the painting of Saint Katherine that hung in the girls' privy at St Wilfrid's.

"I was wondering if…" Flora cleared her throat again, as if trying to remember lines she'd rehearsed. "If you wouldn't *very much* mind"—the words came out with some wincing—"that is to say, if I might be permitted to join you?"

Ivy and Teddy looked at each other, each one reflecting the utter bewilderment written across the other's brow.

"You mean you want a part in the show?" Teddy demanded.

Flora nodded uncertainly.

"Sorry. It's the business of our silly little club only, remember? The one you snitched about to Barney?"

"I don't think it's silly, really. And anyway, I don't care for Barney anymore."

"Oh?" Teddy crossed his arms over his chest. "How's that? Did you find he'd never been to finishing school?"

"No. He was rather rude, that's all. I simply knocked on his door last night to see if he wanted to go for a walk, and he practically shouted at me. Said I ought to mind my own business." Flora looked on the verge of shattering. "Said it was time to play with the other little kiddies and give him some space." She spoke each word as if spitting out a mouthful of bitter medicine.

Teddy raised one eyebrow, then threw his head back with a derisive howl. "Well if you think we're just going to welcome you in, just like that—after you've behaved like a right little git—you've got another thing coming, sister dear."

Ivy's eyes hadn't left Flora's face during this exchange. She couldn't deny there was a change in it. The lily-white neck was flushed; the turned-up nose pointed down; the strawberry mouth quivered. Unbidden, Dr. Briscoe's words flooded her mind: *'What I prescribe is patience and friendship.'* Hadn't she, herself, been shown patience and friendship by Teddy when she least deserved it?

When it looked as though Flora was on the breaking point of tears, Ivy spoke up. "I think we should give her a chance."

Flora raised her eyes. They were swimming with gratitude. Ivy gave her an uncomfortable little smile and looked away.

Teddy eyed Ivy like a doctor might inspect a patient who was showing signs of lunacy.

"She needn't wear *socks* yet," Ivy said under her breath, hoping Teddy would understand what she meant. "But she could help us with the show, couldn't she?"

"Well, it's up to you; but personally, I wouldn't tell her a thing." He spoke to Ivy but directed the words like flying darts at Flora. "After all, she's such a notorious tell-tale."

"I am not! I cross my heart not to tell a soul anything

you don't want me to. Oh, Ivy," she pleaded, "you'll let me join, won't you?"

Teddy didn't give her the chance to answer. "Even so, you won't like this game. You might get dirty and soil your pinafore, and you're much too much of a princess for that."

Once again, Flora looked on the verge of tears.

Moved by a pinprick of pity, Ivy stepped in. "Actually, we do need someone to help with decorations…"

Flora clasped her hands. "Oh, yes! I'm awfully good at arranging flowers. I could pick the wild ones from the meadow and make swags and garlands and… and everything! Oh, I won't let you down. On my honour, I won't."

Teddy gave a derisive snort, but over the next hour, Flora was true to her word. She set about her task with an industrious spirit: picking, arranging, even braving the sheep pasture to retrieve a bundle of Queen Anne's lace for her garlands, and humming a merry little tune while she worked. Ivy could hardly believe Flora had it in her to be so agreeable.

Ivy and Teddy were busy themselves—sweeping the floors, arranging hay bales in rows to serve as theatre seats—but all the while, Ivy kept a watchful eye on Flora. What had brought about her transformation, Ivy could hardly guess. Mrs. Emmett hadn't known what to do with the girl at home, and had given up offering her little domestic jobs when Flora complained she hadn't the constitution for washing or ironing or stitching or baking. Ivy imagined how lonely the past months must've been for the girl, who had nothing better to do than swoon over a grown man who noticed her no more than he might notice a butterfly flitting around his head.

Maybe Father had been right and Flora's frostiness just needed time to melt. But Ivy determined to keep her on a probationary watch before telling her anything about S.O.C.K.s. Maybe, if all went well, she could become their mess sergeant.

Presently, the barn theatre began to take shape. Ivy and Teddy stood back to take in the fruit of the afternoon's labour. Flora, to their speechless astonishment, offered to run into the house and ask Mrs. Emmett for a pitcher of lemonade. As she went, Kenny and Esme came skipping into the farmyard—their pockets bulging and their faces shining.

Kenny plopped his Scout's hat upside-down on the hay bale where the two older ones sat. "Empty your pockets, Pip!" he ordered his sidekick.

Ivy's mouth dropped open as she watched a shower of coins fill up the bowl of the hat.

"How did you do it?" she asked, once the four pockets had been turned out and the final coins tossed into the pile.

"We just told people we were raising funds for Churchill's S.O.C.K.s," Kenny explained matter-of-factly. "Old Miss Paisley said, 'What's our world coming to when the prime minister can't even afford to dress respectably?' and handed us a sixpence. Mrs. Sayers thought we were part of Mr. Churchill's fundraising effort to send socks to boys on the front, and she thought that was a wonderful idea. Started crying and everything, then put a whole shilling in!"

"Kenny, you mustn't lie to people to get money off them. That's cheating!" Ivy cringed to hear Vera's maternal tone coming out of her own mouth.

"But I didn't lie! It's not my fault they misunderstood what I meant about Churchill's S.O.C.K.s."

"And that's another thing. You can't go around using our secret code name!" Somebody's bound to figure it out. You'll have to think of something else."

"Don't think that'll be necessary," Teddy spoke up from behind. He had begun counting out the treasure in the hat. "Forget lemonade and fairy cakes. This lot will buy a banquet!"

Kenny clapped his hands and rubbed them together like a big-city business tycoon. "I know what let's do! Let's buy Ernie a new Spitfire with it! Golly, won't he be tickled?"

Teddy looked thoughtful. "Yes, I suppose he would be. But do you know, I reckon if Ernie were here, he'd tell us to put that money where it will *really* count."

Kenny scratched his head. "Where's that?"

"Why refreshments, of course!" Teddy gave him a gentle slap on the back. "You know what they say, don't you?"

Kenny shook his head.

"Nothing tempts a spy out of hiding like a nice fairy cake. Wouldn't you agree, Freckles?"

Teddy's attempt at a straight face started to crack. Then Ivy lost it, and the two of them laughed until tears streamed down their dusty cheeks. Kenny shrugged at Esme, snatched up his hat with all its bounty, and left them to their hysterics.

22
ANDERSON KNOCKOUT

Though she told herself she was only doing the variety show to rat out the spy, Ivy harboured a secret fluttery feeling of excitement as the day approached. Those final sunny, steamy days of July were happy ones.

Flora kept up her newfound good form, and Teddy's grumpiness towards her slowly cooled into stiff tolerance. He even phoned his aunts at Ashbury Park on Flora's behalf to request if she could borrow their harp for her act in the show.

To everyone's delight, the aunts went above and beyond his request. As it turned out, they had considered sponsoring some sort of entertainment for the troops themselves. They poured all their charitable resources into the S.O.C.K.s show: lights, sound equipment, publicity—they even contacted some friends from London and arranged for the BBC radio network to come along and broadcast, as well as a famous singer to perform as a special tribute to

Johnnie Emmett and all the other men and boys at war who called Ferny Hill their home. But the cherry on top was the Ashbury sisters' offer to host a reception and dance at the Great House after the show for the whole village.

Ivy had never set foot in Ashbury Park, and the thought of actually hosting a grand event there made her heart patter just a bit faster than usual. But of course—she reminded herself over and over—the best of it was, with the Ashbury sisters' help, nobody would miss out on the event… and hopefully, that included the spy. Mr. Blackwood agreed with them on this point when he called in during a rehearsal for a private word with the S.O.C.K.s members.

"Ya. Ya. The bait is set. No infiltrator will be able to resist the opportunity to set foot inside the walls of Ashbury Park." He gently tweaked a ladybird out of his bushy beard and continued. "We'll need a very tight guard on the night, but I'll arrange all that. Never you worry about it. Good work, cadets."

Nothing was left for Ivy, Teddy, and the others to do but rehearse and carry out their usual message-running duties. Ivy looked forward to her morning and nightly rounds more than ever, now things were so busy. She loved having the world to herself and Nelly in the hour just after sunrise, when the dewy meadows shimmered golden, and flocks of geese sounded their trumpets through the mist overhead.

And the night rounds were just as good. The night sky glowed like a blue lantern, bathing the fields and forests below in ethereal light. Her rides were all routine to her now, so her mind was free to roam. Most often, she thought of her father, working tirelessly among the young medics. She wondered what Vera was doing, whether she was homesick for little Ferny Hill. And she thought of Ernie, and how he might be looking up at the very same stars—maybe even watching them from the cockpit of a plane. Maybe he was thinking of home at that very same moment...

It was a nice thought, anyway. It made her feel as if, in spite of the miles wedged between them, their family was all together again somehow.

Were it not for her constant thoughts of her family far away, it might have been easy to forget the reason they were doing all this—that there was, in fact, a war on. And, of course, there were the daily announcements on the wireless—reminders that Hitler's vile intentions were now bent full-force on Great Britain. His Luftwaffe was doing everything it could to seize superiority of the British skies, and destroying RAF airfields was a favourite strategy. Bombs had already been dropped on bases all along the East coast. Teddy had even read that Eton, his own school, had suffered bomb damage. Every night, the news reporters gave the tally of RAF to Luftwaffe fighters down—and so far, by some miracle, the RAF was winning.

But the threat on Ferny Hill was hot as a live wire, and the increasingly regular air raids in the village were proof of it. More often than not, when the air raid sirens sounded, Mrs. Briscoe was out on calls or ambulance duty, and then it fell to Ivy to round up the Imps into the Anderson. Grandmammy was having none of it. When the alarms sounded, she would sit herself squarely down in Dr. Briscoe's chair, her lips set in a defiant line, and work her knitting needles with the fury of a Blitzkrieg.

It so happened that the sirens sounded the morning before the variety show. Teddy stayed on at The Beeches for breakfast once he and Ivy finished transmitting the morning's messages, so they could go over the order of the acts once more. Ivy wished she had gone to the farmhouse instead. The more valiantly Teddy tried to be charming and polite, the more Grandmammy shuffled around in her tartan dressing gown, scowling and muttering under her breath—things like, "What is this, a restaurant?" and "I didn't leave the shores of Ireland to wait on some English politician's son."

"General, ma'am. My father's a general, not a politician," Teddy corrected her cheerfully.

Ivy automatically winced, expecting a knife to come hurtling at her unsuspecting friend any second. But before Grandmammy could retaliate, they were saved by the howl of the air raid siren.

Grandmammy shouted over it. "If that man with the wee moustache thinks he can interrupt breakfast on a whim..." She shook her bowling ball of a fist, as if Hitler were standing right in front of her to see it, then resumed kneading a lump of dough with more-than-usual violence.

"I see where you get it, Freckles," Teddy jested under his breath as he and Ivy hurried to the bottom of the stairs to round up the Imps. She pulled a face and dealt him a jab to his ribs with her elbow before shouting, "Tootles! Pip! This is not a drill. Stop dawdling!"

The Imps, who had been dressing for rehearsal, stampeded down the stairs, Kenny still in his underwear and striped Boy Scout knee socks.

"You're lucky it's not winter, you know," Ivy said, shoving Spud into her brother's arms and pushing them both out the door.

It was rather snug in the Anderson. Flora and the Emmetts came over as well. As they sat in silence and listened, Teddy looked around.

"Where's Barney?"

"Had to make a trip to London," Farmer Emmett answered. "I reckon it's about reportin' for duty. Brave lad. Oh, and he said to tell you young'ns to break a leg with the show. He's sorry he can't be around to help."

"As if we needed *his* help." For the first time in several days, Flora stuck her nose up in her old manner at the mention of Barney.

When the 'all clear' sounded about twenty minutes later, Teddy pushed open the door. He turned and glanced over his shoulder with a smirk at Ivy. "Just as well your grandmother stayed put inside. I dare say her backside alone would fill up half the shelter." Chuckling at his own joke, he turned back towards the door.

His smile dropped instantly. There before him was a wall of tartan—and, at the top, Grandmammy's disapproving face. Poor Teddy hardly had time to wince before the old woman reared back her titanic arm and let her fist fly soundly—*smack!*—into the boy's jaw.

"That should knock some of the cheek out of you, eh laddy?"

Ivy and the other children watched in stunned silence as

Teddy steadied himself. Rubbing his jaw, he answered in a rather slurred accent, "Yes, ma'am. In fact, I believe you've knocked half the cheek right off my face." He shook his head like a wet dog. "I say, Mrs. Kennedy, you do throw a mean right hook. If Jerry thinks he can invade Ferny Hill without a fight, he's got another thing coming."

Grandmammy's fierce bulldog scowl faltered, then it looked like she might be sick. Then, to everyone's disbelief, the corners of her rigid mouth gave way and turned up into something very like a smile.

"That's a clever wee lad." Teddy jumped as her great bear paw of a hand smacked him on the back. "Come in, so. I'll pour ya a cup o'tea."

Ivy sighed out a huge breath of relief. If Teddy could keep Grandmammy sweet, life was going to be a lot easier.

Later that afternoon, Ivy waited behind the stage wing made of borrowed hospital screens, stroking Nelly's neck as the two waited to go on. So far, dress rehearsal had been a breeze: Flora had played Pachelbel on the harp; Kenny sang 'Run Rabbit' with Esme—dressed in homemade ears, whiskers, and a tail—standing in for the rabbit; Spud danced and jumped through hoops; and Teddy did a bit of sharp shooting with Farmer Emmett's rifle, hitting a melon, an apple, and finally a cherry off some upturned buckets. Now he was back on stage, telling a few jokes before introducing the next act: Ivy and Nelly performing a dressage march to 'It's a Long Way to Tipperary' played on the gramophone.

She peeked around the curtain at the small audience that had gathered for the dress rehearsal. Mr. Blackwood and Grandmammy were there, enjoying the show and a pipe together while glancing up occasionally at the dark, heavy clouds pushing in from the west. And Mrs. Briscoe, who had managed to get the afternoon off, was helping Mrs. Emmett set out a picnic lunch for the performers and crew.

"And now, ladies and gents," Teddy belted, "I present to you an act sure to inspire that patriotic spirit: the astonishingly talented Ivy Briscoe and her trusty mare Nelson!"

Ivy looked out and caught her mother's eye as Nelly trotted up the stairs onto the platform. Mrs. Briscoe smiled and gave her a nod of confidence. Ivy smiled back. It was nice to see her mother relaxed and happy for a change, dressed in a comfortable cotton dress instead of her stiffly starched nurse's uniform.

Teddy placed the needle on the gramophone, and the upbeat music began to blare.

March two three four. Nelly's hooves stomped up and down in perfect rhythm at Ivy's prompting. She chanced another glance at her mother just in time to see Alfie Watkins cycle up with the post. He was handing her something. *Why was his head hanging like that?*

Nelly missed a step and got out of time. Ivy's concentration was broken.

"You alright?" Teddy mouthed from the opposite wing.

She nodded, but as she turned her attention back to her mother, her heart stopped. Kathleen Briscoe was holding the open telegram in both hands. Suddenly, she stumbled backwards, grabbing hold of a cherry tree for support. Mrs. Emmett ran over and braced her just in time as she crumpled to the ground.

The music blared on, but Ivy stood still. The whole world stood still; it seemed to press in on her from every side until she thought she would suffocate. And she wanted to suffocate. She wanted anything rather than to see what was in that telegram.

But what difference would it make? She already knew.

23
WE WILL FIGHT

Missing in Action... Pilot Officer Briscoe's plane was hit by enemy fire on a reconnaissance mission to France... last seen going down over Le Mans... Deepest sympathies...

She'd drunk down the words like a poison, feeling nothing at first. Then, sudden as a knife dropping, the pain. Stabbing, throbbing, lethal pain. Then another long spell of nothing, which was almost worse.

How many hours had gone on like that? It felt like days, but it was still the same day... the same day she had laughed and joked with Teddy. But all that felt like a lifetime ago, when there was still sunshine and hope in the world.

That afternoon, almost as soon as she'd reached her mother under the cherry tree, the dark clouds had pressed their attack on the sun with unstoppable force and won. The sky had broken, and the rain had pommeled the earth like a barrage of bullets all evening long, right into the night. Teddy had taken Ivy's night message round without asking. Just saddled up Napoleon and left before she could stop him. They hadn't spoken since the telegram came, but he had slipped her a note under the kitchen door that simply said *"I'm borrowing your ridings socks tonight. See you tomorrow."*

She wished he hadn't. How desperately she'd wanted to *do something*—anything but sit there listening to her brave, strong mother sob like a little child into Grandmammy's chest.

Eventually, Grandmammy had sent them all to bed, as gently as a shepherdess guiding her lambs. Ivy lay in her bed staring up at the ceiling. She could still hear her mother crying through the walls, but more weakly now, like she was crying herself to sleep.

Ivy knew she'd never sleep that night. For hours, her mind churned, trying to make sense of things that would never add up. Before, the war had been exciting: an adventure, a chance of being heroes. But suddenly, a glass had shattered, and all the fun and glory had drained out. She felt empty. How could a world without Ernie be anything but empty?

An air raid siren sounded, but nobody stirred in the Briscoe home. What did it matter? It wailed on and on for minutes. Ivy heard her door creak open and little feet patter across the floor. Esme crawled under the quilt and snuggled her curly head against her sister's shoulder.

"I was scared, and I didn't want to wake Mother," she whispered.

"It's ok. You can stay here."

"Ivy?"

"Yes?"

"When's Father coming home? And Vera?"

"I don't know."

Esme was silent for a moment, and then again: "Ivy?"

"What is it, Ez?"

"If Ernie's gone missing, they'll find him, won't they? Just like we found Spud when he got lost in Marshwood Forest?"

Ivy swallowed hard but didn't answer. She stroked her sister's fleecy head until she was sure Esme was asleep. She thought of Ernie ruffling her hair just before he left, telling her to be brave. But it wasn't bravery filling up her emptiness. It was something strange and new. It was anger. Pure, white-hot anger. Anger like she'd never known in her life, surging up like lava ready to spew from an erupting volcano.

In that moment, she wanted nothing more than to meet a German, a real live German, for herself. She'd feel no fear—only readiness to release all that molten hot anger at the enemy to avenge her brother.

There was no need to wait for the dawn's light. The rain drummed on; the sun, too, was missing in action. Careful not to wake Esme, Ivy got out of bed and tiptoed into Kenny's room. His pocket knife lay on top of the chest of drawers. She took it and put it in her pocket, then crept out and made her way down to the kitchen. She took Ernie's old mac off the hook by the door and pulled on her riding boots. The clock on the mantelpiece in the parlour gonged once. Four thirty. Still an hour and a half before she was due on her rounds. No time to lose if she wanted to find the enemy first.

The silver rain lashed down on her like bullets as she trudged and splashed her way to the stable. The wind did its best to keep the stable door shut, but Ivy's fury gave her unnatural strength, and she heaved it open.

Something big moved in the corner where neither of the horses was kept. There was a wild flapping sound followed by a thud and a grunt, then a torchlight clicked on. Ivy shielded her eyes and squinted into the beam. It lowered, and two startled blue eyes were staring back at her.

Teddy lay sprawled out on a pile of hay on the ground. He had clearly just had a fight with the horse blanket and got tangled up when Ivy startled him. With some effort, he threw it off and jumped to his feet. He was wearing burgundy socks with bits of hay stuck all over. In fact, he was covered in so much hay, from socks to disheveled hair, Ivy figured he must've spent the whole night in the stable.

The two of them just looked at each other for a moment, neither one speaking. Ivy didn't want to hear how sorry he was about Ernie. All she wanted was to get on her horse and ride—ride to vengeance without delay.

Thankfully, Teddy seemed to know her thoughts, but he also seemed intent on getting in the way.

"I thought you might try something... heroic," was all he said at first.

Ivy didn't answer, so Teddy continued. "That's the reason I'm here, see? Ivy, I know you, and I know you want to do something about what's happened. To make it right somehow. But the truth is..." His mouth moved before he managed the words. "You can't."

Ivy winced. His words had struck home.

"Listen," he pressed on. "I know we're equals, but as your friend and fellow soldier, I'm urging you not to do anything rash. Let me run your rounds for you. I can manage them just fine for a few days." He placed his hand on her shoulder.

That was it. He wanted her to sit at home and do nothing after her brother had just been shot out of the sky?

She slung his hand aside. "What's the use of these stupid message rounds anyway? I'm not playing anymore! Don't you see? The war is out there, right now." She pointed towards the forest. "It's real. It's not a stupid game."

"Don't you think I know it's no game?" His voice was steady, calm. "My father is out there too, you know. And I wish I were with him. But why do you think he's fighting in the first place? It's the same reason Ernie put his neck out there. To protect this country from getting squashed like a bug. And that's what we're doing too, because if they fail to fend off the enemy, then it's all up to us. S.O.C.K.s is part of that. We're all in it together."

When Ivy made no reply, Teddy flopped down in the hay and pulled on a pair of Ernie's old riding boots. "Go be with your mum and the Imps. They need you now."

"What about the show?" she asked flatly.

Teddy slapped his legs and stood up. "You really want to know what I think?"

She waited, knowing he would tell her whether she wanted to know or not.

"I think we should go through with the show. It's doing

our part in this war. And I think it's what Ernie would want, don't you?"

Ivy pressed her back against the wall and slunk down. Her mind finally felt the exhaustion of a full night's raging. For once, she didn't argue with Teddy. She would let him take her rounds this time. But her thoughts and plans she would keep to herself.

24
THE SHOW MUST GO ON

The dark sky and muddy ground couldn't keep the crowds away from coming to the Ferny Hill Variety Show. Ashbury Park was an enormous estate, but still, it was hard to believe so many officers had been billeted away in there for almost the past year. The Land Girls, too, seemed to come out of every nook and cranny in Ferny Hill. They filled the farmyard with laughter and merriment, like one large, humming instrument mixed in with the jazz band the boys at Ashbury Park had put together.

The music, the laughter, the festive lights strung up in the trees and the barn rafters… it all belonged to a different world than the bleak, war-stricken one Ivy was living in. Never had she seen such a large and festive crowd; never had she been less keen to be a part of it.

Mechanically, she helped Kenny and Esme get all their props ready and made sure Esme's bunny ears were on straight. Then Ivy hid herself behind the wings to wait with Nelly. She kept her head down when anyone came near.

She didn't want to join the party; but even more, she dreaded having to face the pitying looks and hollow remarks of people who'd heard the news about Ernie, however kind their intentions may be.

Around six o'clock, everybody took their seats on the hundreds of hay bales, blankets, and folding chairs set about the barnyard, and the show began.

Teddy was a first-rate Master of Ceremonies, dressed in his Eton waistcoat and top hat, working a laugh a minute out of the crowd with joke after witty joke. Next, the famous singer had everyone up on their feet, clapping and singing along to 'There'll Always Be an England'; Flora's harp-playing had every old lady dabbing her eyes; and the Imps had the whole lot in stitches with 'Run Rabbit'. All the while, Ivy waited.

At last, applause rang out for Teddy's sharpshooting spectacle, and Ivy knew it was almost time. She watched Teddy run offstage, prop the rifle against the props table, and quickly fix on his top hat again before running back into the spotlight to introduce Ivy's act.

That was her cue. Without a second's hesitation, she grabbed the gun Teddy had left behind and slung it over her shoulder. She also took the box of ammunition, stuffing it into Nelly's saddle bag. Then she mounted the horse, and just as Teddy's introduction began—"Ladies and gents, I now present to you…"—she and Nelly cantered quietly out the back of the barn, breaking into a full gallop just as the crowd's applause broke out. The applause and the blaring gramophone faded away to the war drum rhythm of her horse's hoofbeats as Ivy sped away under a heavy, dusky sky.

This had been her plan all along, ever since Teddy had intercepted her in the barn that morning. It was better this way. This way, he wouldn't come after her. This way, she was armed and ready. She knew in her heart that her enemy was still out there, and—when she found him—she meant war.

She started her journey down the dirt lane that ran between the sheep pasture and the hayfield, then cut across the cornfield, never letting up on Nelly until the forest had swallowed them both up.

The stream had swollen and spilled out over the bank. Ivy prodded Nelly through the water, but the bank on the far side was a steep, slippery incline. The mare struggled to get up against the sliding mud. Her front foot caught a root as she heaved forward, and Ivy lost her grip and fell face downward into the muck. Her knee struck against a sharp stone, and she felt her skin tear. She turned over, gripping the throbbing knee in her hand. When she pulled her hand away, it was covered in blood mixed with mud.

She felt no pity for herself, nor thought for a second of turning back. Her heart exulted in the pain and the blood. The worse the hardship, the better. Hadn't the boys in France and Belgium suffered much worse? She wanted to be a soldier—to feel their suffering… to feel whatever Ernie had felt when his plane went down.

Most of all, she wanted to find the German pilot alive—so she could kill him.

25
MANHUNT

Ivy scrambled up the bank and coaxed Nelly up after her until they both found their footing on level ground. The horse had a scratch where the root had caught her shin. Ivy led her by the reins to give her the chance to catch her breath, and to give herself the chance to find her bearings. She rummaged for the torch she'd packed earlier that day in Nelly's saddle pouch.

It was dark in the forest. The evening air hung with musty humidity; a cloud of vapour appeared in the torch-light with Ivy's every breath. She shut her right eye tightly closed; if forced to switch off the torch to hide herself, she'd want a bit of night sight so as not to be left entirely to the pilot's mercy… as if he had any.

It didn't take long before the torch beam lit up the white patch of parachute. From there, Ivy walked deeper into the wood until the beam of light reflected off the tail of the Messerschmitt. The eerie sight of the Nazi's ugly, crooked swastika made her heart somersault into her throat as goosebumps prickled her clammy skin. She wasn't afraid, yet her hand automatically reached down to her side and touched the barrel of the rifle as her feet took her, step after purposeful step, closer to the wreckage. Her pulse raced like an electric current. Her skin felt the pricks of a thousand tiny needles as every nerve came to attention. This was enemy territory.

It had been more than one full week since she'd watched the dogfight and seen the plane go down. There would be no footprints to follow by now, not after the rain. But she'd come prepared. With Kenny's help over the course of the day, she'd thought back on everything Mr. Blackwood had ever taught his Scouts about tracking, and all his stories of hunting the enemy in the African bush.

"Rule one is to know your terrain," he'd told them.

She reached into Nelly's saddle bag and pulled out the folded map of Ferny Hill she'd taken from Ernie's orienteering case. Crouching down, she spread it out over a log and shone the torchlight over it. With her finger, she traced what she thought had been her course through the forest and across the stream. She tapped the spot that must be the plane crash: her starting point for the hunt.

Now it was time to employ the second rule of tracking: *Know your enemy.*

"Now where would I go from here if I were a pilot downed behind my enemy's lines?" Ivy asked herself.

The closest civilisation was a little pig farm to the northeast. The German surely would've seen it from the sky, but would he remember it once he'd parachuted from a burning plane? The only way to find out: look for signs of his escape from the crash.

She folded up the map and returned it to the saddle bag,

then aimed her beam in the north-easterly direction, not exactly sure what she was looking for. She wiped her face with her palm and smelled the metallic scent of her own blood.

Blood.

That was it. Kenny had said there was blood in the boot tracks.

She bent over as she moved forward, inspecting every plant in her path. Sure enough, after four steps, she came across a fern frond smudged with a streak of rusty brown. She was on the right course.

A few steps further, she inspected a sapling with a broken-off branch. She knelt beside it. The stump where the branch had been had scratch marks across it, like a knife had been used to saw it away. From that point, she discovered a series of round peg holes at intervals in the dirt. They were spaced out about a step's length apart, and between each, the mulch and decay on the forest floor had been swept up, like something heavy had been dragged across the ground.

Only when Ivy came to a decaying log in her path did the clues begin to fit together. A strip of moss had been scraped off the top of the log, and the same rusty brown streaked across it. The pilot clearly had bled from a wound, probably in his leg. Could it be that the leg had been crippled, forcing him to drag it along behind him in his flight through the forest? That would explain the broken tree limb and the peg holes. He'd cut the branch to use as a walking cane.

There was no doubting it. She'd found the enemy's trail. Now the only lingering question was what she would do when she found him. What if he hadn't survived? The thought of stumbling across a dead body sent a chill spreading up her spine despite the mugginess of the night air.

No, she told herself, shaking off the dread that had momentarily gripped her. *He made it out of that plane crash. He's alive. And when I find him...*

Once again, Ivy's hand felt for the rifle at her side. With her forearm, she wiped away the sweat stinging her eyes to clear her vision.

There was no going back now.

26
MEETING THE ENEMY

Just as she'd suspected, the tracks led Ivy north-east through the forest, towards the little farm on the map. The distance was short, but the journey was slow. A few times, she had to redouble her steps when she lost the trail on some bit of hard ground where the stick's imprints were less noticeable. And the forest undergrowth became denser the closer she came to its edge, which made it difficult to lead Nelly along through the briars and nettles.

At last, the tree line broke, separated by a deep ditch from a vast, plowed field. She'd seen ditches like this many times before; it was a *ha-ha,* a farmer's trick for keeping his livestock in his field without fences. But at that moment, it made Ivy think of the hellish trenches where so many men had spent their final days, had their final meal, and said their final prayers during the last war. If her enemy had wished to avoid being seen in the open field, the trench would have provided him with the cover to advance unseen.

She stayed in the shadows of the tree line, following the ha-ha on its course around the field. The wind whipped up off the open field, flinging sharp clods of dirt like shrapnel and whistling in Ivy's ear as she crept along. There was not much she could do in the way of tracking now; there was nothing for it but to follow her own gut as she clung to Nelly's side, letting the horse's barrel belly shield her from the wind's onslaught.

The ha-ha eventually turned a corner, wrapping around the forest to the right. There, a patch of the field had been left to the weeds and grass. Once Ivy had turned the corner, the wind's force died down, and she was at last able to raise her eyes to what lay ahead.

The wild grass grew waist high right up to the edge of the wood. Some way off, tucked against the trees in a sea of overgrown blackberry bushes, was an old grain silo. The years and elements had done their worst to it. Vines snaked up its curved sides; the roof slats looked more rot than wood. And yet, the silo seemed alive somehow. As if the shack were winking its eye, a flicker of light blinked from one of its square cutout windows.

Ivy's breath caught in her chest. She blinked to refocus her eyes, and then she saw it—a thin wisp of smoke unfurling through another opening to ride the breeze, like a spectre setting out on its nightly haunt.

The silo wasn't alive, but someone was living inside it. An abandoned old shack, tucked away from view: this was the perfect hideout for an enemy fugitive. The electric current pulsed up and down Ivy's whole body as the meaning of what she had found sunk in.

This was it.

Quietly, carefully, she led Nelly under the cover of the trees, looped her reins over a limb, and gestured for her to stay. The mare dipped her head as if she understood. Ivy had to carry on alone now, without the mare's great, muscular body to shield her—nor to carry Ivy off if she got into a real scrape. She swallowed and found her throat painfully dry.

Ivy slung the rifle over her right shoulder and gripped the hand guard in her left hand, pointing the barrel downwards but on the ready as she stealth-crept around the bramble that hedged the edge of the forest. The grass was, mercifully, still wet; it made no sound under her boots. As she neared the silo, she caught the smell of wood smoke, but also a hint of something sweeter, like Father's pipe tobacco.

It was strange to think of the German smoking a pipe the way her father did, as if this enemy were just another man. She had pictured eyes full of malice… gritted teeth spitting out harsh words… monsters, not pipe-smoking men. The familiar smell unsettled her, but it gave her the courage to keep walking—step after step, closer and closer, until she could reach out and touch the lichen-covered stones of the silo.

Someone inside coughed. Without thinking twice, Ivy flung her back against the stones as if they would swallow her up and make her invisible. The coughing stopped.

After a heart-thudding moment, she resolved to shuffle around the silo towards one of the square openings where she could get a good look at her enemy—hopefully without him getting a good look at her. But when she tried to move her right leg, a dozen blackberry thorns clung to her trouser like barbed wire. She was caught.

Ivy bent over her leg, trying to unlatch each tiny barb; but in the darkness, it was slow going, and for each thorn she removed, another one caught her or pricked her fingers and arms. But she kept at it with fury. So intent was she on freeing herself, she didn't even hear the booted footsteps against wet earth… didn't notice the dark figure that had stepped across the silo's crumbled threshold to relieve himself in the bushes just a stone's toss from where she stood. It wasn't until he'd finished that his brusque cough made her freeze. At the same time, the figure turned slowly, taking in the night air.

There was nothing for her to do. Still doubled over, still stuck fast, she waited in horror for the white, soulless eyes to find her.

27
UNEXPECTED SYMPATHIES

He found her alright. Looked right at her and didn't budge. But to Ivy's astonishment, his face was not the face of a monster... not even the face of a man. This was a boy's face—a boy no older than Ernie. Although a thick stubble covered the lower part of his face, she could tell he was young from his eyes. Far from blank and soulless, they were dark and bright with youthfulness—and, at that moment, wide with stunned surprise.

Then, as if shaken by a thought, he swung around and looked behind him. He looked wildly in every direction before turning back to her.

"You are..." He cleared his throat and spoke louder. "... in need of help?"

Hearing the Nazi pilot speak English with scarcely any accent shocked Ivy even more than his young, perfectly human face.

"Erm... I..." Confusion blurred her brain. She couldn't remember how to speak.

"Here." He stepped forward, and she noted his heavy

limp as he worked his way through the grass, nettles, and briars until he was kneeling over her. Ivy inhaled, and her nostrils filled with the sharp odour of sweat mixed with the pipe tobacco she'd smelled before. Chances were, he'd not washed since the crash. He wore a thin white vest that was covered in soot and smelled of wood smoke. She breathed in sharply as he reached into his back trouser pocket. When he drew out an object and flicked it with his thumb, her every muscle seized up like a rabbit petrified by the bark of a hound.

It was a pocket knife.

"Do not fear. Look, see?" Slowly, with his free palm open in front of him as if to assure her he wouldn't pull any tricks, he bent down and chopped at the branches clinging to her leg until she was able to pull it free.

Her liberator stood up and faced her. "You haf some bad scratches. Zer is blood." He pointed to her shin. "Come. I can gif you a bandage."

Was this a dream? A fit of fever, perhaps? Her head throbbed with confusion, and yet she found herself saying, "Thank you", and following his lead through the undergrowth, right up to the silo door. She stood on the lopsided stones in the doorway, watching the small fire in the centre of the floor throw strange shapes about the curved walls. Meanwhile, the pilot ducked inside and began rummaging through a pile of cloth against the back wall.

And then it occurred to her. A *bandage?* Where would a fugitive Nazi spy get a bandage? As if he'd remembered to grab his first aid kit before bailing out of his plummeting Messerschmitt. Should she run? Should she shoot? She slowly reached around to pull the rifle forward, but at the same time, the pilot stood up. He was holding a scrap of pale blue cloth and, with his pocketknife, he ripped it in two. He smiled and gestured for her to come closer.

She knew it could be a trap; she hadn't completely lost her wits. But then, if he'd wanted to kill her, why not take his chance while she was stuck in the brambles? It would've been the easiest thing in the world, and nobody would ever have been the wiser. Not only that, but there was something so disarmingly genuine in this young German's eyes. Something—or was she seeing things?—that reminded her of Ernie.

She took a step in, and then a few more, until she could reach out and take the scrap of cloth he held out to her. Now, in the firelight, she realised what it was: a strip of his pilot's uniform shirt. She looked down and saw the same pale blue cloth tied tightly around his own left leg, discoloured by a large blood stain.

He noticed her looking at the wound and smirked. "Yes, I haf got a bit cut up myself." He laughed nervously. "Er, you vish for me to tie it for you?"

"No," she answered abruptly. She bent down and wrapped the cloth around her shin and calf, and as she did so, her eyes glanced over at the jumpsuit splayed out on the floor as a makeshift rug. He'd strung up the remainder of his parachute as a bivouac against the leaky roof. Laid out on the jumpsuit was a gas mask turned over and filled with blackberries, a tin cup, a metal Nazi cross, some cigarettes and matches, a pack of something labelled *Knäckebrot*, and a small, square photograph of a girl. It must've been everything that survived the crash—everything this boy owned.

"Please." He gestured to the jumpsuit once she'd

finished tying the scrap of cloth. "Sit. Sit," he urged, as if she had just stopped by to pay a neighbourly visit. When she didn't move, he crossed his legs and sat down himself, as if to show her how it was done.

Ivy still didn't sit. She stayed on one knee, looking down at the pilot sitting cross-legged in front of her, and noticed his overgrown, wavy blond hair for the first time. She swallowed, then spoke.

"I know who you are. I tracked you from your Messerschmitt."

His blue eyes didn't flinch, but he nodded ever so slightly. "You tracked me on your own? That is very..." He paused. "If you ver my sister, I vould not haf advised that."

His sister? That caught her off guard. She frowned. "Is that why they sent you to spy? Because you speak English so well?"

He cocked his head. "To spy? I think you already know that I am here because my plane crashed."

"But haven't you been sending information to Lord Haw-Haw about Ashbury Park?"

He raised an eyebrow. "Lord Haw-Haw? The English Nazi reporter?"

"He's been reporting all kinds of things about Ferny Hill. If *you* didn't tell him, then who did? You must at least know that. It's someone from your side."

The pilot scratched his stubbly chin. "I'm afraid I know nothing. They tell me nothing. Only that I must fly my plane ofer your county of Sussex and take photographs. I suppose my mission vas to collect information, that is true. But I am no spy, and vatefer information my camera collected, it nefer got back to headquarters."

"So… you just so happen to speak English perfectly?" she asked, trying to sound sure of herself—though she was anything but.

"I speak English so vell because I used to lif in America. My father vas a crop duster in Pennsylvania. He taught me to fly the crop duster plane ven I vas only ten so, ven I grew up, I could follow in his footsteps. It is a beautiful place, Pennsylvania. You haf heard of it?"

Ivy was dumbfounded. This wasn't adding up at all. "Then why did you join the Nazis?"

"I nefer did join them. Not one of my friends joined them. And yet here vee all are, fighting their war."

His eyes flashed in the firelight. He struck a match and lit up a cigarette. After a couple puffs, he sighed. "But you vish to know vhy vee left America. My father had to borrow very much money to keep his plane in the years of Great Depression. So much so that he could not pay his debtors, and vee ver forced to return to Germany to seek help from our relatifs. That vas three years ago, vhen I vas fifteen. Perhaps not much older than you?"

"I'm fourteen, nearly," Ivy answered, immediately feeling shamefully childish.

"Ah." The pilot looked pleased. "The same age as my sister, Marta." He pointed across Ivy at the photograph.

Ivy picked it up and looked at the smiling, dimple-cheeked girl with blonde pigtails standing beside a big, brown horse. "She rides?" Ivy asked in a small voice.

He smiled as he nodded. "Yes, she is really very goot. Much better than me." The smile faded away, and he hung his head. "I don't suppose I vill efer see her again."

Like frost melting, Ivy's heart softened and went out to

the enemy stranger. She knew exactly what he was feeling. "I've got a brother the same age as you. Ernie, he's called."

"Ernie? Short for Ernest? That is the same as my name—only, in German, we say *Ernst*."

"You don't say? And he's a pilot too! I mean… that is..." She tried to stop them, but before she knew it, her vision blurred over with hot, stinging tears. It was the first time she'd cried after all that had happened, and in front of a complete stranger—and a Hun at that! She bit her lip and tried to force the rising lump back down her throat.

"Vat is wrong?"

She wiped her eyes across her forearm. "We got a letter. Yesterday. It said Ernie… it said he's missing in action. His plane went down somewhere in France."

"I see." Ernst was silent for minute, then added quietly, "That explains vhy you haf come looking for me, and…" His eyes moved to the rifle still slung over her shoulder. "… vith that."

Ivy had been holding the weapon limply at her side since their conversation had started. Now she stiffened and held it behind her back before dropping her head. It was shame she felt, and it had nothing to do with failing to accomplish her mission to avenge Ernie. This enemy pilot seemed to be looking right through her, and she felt just like a silly kid, holding that weapon and playing at things too big for her.

Ernst watched her silently for a moment. Then, with a suddenness that made Ivy's head jerk up, he jumped to his feet and slammed his fist into his open palm. "Damn this var, vhen ordinary boys are forced to shoot at other boys just the same as us—somebody's husband, son, brother."

Something fiery hot kindled inside Ivy's chest, and she jumped up too, all but shouting: "It's not the war's fault, you know. It's not like we had any choice about it after all. It's your stupid Hitler's fault. Nobody here wanted it to happen. Ernie went because he had to… because it was his duty to defend our country. And now… and now…"

She dropped the rifle as she sunk to her knees. The torrent of tears was far past holding back now, and she wept with all her heart—wept as if weeping alone would fix all that was broken in the world.

All the while, Ernst said nothing. He just stood there, sober eyes cast to the ground, and let Ivy pour out all the pain and anger she'd carried—like a soldier's knapsack—since that dreadful letter had come.

And somehow, she didn't care if he saw her crying. It was the only honest thing she could do in that moment—the only way she could show how much Ernie meant to her. She wasn't ashamed of that.

At long last, her sobs softened. Ivy sat back on her heels and dabbed her nose and eyes on her sleeve.

Seeing this, the German hastily took a neatly folded handkerchief from his table and handed it to her. Only after Ivy had taken a deep breath, and it seemed the storm had passed, did he speak.

"I think your brother is a very brave man. And do you know vat else? He is a very lucky man to haf a brave sister like you to veep for him."

Ivy glanced up at him through swollen eyes. He squatted down so he was looking directly back at her.

"Vat is your name?"

"It's Ivy. Ivy Briscoe," she whispered.

"Vell then, Ify Briscoe. You listen to me. Don't gif up hope. After all, at this moment, my own mother and sister will haf received a letter to say that I, too, am missing. Yet here I sit, alife and in good company." He smiled with such a kindly smile, she didn't even flinch when he rested his hand gently on her shoulder. "Nefer gif up hope."

28

DUPED

"Good grief, Freckles! Where have you been?" Teddy's eyes moved from the rifle slung over Ivy's shoulder to the light blue bandage wrapped around her leg, then back to her face. His eyes were a mixture of anger and doubt—neither one like Teddy at all.

Ivy shrugged and pushed passed him to lead Nelly into the stable. "I'm sorry," was all she could think to say.

The truth was, she would have liked to tell Teddy everything right then and there—about Ernst and the unexpected understanding they'd come to. But she had made a deal with the German fugitive, and she'd sworn on her honour to keep it. She had wanted Ernst to come back with her. After all, he had said himself he didn't want to fight for Hitler. If he turned sides, he could stay in Great Britain and help the Allies.

But Ernst had explained that it wasn't quite so simple as that. "It is fine for me. But if efer the Nazis discovered I vas liffing among and vorking for their enemies, my family vould pay the price. They vill be imprisoned, tortured, efen killed. How could I do that to my mother and father? To Marta?"

Ivy had to admit, it wasn't as easy a choice as she'd thought; but she had urged him to make it all the same. She told him that if it were her, she would want her brother to do the right thing, no matter the cost.

And so they had left it at this: Ivy would give Ernst one day to think it over and decide whether he would surrender himself or be taken prisoner. She would tell no one she had seen him. When she came back the next day, either he would return to Ferny Hill with her to give himself up, or she would have to tell Mr. Blackwood about him. It was her duty, and he understood that. He swore he wouldn't run. They had shaken on the deal and left each with the other's good faith.

But now she felt she had lost Teddy's faith in her. After all, the variety show had been their mission, with the objective of looking out for the spy. She'd left him in a lurch by running off the way she had.

"Please tell me you haven't used that rifle. You haven't a clue how to shoot it, you know."

"I didn't use it!" She spun around. "Look, I'm sorry, Teddy. I'm sorry I left. I just needed to… to ride."

"So you didn't hide out in the substation?"

She looked at him, puzzled. "Why would I do that?"

His hand flew to his forehead as if some terrible thought had struck him. "If you didn't, somebody else did. I went looking for you and found it wide open: the hens running amok, the privy seat raised up, everything. I couldn't imagine you'd have left it in that state, but I hoped it was you. Otherwise…"

"But who could have opened it?" Her mind raced in panicked circles. "Kenny and Esme aren't strong enough to lift the privy seat on their own. Mr. Blackwood was here, wasn't he? Watching for the spy? Nobody else knows about it. How could they?"

They stared at each other, each one reflecting the other's dawning horror. Teddy sprang first into action. "Come on."

Teddy struck a match as soon as his feet hit the substation floor. He took a candle from the ledge in the entryway, lit it, and held it up to flood the bunker with its light.

"All clear!" he shouted up. Ivy followed down the ladder.

"Did you close the radio room after you messaged headquarters this morning?" she asked.

"Of course I did. Oh, blimey!" Teddy groaned. The map table and benches were folded up against the wall. The radio room was wide open.

"The notebook!" Ivy breathed. The same horrid thought propelled them both forward. Gasping in the muggy, subterranean air, they pushed into the cramped cave of a room. Teddy frantically raised the lantern over the tiny table where the S.O.C.K.s notebook—containing all sorts of top secret information—was kept.

It was gone.

"No, no, NO!" Ivy gripped the sides of her head with clawed fingers. "Everything was in there! The official S.O.C.K.s code key, the map of dead letter drop locations, and… oh no."

She looked at Teddy. He looked as pale as some earth-dwelling creature in the lamplight. "Mr. Blackwood's operation base is on that map."

"Right. We've got to keep our heads about us," Teddy said commandingly. "The spy can't have got far. We need to find him, then work out how to get back the notebook."

"But where do we even start?" Ivy threw up her hands and sank down onto the wooden table. Something light and papery blew off it and floated down to the floor. Teddy stooped to pick up the thing and held it up to the light. It was the discarded wrapper from a pineapple cream.

"Just Kenny leaving his rubbish around again," Ivy grumbled dismissively.

Teddy was still holding the square wrapper aloft. "Kenny's never been allowed in the radio room, as I'm aware."

Ivy's eyes grew wide as she realised what Teddy had found.

He nodded. "Looks like the Candy Man has paid us a visit. I think we've found our spy."

29
THE CANDY SPY

"But why would Barney break in here and take our notebook? He's in the Army. He's on *our* side. And anyway, he's out of town. He's not even in Ferny Hill, remember?" But even as Ivy defended his innocence, images of Barney schmoozing at the bar with those drunken soldiers sowed a seed of doubt in her mind. Now she thought about it, he certainly did ask lots of seemingly innocent questions.

"There's only one way to find out." Teddy stuffed the wrapper into his pocket. "If we find Barney, there goes his alibi. We can ask questions later. I say we try his room first."

Most everyone had gone over to Ashbury Park for the after-party, so there was no one around at Emmett's Farm to see the two of them dash through the barn, dodging hay bales like rats in a maze to get to the rickety old staircase that led up to the loft where Barney's room was. Nor did anyone come running when, after knocking hard on the door and getting no reply, Teddy raised the butt of his rifle and whacked it against the lock, breaking it off. Slowly, he pushed open the door.

The room was empty alright, but a cigarette was still smouldering in the ashtray on the bedside table.

"You check those drawers." Teddy nodded Ivy towards a wooden chest of drawers. "I'll try his suitcase."

Ivy didn't argue or tell him he was being bossy. With military obedience, she went straight to the drawers. There wasn't much—just a leather wallet, a matchbox, and a whole lot of sweets.

So that's *where he keeps his contraband stash.*

She opened the wallet, and a page of food stamps fell out. Underneath those was a pocket containing some other cards and papers. The first one turned out to be an identity card with the name 'Barney Larson' printed on the first line... only the photograph beside the name *wasn't* Barney at all! It was a skinny fellow with buck teeth dressed in an army uniform.

"What on earth?" Perplexed, Ivy looked at the next paper: another identity card. She flipped it open to see a photograph of the Barney *she* knew—the thick eyebrows, the cleft chin. The hair was lighter—the jet black must've been the result of hair dye—but there was no mistaking him. The only difference was the name printed beside the photograph: Walter 'Wally' Winters.

Ivy's lungs deflated in amazement. She hurriedly glanced at the next paper. It was a membership card for the British Union of Fascists, once again with Barney's image pasted on and the name 'Walter Winters' inscribed beside it.

"Teddy, look!" She spun around, holding out her

discovery for him to see. He was bent over a small black suitcase.

"Give us a mo', I've just about got it… there!" He'd been working out a number combination to open the suitcase locks. They both clicked open, and he raised the lid to look inside. "Ha! Would you believe it? Now that's incriminating evidence of being a spy if ever I saw it."

Ivy walked over and knelt down to see for herself what evidence he'd found. She gasped. Inside the suitcase was a radio transmitter—headphones and all.

Teddy looked stunned. "So *that's* how he's been sharing the Ferny Hill news with the Nazis. I hope you're good and convinced now, Freckles? Say, what was it you found there, anyway?"

"I'm convinced alright, but not just because of the radio." She handed him the identification papers.

Teddy's jaw tightened as his eyes flitted over them. "Why, that scoundrel! I knew he hadn't been to Dunkirk! I reckon he stole the name off some poor sod who actually did go over and die fighting, and all the while he's really a fascist! An English Hitler supporter! A traitor! Of all the perverse… the low-down cheap tricks..."

He sat back on his heels and, to Ivy's surprise, smacked himself flat against the forehead with his palm. "We may as well face the facts, Freckles. We've been duped. And I'm the biggest fool of all! I suspected he was fishy… maybe a deserter who thought himself too good for this war, maybe looking to bunker down in a small village and make himself into some sort of local celebrity. But I never in a million dreamed *he* was the spy! After all, he's just so… so English! So very much like us."

Teddy shook his head in self-disgust. "And still he pulled the wool right over my eyes. There I was, simpering onstage to the whole of Ferny Hill in hopes of rooting out the spy—meanwhile, the spy was making the most of a clear coast to weasel his way into our substation! That was his plan all along, don't you see? And I fell right into it like a witless wally."

"But how?" Ivy shouted. She could take her share of the blame later; there was no time for that now. "I still don't understand how he found his way in!"

Teddy rubbed his chin. "Yes, that does still pose a pretty pickle." His eyes narrowed. "Hang on a blithering minute."

"What is it?" Ivy asked, trying to read the thoughts that were at that moment taking shape in Teddy's mind.

He slapped his leg. "I can't believe it. I *am* a fool. Taken in by my own charming baby sister!"

"Flora? What's she got to do with it?" *Couldn't he for once just spell things out?*

A joyless grimace sickened Teddy's face. "Didn't it strike you as odd, the way she suddenly changed her tune towards Barney and became all chummy with us, just like that?"

Ivy thought, then hesitantly answered, "Yes, I suppose it did seem rather sudden. You think it was all just an act? That Barney put her up to it so she could spy on us without raising our suspicions?"

"That's exactly what I think," Teddy answered, pushing himself to his feet. "And a right good little spy she turned out to be, the little leech." He slammed shut the suitcase with the wireless inside and picked it up. "Come on. Let's go see what we can get her to cough up. If anyone knows where Barney… or Wally, I should say, is hiding, it's probably his little sidekick."

"Ted, we can't make a scene over your sister at Ashbury Park!" Ivy protested.

He swung around in the blasted doorway. "We're not going to. Flora was meant to round up the Imps and wait at the Emmetts'. We thought we performers should turn up all as one troop. At least, I *hope* she's still there. Bring those papers, Freckles, and let's go. Not a minute to lose. Every second gives that turncoat Winters a chance of escape."

30
TICKING TIME BOMB

"But I swear, I didn't! I've not even spoken to Barney all week! I thought he was away, just like you did!" Flora choked, tears glistening down her porcelain cheeks.

She'd come out of the farmhouse door to look for the two of them just as they had come looking for her, and Teddy had laid into her like never before, telling her she was as good as a traitor and deserved to go to prison for what she'd done.

"Tell him, Ivy!" Flora pleaded. "Don't *you* believe me?"

Ivy didn't know what to say. The truth was, Flora seemed completely floored by everything her brother had told her about Barney, and especially his accusations that she had been a part of it. But so far, Teddy's record for being right about things was pretty good. And besides that, what other explanation could there be?"

"*Please*, Ivy." Flora begged, weaving her fingers together as if praying. "You've *got* to believe me. I know I was horrid before, but I'm not lying now."

Ivy turned to Teddy. "Maybe she is telling the truth, you know."

"Don't fall for it," Teddy snapped. "Who else could possibly have told Wally about the substation?"

Right at that moment, Esme came skipping through the hedge with Kenny rolling and stomping along behind her. He was still wearing his skates from his last act and struggled to make headway through the grass.

Ivy's inner Vera clicked in. "Where have you two been? You shouldn't be running around in the dark by yourselves. And Ez, where'd you get that enormous lolly?"

Esme lifted up a saucer-sized, rainbow-coloured lolly and smiled with satisfaction before taking a lick.

Kenny crossed his arms. "It's not fair she got one and I didn't. I did more performing than her. And she won't even tell me who gave it to her."

"I told you, Kenny," Esme said between licks. "I'm not allowed to tell. Barney said I could only have the lolly if I kept it secret."

Ivy exchanged a look with Teddy. She crouched down and took Esme by the shoulders. "You saw Barney, just now?"

Esme bit her lip, but her expression confirmed it.

Ivy tried to speak calmly. "Now listen here, Ez. It's important. You *must* tell us what Barney said to you or… or very bad things will happen."

Esme considered her lolly for a moment, then said, "You're sure it won't make me a snitch?"

"It won't make you a snitch. In fact, it'll make you a hero," Ivy assured her.

Esme raised her shoulders and heaved a great, relenting

sigh. "Alright. I went out to pay the rabbits a visit during the show, 'cause I thought the 'Run Rabbit' song might have upset them. And that's when I saw Barney walking 'round the henhouse."

"But I thought Barney was away..." Kenny began, but Ivy hushed him.

"Go on, Ez."

"Well, he said to me that, as the show had been all his idea, didn't that make him part of our club now? And that he especially wanted me to be the one to show him all about our hideouts. Said he'd give me this lolly after! So I showed him about the special lever, and the secret privy door and everything, and I didn't even forget anything!"

Ivy looked over her shoulder at Flora, who was wiping her eyes on a doily handkerchief; and at Teddy, who had his arms crossed over his chest, scowling at the ground rather than looking at his sister.

Ivy turned back to the happy, lolly-licking Esme. "Then what happened, Ez? It's very important," she urged, still as calmly as she could.

"Then we went down into the substation, and I showed him where the special room was, but I said I didn't know how to open it, and only you and Teddy knew. But he worked it all out himself. And then we looked at the notebook."

"Did he ask you questions about it?"

Esme thought for a second. "He did ask me about the marks on the map. Especially Fishpond's Bottom. I told him about how we went to spy that time and found Mr. Blackwood's secret bunker with all the booby traps and the secret tunnel into Ashbury Park."

Ivy sat back on her heels. How could she have been so careless as to entrust so much dangerous information to a seven-year-old? She wasn't angry at Esme. She was just a kid, easily taken in by the lies and bribes of a professional spy. But she, Ivy, a trained Special Duties agent, should've seen it coming.

The gathering dusk spun around her as she stood. She felt like being sick, but she forced her voice to stay steady. "Thank you, Ezzy. Did anything else happen? Did Barney say where he was going next?"

Esme screwed up her face in thought. "He said he'd like to pay a visit to Mr. Blackwood's bunker sometime, that's all. But I told him he would have to ask Mr. Blackwood, 'cause we weren't allowed there anymore 'cause of all the frightful weapons inside."

As the full meaning of what Esme had said sunk in, Ivy felt like the force of a tidal wave hit her in the gut.

"Good God!" she breathed, turning terror-stricken eyes towards Teddy. "If he gets into that bunker, he won't need to sneak into Ashbury Park. He'll be able to explode his way in. What if he uses the TNT to blow up the house while everyone's inside it?"

"Who's going to blow it up?" Kenny asked. He'd been skating around them in circles, hungrily eyeing Esme's lolly, and was only just tuning back into what the others were saying.

"The spy, Tootles," Teddy answered. "Listen, I've got a job for you. Your most important job yet. How fast do you think you can get to Ashbury Park?"

"Why, I can get there in five minutes on these!" Kenny

picked up one of his legs and gave his skate-clad foot a shake.

"Then I want you to go as fast as your skates will take you and fetch Mr. Blackwood. Tell him we've discovered the spy and we're heading him off at Fishpond's Bottom. Come quick with reinforcements. Now say it all back to me."

"Discovered spy. Come quick to Fishpond's Bottom with reinforcements," Kenny recited. "Got it."

"Good. Tally ho, soldier. And don't look back!"

Kenny took just a moment to salute, then spun on his skates and lunged off into the dusk.

"Careful, Ken!" Ivy called after him. Then, to Teddy: "What if he doesn't get there in time? What if Wally finds the dynamite first and blows the whole place to bits?"

"We're not gonna let that happen. We can still outrun Wally on horseback."

She nodded, ready to sprint back to the stable.

"What about me? Can't I help? After all, this is all my fault." Ivy had almost forgotten Flora was there 'til she spoke up.

"But Flora, you heard what Esme said. We know it wasn't you."

"But it is, partly," she whimpered. "None of this would've happened if I hadn't told Barney about your club in the first place. I thought it was all just a game, and... well... I *was* a bit jealous not to be a part. But I never dreamed it was real, or that I was putting anyone in danger. I swear it."

There was no time for another bout of tears now. Ivy quickly interjected, "We know, Flora. You could never have known Barney was a spy. And anyway, it's as much my fault as yours. If I had watched over Esme and Kenny during the show rather than run off, none of this would have happened, either. We're all a bit to blame."

"Speak for yourself, would you?" Teddy butted in. "And let's get going!"

Ivy rounded on him. "You at least owe Flora an apology for accusing her just now." She looked at Flora. "We both do."

Teddy was tapping a perturbed foot. "Look, I promise to grovel down on my knees when this is all over, but can't it wait? We've got a spy to catch—before he blows up an entire RAF airbase, along with the whole village!"

"Right." Ivy snapped her focus back to the emergency at hand. "Flora, the most helpful thing you can do is to stay here and look after Esme." She added over her shoulder as she ran, "Keep cover in case Barney comes back. And pray. Pray with all your might that we're not too late!"

31
MOMENT OF TRUTH

Ivy had never ridden better than she did that night, she and Nelly clipping trees and leaping over ditches like a champion fox hunter on her thoroughbred. Teddy did well to keep up on Napoleon, though he was panting like a dog when they dismounted at the corner of the Ashbury Park estate. They'd get nowhere on horseback through the dense pines and bramble of Marshwood Forest, but they'd ridden as far as they could go down the lane. Now the wall would be their guide into the depths of the dark wood, down to the pond.

Teddy carried the rifle and walked in front. Little did he know that it was the second time that night Ivy had stalked the enemy; and this time, she knew the enemy would be armed and dangerous.

Teddy squatted, scooped up a handful of greyish pond muck, and wiped it across his forehead, nose, cheeks—even his ears, neck, and hands. Ivy did likewise. Only then did she notice he was still wearing his black tailed coat. Though it was dripping in mud, it was just as well he wore it: it made for decent camouflage in the dark. He gave her the signal to follow; and, crouching down low, they crept—just as they'd practiced—along the edge of the pond towards the old Scots pine that they'd marked on the map as Mr. Blackwood's 'Trap Door'.

It was quiet. Only the wind in the pines, the mud sucking at their ankles, and the occasional bullfrog's croak disturbed the silence. Maybe Wally hadn't found the place yet after all…

When they were just down the bank from the Scots pine, Teddy lay down flat on his belly behind a bunch of water reeds and waited for Ivy to come up beside him. He spoke in her ear, barely in a whisper: "We'll hug the wall and approach from the shrubs on the other side. Follow me."

They shuffled along with their backs pressed against the stone wall of the Ashbury Park grounds, then crouched and picked their way—slowly, stealthily—through the tall nettles until they came up under the umbrella-like branches of the Scots pine. Ivy could feel the nettles' stings even through her riding trousers, but she didn't make a sound. They were no more than a yard or two from the hatch.

Teddy held up a hand to signal 'wait here' while he tread cautiously forward. He was out in the open now, and he crouched down to examine the hatch. "Nobody's been here," he whispered hoarsely.

Ivy blew an enormous sigh of relief through her lips. At the same time, Teddy grunted as something big and dark dropped down from the pine tree's boughs and landed flat on top of him. The something, Ivy could see, had jet-black hair.

She shot forward as Walter ripped the rifle off Teddy's

shoulder and tossed it away into the nettles. Ivy made a lunge for the rifle, but before she could get it, Walter shouted, "Stop! Take one more step without my permission, and I'll pull the trigger."

He wasn't bluffing, either. Gripped in his hand, with the barrel jabbed right against Teddy's temple, was a small revolver. With his other arm, he held the boy in a locking brace around the shoulders. Ivy was paralysed. Walter had duped them again and left them utterly defenceless.

The following charade was something out of a nightmare. Sweat stung Ivy's bleary eyes as she followed Walter's every order with shaking knees and trembling hands. He had Teddy sit against the Scots pine, then pulled a kerchief out of his pocket and told her to gag Teddy with it.

"I'd prefer to work without any of this one's chaff," he sneered.

"I'm sorry," she mouthed as she held up the cloth to Teddy's face. Teddy put the gag in his mouth himself, then handed the ends back to Ivy to tie. He made up for his loss of words with eyes that shot daggers at Walter through the sweaty fringe sticking to his forehead. But Walter's spirits weren't dampened. He was smiling his white, movie-star smile—though now it looked nothing but sinister.

He had a long rope looped across his torso which he took off and handed to Ivy.

"Next game: 'tie Teddy to the tree'. You're a Scout, aren't you?" Walter's tone was disgustingly casual, as if he were having a jolly good time of it. "I expect to find those knots satisfactory, or I'm afraid I shall have to punish you both." He gave the revolver a little shake in the air.

While she worked, walking around and around the tree, constricting Teddy in the rope's coils, Walter paced smugly back and forth in the clearing. He was enjoying himself.

"I must say, I knew the British military were inferior, but I never thought they'd be so foolish as to trust a couple of kids to keep government secrets. Ha! Not that I'm complaining. It's made my job as easy as stealing sweets from a baby!"

Ivy carried on with her task, pretending not to hear.

That didn't stop Walter from speaking his mind. "I admit, I was a little perturbed when you two interrupted my interview with Private Tibbs at The Rifleman that day. He was on the verge of telling me some very interesting information about the top secret work they're doing at Ashbury Park. But then you came along and gave me a better idea. When one door closes and all that. Anyway, I knew you kids were up to something… part of some kind of Resistance, something Gubbins and your old man put you up to."

At the mention of Gubbins, Ivy looked up involuntarily. *How could he know?*

Walter seemed amused by her surprise. "Yes, I know all about the colonel's visit. I knew a truckload of sappers were cooking something up in your garden, and I assumed it was more than a new bed of pansies. You see, I have a very good vantage point from the Emmetts' loft. Most convenient. But, where was I? Ah yes. So instead of getting angry at the pub, I thought to myself, 'Wally, you genius, why not kill two birds with one stone? Find out what these kids have been put up to *and* gain full run of Ashbury Park in one go!'

"I'd already tried to get information out of that little

blonde twit of girl, but it was clear she had nothing but butterflies in her head. She did tip me off about the henhouse; all I needed then was the time and space to poke around a bit. And that's why my idea was so ingenious! With the whole village rounded up like a bunch of dumb sheep to watch a bunch of dumb kids sing and dance, I'd have all the time I needed to find out your little secrets, then pay a visit to Ashbury Park and see what the RAF has been getting up to."

But you didn't manage it, did you?" Ivy growled through gritted teeth. "You'd have got nowhere if you hadn't manipulated my little sister."

"Ah, little Esme. Sweet kid. Especially sweet for telling me about this bunker of your friend's… Mr. Blackwood, is it? Ex-military, I believe? He's Resistance too, eh? Oh, now don't look at me like that. Of course he is. This quaint little place is crawling with government secrets. Why else do you think they sent me here? Not for the company!"

"'They?' You mean your stupid little club of Hitler supporters?" Ivy had finished the knots, tying them as tightly as her fingers could pull. Now she was buying time. If she could just keep him talking a little longer 'til help arrived...

"Club? Ha!" His smile transformed into a snarl. "The British Union of Fascists is no social club, doll. After Hitler gets ahold of this over-confident little island called Great Britain, guess who's gonna be in charge?" He pointed to his own chest. "That's right. Yours truly and his 'little club'. So you can start practising taking orders right now. Get over here and show me how to open this thing up." He stomped his foot twice on the trapdoor.

"I… I don't know how. I've never done it." Ivy tried to sound convincing.

"Well, I suggest you figure it out. Or would this help you?" He extended the hand with the gun so it was pointed at Teddy, right between his eyes.

"OK, OK! I'll try." She shuffled around in the pine straw for a few seconds before her hand brushed against the pole that opened the hatch. With her heart in her throat, she placed both hands on the pole and gave it a wrench. Behind her, the hatch door lifted and swung open.

"Ah, very good," Walter said through his teeth. She turned to find him holding a cigarette between them. He struck a match, lit the fag, shook the flame out, and tossed the match over his shoulder.

Without thinking, Ivy flew to where the match smouldered and stamped it out with her foot.

Walter was looking at her with one thick eyebrow raised.

"You could start a forest fire that way," she said quickly.

"Yes, in a damp marsh. Aren't we conscientious. Now come here, would you?"

She obeyed. He blew a puff of smoke in her face, making her blink; then all of the sudden he grabbed her, spun her around, and clasped his hand over her mouth. He still had the gun in the other hand, but it was the cigarette between his teeth that frightened her most. Teddy had said it: one single spark could set off the whole bunker full of TNT.

"You're going down with me, sweetie," he said in her ear as he pushed her right up to the edge of the opening. She knew if that happened, they'd all be blown to bits, then and there. But what could she do? It was a terrible choice: she could struggle and wind up getting shot, or she could let him blow the place up, himself included. In the split second when she'd decided she would risk the struggle, a voice from behind froze them both.

"Achtung!"

Walter let go of Ivy and swung around. At the same time, someone's fist swung forward and met him square in the eye.

Ivy turned around expecting to see Mr. Blackwood; but the person straddling Walter on the ground was thin and blond-headed.

"Ernst!" she screamed.

Ernst pinned Walter's arms down on either side of his head before answering.

"Take his gun, Ify. Throw it into the vater."

She did. "How did you get here? How did you find us?"

"I realised you ver right as soon as you vent avay," he panted. "So I followed on foot. I saw your horse on the road with another horse and heard voices." He was wincing and gasping, clearly in pain from the journey and the struggle with Walter.

Walter, too, was out of breath, gaping with amazement at his attacker through the eye that wasn't swollen. "A Luftwaffe uniform! You're German?" He laughed hysterically. "This is good fortune! We are on the same side!"

"Vat side is that?" Ernst asked, still keeping a tight grip on Walter's arms.

"Your Führer is my Führer. I fight for Nazi domination of Great Britain—of the world, in time—just like you." Now his smile had a maniacal hunger about it. "Lend me your hand, Freund, and tonight, we'll make history together."

"And vat do you suggest vee do vith these children, *Freund*?"

"As the Führer says, 'He who owns the youth gains the future'. They can either help us achieve the future, or we eliminate them."

Ernst was silent.

To her horror, Ivy saw him loosen his grip on Walter's arms.

"We will never help you!" she cried. "And you!" Ernst looked straight ahead, his eyes inscrutable. "I trusted you!"

"Let me up, will you? I'll deal with the brats," Walter said, squirming to free himself.

Ernst's eyes narrowed on Walter. His knuckles went white as his grip tightened on the man's wrists, his jaw clenched.

"Vith your side, children are nothing more than instruments... just veapons. Vith your side, there *is* no future—not for Great Britain, not for Germany, not for me or for Marta. I tell you, I haf had enough of your side."

Ivy could have jumped up and down and 'hurrahed' for Ernst in that moment—but before she got the chance, some great, motorised monster burst through the underbrush and hurtled down the bank, the two beams of its headlights flooding the clearing as it ground to a halt. Ivy did a double take, squinting into the headlights. In the truck's driving seat, looking fiercer than ever, sat Grandmammy! Kenny was beside her, looking both terrified and absolutely exhilarated at the same time. Mr. Blackwood and two armed soldiers jumped out of the back and took position with their rifles, aimed and ready to shoot.

"Leave the Hun to me, ya!" Mr. Blackwood ordered.

He cocked the gun, and—before Ivy could move or breathe or make a sound—he fired.

"No!" Ivy screamed, running forward and dropping to where Ernst had fallen. Walter scrambled free, but she didn't think about him. Ernst's bare shoulder was bleeding, but the bullet hadn't struck home—only skimmed him.

"Ivy, move back!" Mr. Blackwood ordered, coming closer and raising the gun to shoot again.

"No, Mr. Blackwood, you've got the wrong man! He's on our side! It's Barney, Barney's the one! He's really Wally Winters!"

"Wally Winters? The wanted fascist?"

All eyes turned on the man standing in the clearing, making ready to run. Would he try? There was nowhere for him to go. He must have realised it, too, because he quickly changed tactics and laughed hysterically.

"These kids, eh? I find 'em and try to rescue 'em from this good-for-nothing Kraut, and how do they repay me? They tell lies about me and make friends with the enemy! Well, I'll take care of him once and for all."

Only then did Ivy notice with horror that Walter had Teddy's rifle in his hand. He must've picked it up when he scrambled away from Ernst. As he raised it to his eye, Ivy didn't think. She threw herself over the German pilot as if he were Ernie lying there, defenceless. She clenched her eyes tightly shut just as a deafening *crack!* split the air.

There was a cry and a thud. Ivy opened her eyes to see Walter writhing on the ground, clasping his foot. She whipped around to find out who had fired the shot. Everyone else was looking at Grandmammy. The brick of a woman stood beside the truck, a pistol—barrel still smoking—in her hand.

"That'll teach ya to aim a gun at my granddaughter, you big eejit!"

Ivy beamed at her with awed admiration. Maybe taking after Grandmammy wasn't so bad after all.

32

UNSUNG HEROES

Everything happened in a bit of a blur after that. The soldiers bandaged up Walter before handcuffing him and loading him onto the truck. Thankfully, he was in too much pain to protest. Kenny pretended to help Mr. Blackwood tend to Ernst's shoulder, pestering the Scoutmaster all the while. "Does this mean I'm a First Class Scout now? Do I get my badge?"

Ivy looked around for Teddy and remembered with a gasp that he was still gagged and bound to the Scots pine!

"Ken, have you got your pocket knife handy?" she asked.

"'Course I got it! Always be prepared, you know." He reached into his back pocket and looked confused. "Er... wait a second."

Then Ivy recalled how she'd borrowed the knife that morning. "Hang on. I've got it."

Without giving Kenny an explanation, she ran over to Teddy with the knife and got down on her knees to untie the gag first, then sawed through the ropes until they snapped one by one. Teddy sputtered like he'd just got a worm in his apple, then rubbed his wrists and sighed. His eyes met Ivy's. Without the slightest warning, he grabbed hold of her shoulders, yanked her towards him, and planted a kiss flat on her cheek.

When he let go, they both looked in unison at the ground, avoiding one another's eyes.

Teddy cleared his throat and said, a little stiffly, "Er, good show, Freckles. You really were marvellous out there. If it hadn't been for your running off to fraternise with the enemy earlier, we'd all be blown to bits by now. You did it. You saved the day *and* caught the spy."

Ivy blushed as she stood up and offered Teddy a hand. "*We* did it, thank you very much." She smiled. "Come on. I'll introduce you to Ernst."

But her face fell when she turned around. Ernst was on his feet, his shoulder bandaged up; but his hands were cuffed behind his back, and one of the soldiers was leading him away to the truck.

"Wait!" She bolted over to where Ernst had been lying. Mr. Blackwood was packing up his first-aid kit. "They can't arrest him! He saved our lives!" she pleaded.

"Ya, but I'm afraid he is *still* a warranted enemy, all the same." Mr. Blackwood placed a heavy hand on her shoulder. "He'll go through due process, and I'm sure his judges will take into account his actions today."

"We'll testify on his behalf," Teddy said to comfort her. "Anyway, it wouldn't be the first time an enemy turned into an ally agent." He stood up straight. "Mr. Blackwood, I should like to thank our rescuer, if I may."

"Ya. Go on."

At the truck, Grandmammy was standing over Walter with pistol still in hand. The soldier who had arrested Ernst opened the door for the prisoner to get in, but Teddy stopped him.

"One moment, Corporal. We'd like a quick word, if we may." The soldier nodded, and Ernst looked from Teddy to Ivy expectantly.

"Ernst, we owe you our lives." Teddy automatically thrust out his hand; then, realising Ernst's hands were cuffed behind his back, hastily withdrew it and patted him on the arm instead.

When he moved aside to let Ivy say her farewells, she found the dreaded old lump rising up her throat again. She swallowed it down, but the tears she couldn't keep at bay. "I'm so sorry, Ernst."

Though the tears blurred her vision, she could still see that he was smiling. It was a genuine smile—the kind you might expect to see on someone's face who has just escaped disaster, not someone who has just been arrested as a prisoner of war.

"Ify, it is best this vay. Now, if the Nazis learn I am alife, they vill hear that I haf been shot and arrested. This vay, maybe I can help the Allies and still my family vill remain safe. Vatever happens, at least I can lif vith peace knowing I haf chosen the right side… This is for the best, efen if I nefer see Marta again. Perhaps one day she vill know that her brother chose the right side to fight for."

Ivy wiped her arm across her eyes. "But you may see her again, when this is all over and we've won the war. Never give up hope, remember?"

He smiled and nodded. "Yes. And you also. Nefer gif up hope."

Two days later, Ivy, Teddy, Flora, and the Imps were sitting under the copper beech trees in the back garden at The Beeches when Grandmammy called from the house, "Come along and get your wee backsides inside. There's a colonel here to call on you."

Ivy shared a look of surprise with Teddy before shouting back, "Thank you, Grandmammy! We'll be right in!"

Mrs. Briscoe was sitting and talking with the colonel when they walked into the sitting room. He stood to greet them, and once again, Teddy's hand raised automatically into a salute. This time, Ivy followed suit without feeling silly and waited, the way Teddy had taught her, for the colonel to return the salute and lower his hand before lowering her own.

"Cadets, in light of the events of the previous few days, I felt it fitting to pay you a personal visit in order to congratulate you on bringing in a very dangerous enemy spy, as well as the German pilot—who, it seems, will turn out to be a great asset to us. The damage to the safety of human life as well as military intelligence would have been incalculable had it not been for your bravery in action."

Ivy felt her chest swell up a little at his words, but she modestly mumbled the words "Thank you, sir" in unison with Teddy.

"There is another matter I wish to discuss with the three of you, if I may..."

Mrs. Briscoe took Esme by the hand and put an arm around Flora's shoulder to lead them from the room. Grandmammy, hovering in the doorway, dusted her hands together. "I'll get the tea, so. Do ya take cream, Colonel?"

"Yes, thank you, Mrs. Kennedy. Now," he said, instantly resuming business once the room had been cleared. "Please take a seat, all of you." He did so himself—a bit stiffly, Ivy thought, as if he were uneasy about what he had to say. "As I've just expressed, I could not be more satisfied with your dedication to your task as Special Duties cadets. You've manned your station well and gone beyond the call of your duties. So do not think that what I'm about to say has any bearings on your performance."

Ivy picked at her thumbnail, wishing he would spit out what he had to say already, but she nodded politely.

He returned the nod and continued. "I've decided to disband the Ferny Hill substation. Though the threat of invasion still exists, it is growing less likely by the day. Hitler is learning that our pilots are made of tougher stuff than he imagined. Also, I fear—with Walter Winters reporting directly to Germany—it is likely that the location of your station has been compromised, even if he was not fully aware of its purpose. It would be too risky to allow you to continue. And so,"—he sat forward, touching his fingertips together—"I am issuing you honourable discharges from this operation. I only wish others could know the full extent of your courage; but of course, as you know, your part in this war must remain a secret."

"Yes, sir," Teddy acknowledged. Ivy nodded again. Kenny was looking out the window longingly.

"There is, however, one way I might give you some of the public recognition you deserve—not as Special Duties agents, but merely as three gallant young people. In light of last night's events, I am nominating each of you for the Albert Medal for saving lives whilst putting your own at risk."

Ivy didn't know what to say. Even Teddy only managed a "Sir, what an honour."

Kenny, however, who had never experienced a tied tongue, raised his finger and cocked his head. "Is that better or not as good as First Class Scout?"

Colonel Gubbins looked confused at first. Then he threw his head back and laughed. "My boy, it's worth a hundred First Class Scout medals."

Kenny jumped to his feet, punched the air, and shouted "Yippee!"

Ivy wished she could feel as happy about it all, but the first thought that had entered her mind overwhelmed the sweetness of the moment with a deep, throbbing ache.

I'd rather have Ernie back than all the medals in the world.

33

HOPE

The mantle clock downstairs clanged twelve times. Midnight. It was officially the second of September: Ivy's fourteenth birthday. She lay awake, watching the sliver of moonless sky through the curtains. Vera snored her same old elegant, little snores from her bed in the corner. Ivy used to put her pillow over her head to block out the sound, but now she didn't mind it.

It was the first time her sister had come home since the fateful day she'd brought home a tall, dark soldier called Barney Larson. She hadn't even been able to get leave when the news about Ernie came, but she'd got special permission to get a couple days off for Ivy's birthday as a surprise.

"I wasn't about to miss my baby sister turning fourteen!" she'd exclaimed when she turned up at the door. "Especially when she's a celebrity and winner of the Albert Medal. I showed everybody the paper and told them that brave little girl on the front page was *my* sister, thank you very much." And she'd hugged Ivy as if she'd never let her go.

Ivy wondered if perhaps Vera felt responsible for the danger they'd all been in because of Wally. Hoping to put her sister's mind at ease, she plucked up the courage to bring it up later when they had just finished a game of snap.

"Vera, I'm sorry about Barney… I mean Walter."

Vera shuffled the deck of cards. "Oh, him? No loss to me. I didn't care a jot for him. Only brought him down here to get rid of him, in fact. Of course, I had no idea he'd turn out to be so dangerous."

"You mean he wasn't really your beau?" Kenny butted in. He'd been reading a comic on his belly beside them on the hearth rug.

"Goodness, no. I hope I have better taste than a Nazi spy for a beau! No, I've been seeing a lovely army captain called Desmond. You know, he was just about to propose to me while he was on leave last week, and an air raid started! I could've killed those Germans!"

Vera hadn't changed much, and Ivy was glad of it.

Especially when so much else had changed. Just one short year ago, things had been so very different. Ivy remembered herself then—on the verge of thirteen, giddy to stay up late for the news and to sip her first taste of sherry. That silly, naïve child seemed… not a stranger, but like a younger sister one pities for her simplicity—and, at the same time, envies because she is so blissfully unaware of how cruel the world can be. *That* girl was happy, never guessing how her life would shift—how a war would turn it all on its head, scattering her family and shattering her safe little world.

But that girl was also unaware of the unlikely friendships that would come to mean the world to her—of Teddy, and Ernst, and even Flora!—and the things they would teach her.

And Ivy knew that, if given the chance, she wouldn't go back to being that girl. Not even to take away the pain. Through all that had happened, she had grown up; and she was sure—as sure as she knew the sun would rise again at dawn—that Ernie would be proud of her.

That thought settled her mind like warm milk settles a restless child. She closed her eyes and drew in a long, deep breath.

Bang Bang Bang came a knock on the door downstairs, urgent and unapologetic. *What now?* Ivy threw off her quilt and swung her feet around to the floor.

"Ivy? What's that racket?" Vera asked groggily with one eye open.

"Someone's at the door," she answered, pulling on her dressing gown. She could hear stirring in the hallway and Grandmammy's galumphing footsteps above. Her mother was on the landing at the top of the stairs, Esme tucked up under her arm like a baby chick under a hen's wing. Kenny stood there too, looking sleepy, with a cricket bat over his shoulder. They all listened silently as the door downstairs creaked open, then shut again. Light footsteps crossed the floor. Someone was in the kitchen.

"Step aside, Kathleen," Grandmammy ordered, creaking down the top set of stairs. They all moved aside to let her—

along with her trusty pistol—go down first. A light switched on. A moment of silence.

Then, "Why of all the harebrained tricks, to come breaking into your own home in the middle of the night without a word to your wife! I might've shot you, don't you know, Noel!"

The voice that answered made Ivy's heart leap for joy. "I'm truly sorry, Mrs. Kennedy. I came on the late train direct from Norfolk and didn't get the chance to phone Kathleen. But I'm more grateful than I can say for your astute care of my family."

Mrs. Briscoe gripped the banister, her face flooded with relief. "Noel?" she whispered, as if she couldn't believe it; then cried out, "Noel!" and ran down the stairs with Ivy, the Imps, and Vera flying after her, all fear and sleepiness forgotten.

The Briscoes' home was a scene of happy chaos. Spud howled and danced around Dr. Briscoe's ankles while everyone else hugged and tried to talk all at once.

"We got rabbits, Father! Real ones!"

"Did you, Ezzy? I can't wait to meet them."

"Father, Mr. Blackwood says he reckons I'll get First Class Scout now. Oh, and we got a medal called Albert."

"Yes, I know, Kenny! I've heard all about it, and told everyone up in Norfolk. You three are practically famous!"

Ivy didn't have anything particular to say. She just hugged her father with all her might and hoped that would say enough.

He kissed the top of her head and stroked back her curls so she was looking up at him. "Happy Birthday, my Ivy. How you've grown. I'm prouder of you than I can say," he said quietly, so only she could hear. Then he raised his voice so everyone could hear him. "Now, if I can have all of your attention, I haven't come home in the middle of the night simply to frighten you all to death. I received news some hours ago… such wonderful news, I managed to get permission to deliver it to you myself. Kathleen, you'd better sit down."

He led her to the settee and held her hand as she sat. "Just this evening, I received a call from France. It was Wing Commander Simmons. He told me that our Ernie…" His voice broke, but he recollected himself. "Our Ernie has been found."

Mrs. Briscoe gasped. Ivy felt her legs go limp as she sank to her knees.

Dr. Briscoe wasn't finished. "He's alive, and mending from some pretty bad injuries. He took a blow to the head that knocked him out for a fortnight; but thankfully, after the crash, he was rescued by some country nuns and brought to a little French hospital. The hospital managed to make contact with Wing Commander Simmons yesterday to inform him that Ernie was there and, under the tireless care of one particularly special French nurse, he's making a splendid recovery. He should be able to return home within three weeks."

There was one long moment when nobody spoke and all Ivy knew was the pounding of her heart in her head. Then, all at once like a dam breaking, there was a deluge of hooting and hugging and happy tears that flowed on into the early hours of the morning. It was a birthday like no other—like a thousand Christmas mornings rolled into one.

Grandmammy traded out her pistol for a tea tray and

passed around mugs of hot chocolate. With one arm tight around Ivy's shoulders, Dr. Briscoe raised his mug as if to make a toast.

"This war is far from over. There are yet difficult days ahead. But today is a day to give thanks, for I believe we can say with confidence that God and hope are on our side."

Ivy raised her mug and filled her mouth with the warm, sweet cocoa to mix with the tears she hadn't even tried to hold back.

She wished she could tell Ernst the good news. She wished she could write to Marta and tell her that her brother, too, was alive and safe. She felt surer than ever that her father was right. They *would* win the war. There was a future to look forward to. And they would have a story to tell their children and their children's children, for a hundred years and more.

Ivy had heard a speech by Mr. Churchill on the wireless months ago, when she and Teddy and the Imps were still busy with S.O.C.K.s. His words had struck her then like a rally cry, revving up her heart like the engine of a Hurricane, and she'd never forgotten them. Now, those same words echoed softly, like a still small voice in her mind, but with a force that could move mountains:

Let us therefore brace ourselves to our duties, and so bear ourselves that if the British Empire and its Commonwealth last for a thousand years, men will still say,

'This was their finest hour.'

EPILOGUE

Ivy looked up from the yellowed pages of the notebook at the sound of the door opening and closing. A tall man with thick grey hair appeared in the doorway. His limbs were long and lanky, and a mischievous twinkle danced in his sharp blue eyes.

"My, but it's quiet in here. Don't say you've been telling them ghost stories, Freckles? Their parents will never forgive us!"

The littlest girl, who had snuggled against her grandmother's side to have the best view of the old notebook, now slid off the couch and bolted over to throw her arms around the old man's knees. "Grandaddy Long Legs! Granny's showed us your old secret book and told us the story of when you caught the bad man."

"Has she?" He looked at Ivy, and she read his mind in his eyes. He was surprised, but not displeased. With the little girl still clinging to one of his knees, he lumbered over to the couch and craned his head to get a look at the open page of carefully sketched and labelled military vehicles. "I say, I've not set eyes on that little beauty for at least forty years. Must've been a fiercely clever chap who drew all those." He winked at Ivy.

She just shook her head. "These three Imps did a bit of digging in the garden this morning, Ted, and found rather more than they'd bargained for."

Teddy put his fists on his waist and eyed each of his three grandchildren playfully. "Is that all? I saw that great dirty hole coming back from Uncle Kenny's farm a moment ago, but I put it down to a mole infestation. Turns out it was Imps!"

"We're sorry for the mess in the garden, Grandaddy, but boy was it ever worth it to find all your old stuff from the war!" Dan said, brushing the hair out of his eyes.

Susan looked worried and laid a hand on her grandmother's arm. "But was that the end of the story, Granny? I mean, didn't the two of you ever do any more spying?"

Ivy exchanged a smile with Teddy—a cover-up for some secret joke they shared. "Well, I can't very well give away all my secrets in one go, now can I? *But,* if you have a look in the top drawer of my writing desk, you might just find two Albert Medals in need of a polish."

The children were off in a flash, racing each other up the stairs to see who could find the medals first. Teddy sank down onto the settee beside Ivy and put his arm around her shoulders. He turned over the page of the notebook. On the next page was pasted an old sepia photograph under the hand-written label *S.O.C.K.s MEMBERS.* In the picture was a curly-headed thirteen-year-old girl and a skinny fifteen-year-old boy, each holding the reins of a horse; and in front of them, a snaggletoothed boy in roller skates and a little cotton-haired girl cradling a white rabbit. They all smiled, squinting against the summer sun like a bunch of happy-go-lucky kids.

Teddy chuckled. "Those were good days, my dear. I enjoyed every minute of your volcanic temper tantrums. They only made me love you all the more."

She gave him a look, then rested her head on his shoulder. "We did make a good team back then, didn't we?"

He squeezed her hand and said softly, "We still do."

ACKNOWLEDGMENTS

A bit like running a spy operation, writing a book requires an immense amount of teamwork if it is to really succeed. It is thanks to the contributions of a first-class team that you hold this book in your hand now.

The first mention must go to the person who planted the seed of curiosity in my mind about the Special Duties Branch: my husband Gordon. How fortunate I've been to have you by my side on my quest to dig up this fascinating piece of the past!

That quest led me to two individuals, without whom this book would never have gotten very far: Bill Ashby and Roger Green. Your incredible depth of knowledge and passion brought history up-close and personal, and this book owes its authenticity almost entirely to your input. Nina Hannaford (British Resistance Archive) connected me to these two gentlemen, along with a wealth of primary sources. Coleshill House (the *real* Ashbury Park) kindly permitted me to visit and explore an actual substation—an experience I shall never forget!

When it came to packaging all that wonderful research into a book, I had the enviable privilege of working with the illustrious Roison Heycock, whose instinct for storytelling was invaluable.

Ruth Nelson, my comrade-in-story, expertly polished up my wild fits of writing. Now I can feel as proud of the presentation as I am of this story itself.

The cover design and map of Ferny Hill are the creation of Edward Bettison, whose attention to historic detail communicates the book's spirit at a glance.

Tamsyn Alston gave superb recommendations on the best WWII books to read. Knowing that an expert in the genre loved this book so much gave me the boost of confidence I needed to put it out in the world.

And knowing Bri Stox liked the book, despite not being a fan of war stories in general, gave me even more confidence that *this* story was worth the telling.

My parents—Jim and Mary—have been wonderfully supportive early readers and reviewers, as ever.

Finally, I owe immeasurable gratitude to the real people who inspired this story—real families and real children who sacrificed comfort and safety for God, King, and Country.

To the two people to whom this book is dedicated: I am grateful to Grandpere—the inspiration for Kenny—for childhood tales of adventures with his sister, Ivy (especially the one about his mother throwing a knife at him when he pulled her pigtails!); and to my dear Aunt Terry—the inspiration for Esme—whose tender heart expressed itself in a love for all things four-footed, and who once really did hide a cat in her closet.

when you unlock the

Do you have what it takes to join the Special Operations Cadet Kids?

- *Discover the real history, heroes, & villains that inspired the book*
- *Decode secret messages*
- *Identify ally & enemy aircraft*
- *Make your own rations recipes*

... and much more!

REPORT FOR DUTY AT

MezBlume.com/ SOCKS_Substation

ABOUT THE AUTHOR

Mez Blume is the British-American author of the celebrated *Katie Watson Mysteries in Time* series. A lifelong explorer of History, Mez writes to transport readers to the Past, that they too might discover its inspiring characters and evergreen adventures.

Get the latest news on books, bonus features, and events when you sign up for Mez's newsletter at
MezBlume.com

facebook.com/mezblume
instagram.com/mez_blume
amazon.com/Mez-Blume

Printed by Amazon Italia Logistica S.r.l.
Torrazza Piemonte (TO), Italy